THE PLEASURE OF A KISS

Alexander straight[ened] from the desk and st[ode toward] her, determined to [make her want] through him. A desire [in his] body or his mind to re[sist] and [do] something about it. And knowing how Charlotte had responded him that day in the carriage, he was damn well certain that she wanted to indulge in him as much as he wanted to indulge in her.

She quickly stood, sending the chair tumbling backward and scrambled toward the opposite side of the desk. Away from him. "What are you doing?" she demanded, holding up a hand. "This is a business relationship!"

"I couldn't care less." He stepped over the toppled chair close to her and grabbed hold of her corseted waist. Though she tried to wiggle out from his grasp, he held on and dragged her toward him. He firmly pressed her warm softness against his body, which in turn only tightened the grating need within him. She ceased struggling against him.

Releasing her waist, he dug both hands deep into her soft, thick hair. He tilted her face up to him, though he was rather surprised to find that she herself was already lifting her face to his. As if she wanted this as much as he did.

It had been far too long since he had given himself over completely to the wants and needs of his body. And he was damn well tired of resisting. Tired of denying himself. He deserved this one pleasure. This one kiss.

He pressed his lips against hers and closed his eyes, giving in to the sensation . . .

Books by Delilah Marvelle

MISTRESS OF PLEASURE

LORD OF PLEASURE

Published by Kensington Publishing Corporation

LORD of PLEASURE

Delilah Marvelle

ZEBRA BOOKS
Kensington Publishing Corp.
http://www.kensingtonbooks.com

ZEBRA BOOKS are published by

Kensington Publishing Corp.
119 West 40th Street
New York, NY 10018

All Kensington titles, imprints and distributed lines are available at special quantity discounts for bulk purchases for sales promotion, premiums, fund raising, educational or institutional use.

Special book excerpts or customized printings can also be created to fit specific needs. For details, write or phone the office of the Kensington Special Sales Manager: Kensington Publishing Corp., 119 West 40th Street, New York, NY 10018. Attn. Special Sales Department. Phone: 1-800-221-2647.

Zebra and the Z logo Reg. U.S. Pat. & TM Off.

ISBN-13: 978-1-4201-0449-3
ISBN-10: 1-4201-0449-7

First Printing: August 2009
10 9 8 7 6 5 4 3 2 1

Printed in the United States of America

*For Maire, who read the first chapter of this book
in its ugliest and most pitiful stage,
then glanced up at me and said as lovingly
as she knew how, "Oh, honey, no."
Thank you for ALWAYS being that
beautiful voice of reason.
At least with regard to writing.
<big grin>
You're next.*

Acknowledgments

Embarrassingly enough, I had forgotten to
thank the beautiful and glorious Sue Lute in
my last book (I could blame age, but well . . .).
Thank you, sweetie, for not only always having
a smile for me, but for all your words of
encouragement throughout the years, and
for coming to my rescue that one night in
New Orleans at Nationals when I was sorely
outnumbered by men (ehm), and also for
recommending your oh-so-fabulous agent,
Pam Hopkins. You have really good taste.
And I'm so glad to have discovered that.

Thank you to the Beau Monde and Hearts
through History, but especially Nancy Mayer,
whose endless waterfall of historical information
not only astounds me, but bloody scares the
wits out of me. I bow to you and everyone
else who goes out of their way to historically
seize each and every single day.

A massive thank-you to my editor,
John Scognamiglio, for giving me the creative
freedom to write the way my heart longs to.
You have no idea how awesome that is.
You freakin' rock.

Lesson One

'Tis truly a curse
to have no coins in your purse.
For you lose sight of all pleasure
and all means of leisure,
which makes life all the more worse.
                    —The School of Gallantry

London, England
January 1830

Being a self-respecting lady born of impeccable culture and lineage—at least on her father's side of the family—Lady Charlotte knew all too well that she was not supposed to wink, wave, smile, or nod in the direction of any man as a means of gaining attention. Especially from a hackney. But the pathetic jangling of the few coins that remained in the folds of her ribbon-drawn reticule reminded Charlotte that respectability was not only sorely exaggerated, but outright cumbersome.

Though she had tried these past few months

through various means to earn her wage most honorably, it was quite pointless. For it all ended the same. In her dismissal.

As a kitchen maid for a banker, she'd been repeatedly propositioned by his scruffy, pudgy-fingered chef to hitch up her skirts. For better pay. After she had rejected his *tasteless* advances, he eventually claimed to the mistress of the house that she always burnt the soup, curdled the milk, and evaporated the tea. All of which, of course, was untrue, but all of which, of course, had still led to her dismissal.

As a house maid for a naval captain, she'd been further humiliated and fondled in close quarters by the butler, who was as determined as he was gangly. When she grew rather tired of dodging his eager hands and threatened to report his behavior to their employer, his retaliation resounded in her ears as he marched straight into the parlor and smashed an entire collection of vases. His accusatory finger not only resulted in the loss of her pension, but also all of her references.

And, yes. It ended in her dismissal.

Sadly, the reality of her situation was this: she had no further means of earning a penny, her scoundrel of a husband was dead, and due to his overly inconsiderate nature, his entire family—including his four mistresses—continued to be well-coddled by his estate.

While she? She was left to languish in her father's unfurnished townhouse with absolutely no annuity, still waiting for the cursed Court of Chancery to award her the one-third of her husband's estate that was legally owed her. A portion of which she had brought into the marriage to begin with.

In the end, contesting her husband's will had been more of an expense than she'd expected. It wasn't until she was forced to pawn off her only corset (indeed) that she realized her financial situation was quite pressing. Not to mention depressing.

And so it was, the moment her hired carriage rolled into the most respectable part of the city, just outside of Hyde Park, Charlotte knew it was time to set aside her remaining pride and introduce herself to the genteel masses as being on the market. With all the advances she had fostered since the death of her husband, she was certain an open invitation would secure much better payment.

Or so she hoped.

Charlotte shifted toward the carriage window and nervously eyed the approaching promenade. There were worse things than selling off one's virtue. Like selling off one's only home, which had been in the family for over a hundred years. Or having to beg to her husband's family—or, heaven forbid, one of his four mistresses—who had inherited everything, knew of her plight, and yet offered nothing.

"Lord save me from myself," she muttered, glancing toward the ceiling of the carriage. "For in my desperation I know not what I do."

Pushing aside the faded wool curtains, she unlatched the small glass window and thrust it wide open, allowing a burst of frosty air to blow in. The biting gust slashed at her face, bestowing

yet another chiding reminder of how cruel
the world truly was. Fortunately, it wasn't raining.
Or snowing.

Grasping the sides of the window with her
gloved hands, Charlotte leaned out. Her large
pleated bonnet bumped against the frame of the
small window as she eyed her prospects alongside
the promenade.

She glanced in both directions, her brows
coming together. Empty? Now, how could the
promenade be empty? There had to be *some* men
left in the city. And though, yes, she knew full
well that most of the wealthy men of great import
were still in the country, she was not in any position to wait for the Season to begin.

She needed coal. And food. And needed to
pay the window taxes on her home lest the house
itself was collected. None of which even included
the long list of legal fees she still owed her lawyer.

Spying a brisk movement up ahead, Charlotte
straightened. It was a man! She prepared to
signal the driver. Then paused.

A portly old gent marched steadily along, a
polished ivory and gold cane clutched in his gray-
gloved hand. His large top hat was pulled low
against the wind, and his gaze was fixed stead-
fastly before him. As though he were charging
into battle.

Charlotte grimaced, shrinking back slightly,
and readjusted her grip on the sides of the open
window. Truth be told, debtor's prison seemed
far more appealing. Aside from the man's appearance and scowl, what concerned her even
more was the pronounced manner in which he

slammed his cane into the pavement after every other marching step.

She had no doubt that he frequently used that cane on his servants. As well as on anyone else who annoyed him. He probably also held on to his assets in the same manner in which he held on to his cane. Most possessively. Which, of course, would do her no good.

Charlotte blew out a ragged breath, sending forth a white, frosty cloud into the frigid air. To be sure, her father—God rest his soul—would be aghast. Though her mother, who had all too recently joined him, would have been rather proud of her being an opportunist. Though perhaps not too proud. Considering.

The icy wind whipped hard at her face, forcing the loose ends of the gauze ribbons tied at her chin to fly up toward the rim of her pleated bonnet. Charlotte ignored the relentless assault and leaned farther out of the swaying carriage, trying to better see down the promenade.

Two young, dark-haired bucks strolled in her direction. Oddly, both were dressed in identical outfits, with matching morning suits, cravats, boots, cloaks, and top hats. And neither seemed to notice her approach, mostly due to the fact that they were much too engaged in their conversation with one another.

As the carriage drew steadily closer, her brows rose, and she noted that their attire wasn't the only identical thing about them. Even their faces were identical. Why, they were twins!

Though the revelation should have increased her hopes, not to mention her chances, she wondered if it also increased the likelihood of a complication. She cringed, knowing she couldn't possibly take on more than one man at a time.

Before she could altogether retreat, however, the two men caught sight of her not only leaning out of the carriage window, but observing them. They instantly ceased their conversation and gawked at her. As if she was being rude.

Which she supposed she was.

Heat splashed across her chilled face. She counterfeited a smile and enthusiastically waved a gloved hand in their direction as if every respectable lady always leaned out of carriage windows. "Good day, gentlemen! Brisk morning, isn't it? Do try and keep warm." She waved again, gallantly holding on to her smile.

Both gents halted, stumbling into one another in a scrambled effort to observe her audacity, but the hackney simply rolled on, leaving them far behind.

Fortunately.

Her smile faded as she glanced about. *Unfortunately,* the promenade had come to an end and the carriage was now being directed down another empty cobblestone street.

As the last of all the wealthy homes wobbled by, Charlotte was about to direct the driver to Pall Mall—for there were always men on that street—when she glimpsed another man much farther down.

Even from the notable distance, she could tell he was a man of great import by the manner in which he carried himself. His overall demeanor demanded not only satisfaction, but the world's complete attention.

Fixing her gaze on the man, Charlotte frantically knocked on the roof of her carriage, urging the driver to desist.

The carriage came to a rapid halt, jerking her far forward and to the side. Charlotte's stomach flipped as she frantically seized hold of the sill, her feet scrambling and slipping against the carriage floor in an effort to remain upright. After a few huffing breaths, she eventually steadied herself into a stable position.

Tinged with a sense of self-consciousness, she prayed that the man hadn't witnessed her absurd theatrics and noted that he had already closed off much of the span between them, allowing her a much better view.

Charlotte couldn't help but stare as she sucked in a slow, disbelieving breath. Who knew such glorious men actually did exist?

His broad upper frame was elegantly pronounced by the exquisite cut of his double-breasted waistcoat. About a dozen brass buttons gleamed, as if very proud to be worn by such a grand species of a man. The silk gray cravat that was bound high around his neck not only framed his masculine, smooth-shaven face, but emphasized it.

His long, athletic legs, which were well fitted into a matching pair of dark wool trousers, were displayed quite delectably by the self-assured, uniform stride he kept. And on occasion, the wind treated her to a bit more by plucking up his black unfastened ankle-length coat and sending it flowing about his large, debonair frame.

Thick bronze hair, scattered by the wind, peered out from beneath his angled top hat. Although she couldn't make out the color of his eyes, she sensed they'd be as striking as the rest of him.

Charlotte tightened her grip on the windowsill until the insides of her palms ached from the pressure. If she did this, if she invited this man into the hackney—assuming he wouldn't laugh her off into next week—there would be no taking it back.

Regardless of her dire monetary situation, this would forever brand her a wanton. But then again, if there was ever a time to *be* a wanton, and in turn financially profit, it was now. With this man.

The gentleman she'd been blatantly spectating suddenly paused in his firm stride. And stared straight at her. His brows rose beneath the brim of his top hat as he glanced over his broad shoulder behind him and then back at her. He resumed his steady pace, only this time he was decidedly heading toward her. And what was worse, he looked quite determined to see what she was about.

Panic quaked through her. No. She couldn't do this. She simply couldn't!

Charlotte scrambled back into the safety of the carriage and stumbled onto the cushioned seat beside the window. She snapped up a gloved hand to send her driver off, but paused, her hand remaining stiffly poised in midair.

Her reticule slowly slid from her wrist down the length of her arm toward the puffed bombazine sleeve of her elbow, the sparse coins within chiming in reminder. She stared up at the ceiling, noting the small distance remaining between her hand and her departure. Why did a part of her wish to stay and engage him?

Because it is far better to secure this man than the next, who may resemble the foot of a horse. Charlotte sighed and dropped her hand back to her side, her reticule hitting her thigh. The truth was, there was nothing left to sell. Nothing but the house. A house she refused to part with, as it was all she had left of her parents.

Her stomach gargled. Then grumbled. Loud even to her own ears. She glared down at her uncorseted belly hidden beneath her bombazine gown. "Oh, hush," she seethed. "You had bread last night."

"I take it you scold your stomach often?" an amused, deep voice drawled through the open window of the carriage.

Charlotte froze, her eyes widening as dread overtook not only the beat of her heart but her entire body. From the corner of her eye she could see the man's well-fitted black leather glove gripping the sill of the open window.

She dared not move or face him for fear that she would encourage him out of her own desperation.

"Forgive the intrusion, Miss." He leaned in closer, his top hat preventing him from completely fitting through the window. "Was there something you needed?" His deep, low voice was now edged with genuine concern. "Assistance of any sort?"

How utterly unfair. Even his voice was divine.

Send him away, Charlotte. You needn't do this. Your virtue is worth far more than any man can pay.

Sensing the gentleman was still waiting for a reply, Charlotte turned her eyes in his direction, determined to send him off. But the moment her gaze met his striking green eyes across the small expanse between them, she knew her virtue had found a price.

For few men resembled the perfection of a Greek statue. While he? He was by far the most splendid of replications she'd ever come upon. Utter perfection, with full lips and the most incredible eyes she'd ever seen on a man.

"How much will you offer for me, sir?" she blurted out.

The moment the words tumbled from her lips, she wished to the high heavens that she could somehow retract them. For they weren't in the least bit intelligent.

Her cheeks burned. Like the rest of her.

The man's jaw tensed as his black-gloved hand slipped away from the sill and dropped to his side. He stepped back toward the pavement and into full view. His green eyes sharply penetrated her own, challenging her to recant her inquiry.

Her resolve, however, did not need to be challenged. And neither did her growling stomach.

"I was hoping you'd join me, sir," she offered again, only this time more firmly. More definitively. To show him that she was quite serious and capable of being steady minded.

His bronzed brows rose a small fraction as he glanced left then right, clearly in disbelief of his situation. He blew out a slow, pained breath, as if arguing with himself over the matter, then straightened the curved brim of his hat and turned fully in the direction opposite to which her carriage was heading. Then disappeared from view by walking on.

Charlotte lowered her eyes to her gloved hands, which continued to lay limply in her lap, and stared at the reticule dangling from her wrist. The one she had hoped to fill. At least he hadn't laughed her off into next week. Which he could have. And should have.

She pinched her lips together from the humiliation of her predicament and blinked back the tears stinging her eyes. No. She would not give in to her emotions. She would find a means to survive without selling her home. No matter what. Charlotte lifted her hand and rapped on the carriage ceiling.

"Hold!" a man yelled from outside.

The side door suddenly jumped open and the carriage tilted slightly to one side. Charlotte's eyes flew up in astonishment. It was him!

Lesson Two

When a man proclaims to be a gentleman,
you'd best gather up your skirts and run.
For what he truly seeks in turn
is what I call a bit of fun.
Now unless both parties are full
aware of this and willing,
in the end, I guarantee you,
it won't be worth a shilling.
                    —The School of Gallantry

Charlotte grabbed on to the upholstered seat of the carriage to steady herself as the man, who had earlier walked on, snatched off his hat and climbed inside. The expanse of his tall, muscled body within the small confines of the carriage was as shocking as realizing that the man was in fact accepting her offer.

He tossed his top hat onto the small seat across from her, and with an equally quick movement, slammed the carriage door shut. After latching the window, he tugged the wool curtains closed on both sides, encasing them in dull darkness.

He sat directly across from her and knocked on the roof of the hackney. As they rolled forward, Charlotte found herself practically gasping for air. She'd never done anything like this before and had certainly never been with any man aside from her husband. Though clearly, the sands of time were about to fill his absence. And how.

The tantalizing crispness of lemon and leather lingered in the air of the carriage. His scent. It tinged each and every shallow breath she drew. She stared back at the blurred outline of his body and face, knowing full well, despite the lack of good light, that he was watching her. Weighing her.

"What is your name?" he finally asked, his timbered voice filling the carriage.

She blinked, stunned by the sound of his attractive voice. "You may call me Charlotte," she replied, not wanting to disclose too much, but not wanting to lie, either.

"Charlotte," he repeated, as if enjoying the taste of her name on his lips. He shifted in his seat. "I suppose that leaves me to introduce myself in the same manner. The name is Alexander. A pleasure."

"Likewise." Alexander. Such a noble name.

He was quiet for a long moment. "I could not help but notice that you are wearing bombazine."

She swallowed and tried to quell her nervousness by smoothing the said-fabric of her gown against her knees. It was a horrid dress, she knew, that did justice to neither her face nor her figure, but it was also the best of what she owned. Sadly.

"Are you a widow?" he pressed.

She eyed him in the dimness. Something about this Alexander lured her toward a place she did not wish to be. For without a touch, he was making her stomach squeeze in anticipation. And without even being able to clearly see his face or his eyes, she found herself wanting to indulge and lose herself to him. Completely.

She eventually nodded in response to his question, only to realize he probably couldn't see her all that well. "Yes. I am. A widow." Though she wasn't by any means in mourning for the bastard. Rather, for her mother.

Silence settled between them as the carriage wheels clattered and droned relentlessly against the cobbled street. What unnerved her most about his overall presence was not knowing what he was thinking. Or what he had in mind for her.

He leaned forward in his seat, the heat of his body drifting toward her in the small space of the carriage. "Am I to be your first? Or do you proposition others often?"

Much to her annoyance, Charlotte felt herself not only blushing but outright trembling. What sort of questions were these anyway? This was *not* what she had volunteered herself for. She needed money. Not more drama.

She set her chin. "I apologize, but I am not interested in becoming any more acquainted than is necessary. I am asking for twenty pounds. Now either get on with it, or I shall have to ask you to leave."

"You should be asking for more than twenty pounds." He rose from his seat and, after a small pause, turned and settled himself unnervingly close beside her, making an already small space even smaller.

She jolted backward, instinctively wanting to escape him. Her head bumped the side wall of the carriage, causing her to wince. In turn, her bonnet shifted to one side, exposing not only her neck to him but also the side of her face and her dark, coiffed hair. She remained frozen as his large body further cupped her into the corner seat.

"So, what is your definition of getting on with it?" he whispered into her exposed ear, his warmth sweeping her entire cheek. "I, for one, would love to know."

Her eyes widened and her breath now escaped in a panicked stream. It was obvious he knew her bonnet was ill placed and that he was enjoying it. Though, oddly, not half as much as she was.

"Whatever would give you the most pleasure," she managed, astonished that she could actually form a coherent, not to mention sincere, reply.

"My dear, dear Charlotte." His heated breath caressed her ear. "I do believe I fear for you. Because more than one definitive form of pleasure comes to my mind whilst in your presence."

More than one definitive form of pleasure? She swallowed. How many did he have in mind?

"However," he continued ever so softly, "I confess that I am far more interested in understanding what your needs are and hope that you'll indulge my curiosity."

His hushed voice entranced her and captured whatever was left of her sanity. She wet her lips but otherwise dared not move for fear that she would somehow bring an end to these delicious sensations swelling within her. "My needs are . . . quite basic, really."

At that moment, she couldn't define her needs aloud. Even if she'd tried. He was blurring everything. Her sight, her thoughts, her senses. The reason why she was even doing this.

His large hand brushed the length of her thigh, ever so gently. Ever so playfully. The heat of his attentive fingertips, which continued to rub her thigh, seared straight through the layers of her gown, chemise, and stockings. "A beautiful woman such as yourself should be demanding far more than mere basics."

Charlotte felt herself fading to his touch. It was so overwhelmingly tender, yet firm, promising to offer so much more than she could have ever imagined from a stranger.

His hand slid up slowly toward her waist. And paused. "No corset?"

She would have gladly explained the demise of her poor corset, but couldn't seem to form anything outside of a monosyllabic word. "No."

His gloved hand continued up toward her right breast. "Less interference is always good."

He provocatively grazed her nipple. It hardened at his touch beneath the fabric of her gown and sent a shiver through the rest of her. She bit her lower lip to prevent herself from gasping. It had been far too long since she'd been touched with such purpose.

His hand traveled farther upward and did not pause until it reached the tied ribbons beneath her chin. He slowly tugged them loose. Both tumbled down, brushing the hollow of her neck in their wake.

The feathery touch of cool leather met her exposed skin, sending countless sensations not only throughout her entire body, but *there*. It was as if he knew that every deliberate touch he bestowed upon her was capable of unlacing both her body and her mind.

He bent his head toward her as his hand nudged her bonnet from her head. Her bonnet dropped onto the edge of her lap, then slid away and vanished into the darkness at her feet.

Before she could entirely recover, his hot, moist lips grazed her forehead. Then moved on to the bridge of her nose. How divine that he'd consider her forehead and her nose above anything else.

Charlotte closed her eyes and waited in a mind-whirling daze for his trailing kisses to lead to her lips. The anticipation of having his lips upon hers left her all the more breathless, and in some way she could almost consider it payment enough. Almost.

He descended with his lips again and kissed her . . . *cheek?* She frowned and opened her eyes, not knowing why she felt so disappointed. This was supposed to be a mere business transaction, after all, and yet . . .

"Close your eyes," he murmured from beside her on the seat.

Her frown deepened. How did he know her eyes were open? She herself could barely make out the fuzzy outline of his face.

"Close your eyes," he urged again. His other gloved hand grasped her waist and dragged her closer to him. If that was even possible.

The scent of lemon and leather coated her skin and pulled her deeper into a heated, swirling world of pleasure. He pressed his body against hers, his muscled arms tightening. She felt herself drowning in his strong, possessive embrace.

Charlotte instantly surrendered to the over-whelming sensation of his warmth and allowed her eyes to flutter shut. Though she was by no means innocent of the ways between a man and a woman, and had experienced moments of marital pleasure at the hands of her own husband, this moment between them was sinfully unusual. For it felt sincere and tender. Yet so breathtakingly intense.

"Where do you live?" He kissed her cheek.

"Live?" The question drifted from her mouth as she longed for more of him. Somehow, nothing he could ask of her would be too much. "Berwick," she breathed.

"And the number, love?"

As his tongue slid down the side of her cheek toward her neck, she fought back a moan and melted against him.

"I . . . forgive me," she murmured against him, trying to remain coherent. "But I . . . I do not know you well enough to trust you with it."

He slid his tongue down toward her lips and licked her lower lip hard, completely soaking it with his warmth. "Would you like to know me well enough?"

"Eleven." Did she actually say it or was that a

faint echo in her mind? Nothing in that moment seemed real.

He flicked his tongue across her upper lip, sending a delicious shiver throughout the length of her body, down to the tips of her fingers and toes.

"You wouldn't lie to me, Charlotte? Would you?"

She tilted her face more toward him, hoping he would end her misery once and for all and simply kiss her. Hoping he would completely cover her mouth with his and ignite more of these wild sensations that were reaching an unsurpassed height. "I do not lie."

"Good." He leaned far back, snatching away the heat she'd grown rather fond of, and blew out what sounded like an exhausted breath. Rising, he flung open the curtains of the carriage on both sides, unlatched a window, and yelled out, "11 Berwick Street! And be quick about it!"

Charlotte sat up against the seat in complete horror, her lips parting as light splashed across her eyes and reality set in. Brainless is what she was. Brainless. "What are you doing?" she demanded.

"Be still." He snatched up her bonnet from her feet, leaned toward her, and dropped it gently onto her head.

She blinked up at him in disbelief as he proceeded to not only straighten the bonnet against her head, but tuck loose locks of her dark hair back into place. He leaned in closer, his handsome shaven face now merely inches from hers, and appeared genuinely occupied with gathering up the gauze ribbons. As if he tied bonnets on a regular basis. His large gloved hands worked beneath her chin, attempting to secure them in place.

"What are you . . . *Enough!*" She shoved his hands away and pushed him back, sending him stumbling rearward into the upholstered seat across from her. "You are *not* inviting yourself into my home."

His hard landing sent them both bouncing within their seats. He adjusted his long coat about himself, then smacked his top hat down onto his lap and glared at her.

"I have absolutely no intention of inviting myself into your home," he snapped. "I am merely *escorting* you home to ensure that you don't offer yourself up again to the next man on the street. Do you have any idea how stupid and dangerous that is?"

A gasp escaped her, and all she could do was gape at him. Why, he had meant to escort her home all along. And she didn't know whether she was supposed to be insulted at the idea of being treated like a naughty child, or grateful at the idea that he cared. That is, cared after taking great liberties with her person!

He shook his bronzed head, causing his combed hair to fall out of place. "A woman of your good breeding ought to know better."

She narrowed her gaze and refrained from outright slapping him. "And what would you know of my good breeding? I hardly supplied you with a list."

"Your speech, your mannerisms, not to mention your level of experience, betray you. You, love, are no widow. Merely parading yourself as one. Though worry not." He leaned forward and winked. "Your naughty little secret shall rest well with me."

His astonishingly rude assessment of her situation strangled the last bit of patience out of her. "I refuse to be insulted by your twisted sense of judgment. You know nothing of me or my situation." She pointed toward the door. Repeatedly. "Now get out."

He laughed, amusement flickering within his eyes. "Or what?" He held up his gloved hand and grew theatrically serious. "You'll ravage me?"

"Remove yourself at once!" She pointed toward the door again, still hating the fact that she had actually enjoyed his devious hoax of an advance. "Before I have the driver toss you into a pile of rubbish where you belong."

He dropped his hand back to his side, leaned far back into his seat, making himself quite comfortable, and eyed her. "Let us say, for a moment, that I believe you. Which I don't. Whose widow are you? Would I know of him?"

Everyone in the upper crust of London society knew of Chartwell. Just as everyone also knew how he'd been shot through the heart—and rightfully so—by one of his many jealous mistresses while at the opera with his latest coquette. The poor, misguided woman was promptly hanged, and Charlotte's life forever changed.

"No," she said in a firm, clipped tone. "You would not know of him."

He smirked. "Because he doesn't exist. Does he?"

Charlotte set her lips into a rigid, thin line, the heat of her body reaching a level it had never reached in her entire life. She'd had enough of this. Of him.

"It is time for you to leave." She snapped up her hand to knock on the roof of the carriage.

He jumped forward and caught hold of her wrist. "Not until we get you home."

Charlotte yelped as he yanked her by the wrist, forcing her forward in her seat. He pressed her gloved hand tightly against his knee, against his warmth. Though she tried repeatedly to pry herself loose, he continued to hold her wrist firmly in place.

She glared up at him. "How dare you! Unhand me!"

He leaned toward her, trying to level himself to her lowered height, but the top hat sitting on his lap prevented him from doing so. His playful gaze searched her face as he continued to closely hover above her. "Why are you so miffed? I am merely a gentleman seeing to your virtue. You ought to be thanking me. Not verbally spanking me."

Such charm. Such wit. Or so *he* thought. She mocked a laugh. "I'll have you know that a real gentleman would have never taken advantage of a lady the way you did. I think you rather enjoyed yourself."

He coolly stared down at her, not at all budging from the close, awkward position they continued to share. "Actually, yes. I did enjoy myself."

His eyes trailed down to her lips before meeting her gaze again. "Which is why it is absolutely imperative we remove you from my presence at once. Otherwise, I'll not be held accountable for what I *really* have in mind for you."

Her breath hitched in her throat, and for a moment she could have sworn her heart had stopped beating altogether. For he said it as if he meant it.

The carriage rolled to an unexpected halt, sending her flying toward him. She jerked back, trying to distance herself from the alluring warmth of his body, but found herself stumbling back at him.

She glanced down at her wrist. Her eyes widened, realizing he was still holding on to her.

"Eleven Berwick Street!" the driver called out in a muffled voice.

Her gaze snapped up and met his alluring green eyes that boldly and silently challenged her to indulge in what he had to offer. Although a part of her was rather curious as to what he was physically capable of, a much larger part of her knew she might not survive.

A sense of panic settled in on her. "Unhand me," she hoarsely whispered. She commenced to rigidly strain against his firm grip. "Unhand me!"

He grinned. Then released her hand.

"*Oh!*" Charlotte stumbled back from her own momentum and lost her footing with a skid. Her bum bounced down onto the hard carriage floor, scattering her bombazine skirts up and around her.

"Why, you knave!" she huffed out, tucking her

skirts around her exposed legs. "You *meant* to do that!"

"Learn from it. Had you engaged anyone else, it might have ended differently." Grabbing hold of her waist, he plucked her up off the floor as though she were a mere doll and set her back up into the seat behind her. He pointed at her. "Now do something with your bonnet. We can't have your neighbors thinking you're on the market."

The way the man carried on, she was beginning to believe he was used to dusting off paths after himself.

He turned and snatched up his hat from the seat. As he brushed past, his gloved hand came down and out and purposefully grazed the side of her thigh hidden beneath the layers of her gown. He smiled down at her.

Her heart skittered as she froze against the seat.

Without sparing her another glance, he threw open the carriage door and jumped out. The cool air from outside the carriage whipped in, shocking her overheated body.

His black-gloved hand snapped back inside, toward her, offering his gentlemanly mannerisms to the end.

As if she were going to take it.

Tying the ribbons beneath her chin, she jerked the bow tightly into place and gathered up her gown from around her feet. She moved for the door, jumped down onto the cobbled street, and hurried past him and his extended hand.

She paused and peered up toward her townhouse. Sure enough, the unpainted house, and all of its blasted windows she had yet to pay taxes on, loomed before her. Though the window tax was the least of her worries. Her lawyer was going to be demanding legal fees again. Fees she could no longer afford.

Charlotte blew out a disgusted breath and shook her head. What an utter waste of a day. She turned and marched toward the front of the carriage, where the driver sat, knowing she had no choice but to pay for her ride, as she certainly wasn't going to allow this *Alexander* to pay.

The bearded driver reached out a dirty, wool-covered hand and knowingly grinned down at her from his seat, showing off sparse, yellow teeth.

"I'll mind you to keep all that happiness to yourself, sir," she snapped up at him. Gritting her teeth, she dug her fingers into her reticule, loosening the ribbon that held it shut.

"Here." Alexander stepped between her and the driver and offered up a banknote. A ten-pound banknote, to be precise.

She glared at him. "A tenner? Are you mad? I wasn't driving about all year."

He bit back what she knew to be a smile. "One would hope." He reverted his gaze to the driver, still holding up the banknote. "Your silence is much appreciated, sir."

The driver reached out and snatched up the money. "I be appreciatin' me own silence more than you, governa." He winked and tipped his dusty hat at them.

"Good man." Alexander pointed toward the

opposite direction. "Take me to Brooks's and your day is done."

The man nodded and shifted in his seat.

Alexander turned back toward her. The way he continued to silently stare down at her, with that firm stance and set mouth, she half expected him to start preaching to her about the sins of the world.

She smirked up at him, noting how lopsided his top hat was, despite his serious gaze. "Your hat is crooked."

"I like it crooked. It's more comfortable." With that, he stepped closer and, to her surprise, grabbed up her gloved hand.

Though she tried to pull it away, he tightened his hold and brought her fingers up firmly to his lips. Then kissed them.

Her heart jumped from the applied pressure of those lips as their heat seeped through her glove and into the skin of her hand. How and why did this man continue to affect her so? It defied all common logic.

"Hold on to your virtue," he murmured over her fingers. His gaze intently met hers. "It's worth far more than I or any other could ever afford to pay."

He released her hand and touched the rim of his hat in salutation. He then spun away, climbed back into the carriage, and slammed the door shut behind him.

The driver snapped the reins and off they clattered.

Charlotte swiped at the top of her hand, where his lips had been, wishing she could remove the very thought of him as easily as she could remove her glove. Him and his insufferable ways. Why, he gave the driver ten pounds. And her? Mere advice. After a bit of indulging!

A gentleman? No. He most certainly was not.

Lesson Three

Many times the past has an odd way
of making its way into the present.
And many times, I confess,
the results can be quite pleasant.
—The School of Gallantry

11 Berwick Street
Late morning, the following day

"Is anyone at home?" The pounding against the front door continued. "Anyone? *Anyone at all?*"

Charlotte tightened her grip on the iron poker she'd snatched up when the man first came to the door. For some impertinent reason, he refused to leave. She was certain that the lawyer had sent him to collect the last payment she'd missed. Quite certain.

"What is it that you want?" she finally yelled through the bolted door. "My employer doesn't permit me to associate with anyone who doesn't have an appointment." A fib, for she lived entirely alone, but much warranted. She knew better than to open the door to every Jack who wanted in. Especially when said Jack was being sent by someone who wanted money. Money she did not have.

There was a pause. "I certainly hope this here delivery counts for an appointment, Miss!" the man hollered back.

Charlotte frowned and edged closer to the smooth surface of the door. The good news was that he wasn't looking to collect money. The not-so-good news was that she hadn't ordered anything. Which meant that most likely he would still be looking to collect money.

"What is it?" she demanded through the door. "Is it paid for? Because if it isn't, take it away!"

The man grumbled on the other side. "I don't know what it is, Miss!" He was clearly losing his patience. "Though, yes, it's been paid for! It be urgent, I was told! Ain't allowed to even set it down! Now, be a good lass and open this here door! I don't get paid until it's delivered, and I've six mouths to feed!" He pounded against the door again, with what had to have been his foot.

Though she was hesitant to open the door, she sensed that the man was in fact genuine. Otherwise he wouldn't be so rude. Or persistent.

Shifting the poker into her other hand, she quickly unbolted the door, edged it open, and peered at the mustached man whose face was bright red against the strain of the large trunk he held.

"Forced to use my damn boot to knock, I was," the man grumbled on, shifting beneath the weight of his delivery.

"My apologies, sir. My employer refuses to be disturbed when unnecessary." Charlotte threw the door farther open and stepped back, hiding the iron poker behind her while taking on the persona of a humble maid. "Set it right here in the corridor."

The man stumbled forward with the trunk then set it on the floor. Blowing out a breath, he glanced about the bare corridor and the adjoining empty parlor. "Your employer just moved in, did he?" He glanced toward her.

"Uh . . . yes." She smiled tightly and gestured with her free hand to the door. "Thank you."

The man nodded curtly and hurried out.

Charlotte slammed the door behind him, thankful to be rid of him, then set the poker into the corner next to the door and bolted all four locks. Leaning her forehead against the cool surface of the wood, she huffed out a breath, hating how utterly defenseless she always felt. Even in her own home. There had to be a better way to live. There simply had to be.

She pushed herself away from the door and slowly turned toward the large leather trunk at her feet. What could possibly be in it? And who could it be from?

Kneeling, she ran her bare hands along the length of the thick, leather straps holding it shut. The trunk alone was worth a solid pound.

She tilted her head to the side and slowly unbuckled each strap. She then pushed the lid back and let it fall open with a thud. Charlotte blinked. Several embroidered full muslin gowns, trimmed with lace and satin, were neatly folded atop one another, creating a contrasting array of lovely pastel colors.

A folded parchment sealed with red wax had been set on them. She caught her breath and plucked up the letter. She had an inkling as to who they could be from, yet refused to acknowledge it.

The letter *H* was deeply embedded into the pressed, hard red wax. Cracking apart the seal, she hastily unfolded the parchment and was surprised to find only a single sentence neatly scribed in black ink.

"More to come," she read aloud. "Sincerely, H."

More to come? She gurgled out a laugh. She needed money for legal fees, taxes, coal, and food. Not bundles of silk and lace to flounce about in.

Charlotte slowly turned over the parchment paper, wondering if it was from *him*—this Alexander. Though there was no other written form of correspondence inscribed upon it, she knew it was him. Who else would be so bold and cheeky?

She flung the letter aside and hovered over the large open trunk, examining the dresses without touching them.

The amount of detail embroidered into the pale pink muslin of the most visible gown was astounding. White and yellow stitched flowers, both small and large, lined the long sleeves and tucked waist. The collar was trimmed with matching pale pink satin and yellow lace. All signs of expensive tailoring. Even the buttons trailing down the sleeves were made from teardrop pearls. None of which could have been tailored overnight.

Which only meant . . .

Dread swept through her as she continued to stare at the dresses. What if these were his wife's gowns? It would certainly explain his hypocritical behavior in the carriage. Yes. *H*. For hypocrite.

He'd been guilt stricken and thought it best to humiliate her with a scolding, though not until after he'd helped himself to a bit of this and that. She should have known such a good-looking man would have already been spoken for.

Charlotte sifted through each and every gown, searching for proof that they indeed were secondhand garments. Initials, perhaps. A subtle stain. A small tear. But there was nothing. Not even a hint of female perfume.

Agitated, she tossed all eight gowns aside, onto the back lid of the trunk. And paused. For there, at the bottom of the velvet–lined trunk, was a beautiful rose-colored corset made of satin. All the busks were perfectly tucked into place, as were the set of matching laces.

He would remember.

Charlotte reached in and poked at it, shifting the corset and rustling something beneath it in the process. She poked at it again, curiosity sparking her, and eventually exposed what lay beneath. Her hand stilled and her eyes widened at the tidy pile of crisp-looking banknotes. At least a dozen of them. At about ten pounds each.

Charlotte jerked her hand away from the trunk and wiped it against the side of her bombazine gown. This could only really mean one thing. He intended to collect in one form or another. For no man ever offered such blatant generosity without asking for payment in return.

"*Hold on to your virtue,* says he," she grouched aloud. "*It's worth far more than I or any other could ever afford to pay,* says he. I am not a charity case, Mr. H."

Though she was by no means a fool, either. She needed this. Which is what agitated her most. She hated the idea of being at the mercy of others.

Pinching her lips together, Charlotte reached out and angrily forced every dress back into the trunk, not at all caring that they were being brutally mangled.

She'd simply sell them all. For each and every touch and kiss he'd claimed under false pretenses. And if he thought that his trunk of charity was going to earn him a place between her legs, there was an iron poker waiting for him. For she was more than done meeting the needs and pleasures of a man. She had her own needs to focus on. And that is exactly what she meant to do.

A loud thud resounded from deep within the walls.

Charlotte's gaze snapped up, her pulse fluttering. She stared down the length of the narrow, shadowed passageway before her, just past the staircase, where the dull, gray morning light from the windows did not reach.

She slowly stood and eyed the walls around her. Was that the movement of . . . *rats?* Oh, how she hoped not. They sounded about the size of raccoons.

Dragging in a harsh breath, she inched backward, toward the door, then reached out behind her and snagged her trustworthy weapon from the corner.

Another thud resounded in the corridor, this time vibrating the floorboards beneath her slippered feet. She glanced up toward the ceiling and noticed dust particles floating down from the empty space where the crystal chandelier that she had sold off had once been. They drifted down like snow.

Panic swelled her throat shut. The house! What was happening? What—

The sharp cracking of splintering wood roared against her ears, and the next thing she knew, part of the oak-paneled wall on the far end of the corridor flew off and crashed against the opposite wall beneath the staircase. A giant, heavyset man with a mop of curly hair, dressed in full dark livery, stumbled out of the wall and into the corridor.

Charlotte released a high-pitched scream and blindly raised the poker up over her head, waiting for the beast to rush at her.

Yet the giant merely stood there, looking quite dazed himself as a plume of dust floated and settled in around him. He rubbed at his head with a large hand and glanced about. "Where am I?"

Charlotte refused to lower the poker wavering above her head. "What do you mean where are you?" she choked out. "You're in my home, is where you are! In. My. Home. Now get out! *Out!*"

"*Harold.*" A heavy French-accented female voice drifted out toward them from somewhere within the gaping hole in the wall. "*Mon Dieu!* What did you do?"

Charlotte's brows shot up in continued disbelief as a beautiful, silver-haired, voluptuous woman dressed in a pale blue morning gown breezed out of the wall and into the corridor, holding up a glass lantern. She delicately coughed and waved away the settling dust, the glowing lantern swaying in her gloved hand.

Merciful heavens. Where were these people coming from?

The giant reached out and took hold of the woman's lantern, looking rather sheepish.

The older woman set her gloved hands onto her corseted waist and glared up at the giant. "I asked that you find a door. Not make one." She gestured toward their surroundings. "Och, look at this mess. Terrible. Terrible."

The giant winced. "My apologies, Madame. I misunderstood."

The woman sighed and shook her head, her silver chignon bobbing. "Gather it. Make it tidy." She then glanced at Charlotte and halted. An arched silver brow went up as she gracefully turned in her direction.

Charlotte blinked and lowered her weapon, still somewhat stunned by the unfolding scene.

"*Bonjour,* Mademoiselle. I am Madame de Maitenon."

The woman sashayed toward her, her full skirts rustling and shifting elegantly around her as the tips of her powder blue satin slippers occasionally peered out. She paused at the foot of the large trunk that sat between them. The woman, standing about a head taller than Charlotte, swept a rather appreciative gaze across the length of Charlotte's figure.

Charlotte tried not to squirm beneath the blatant scrutiny of those firm, blue eyes. The woman's presence, though not in the least bit intimidating, was rather overwhelming. Something about her reminded Charlotte of music, champagne, wine, and chocolate rolls. All of which she had once loved so dearly but could no longer afford to indulge in.

"We French usually have more manners than this, I assure you." Madame de Maitenon waved her hand about, sending a waft of crisp mint in Charlotte's direction. "You see, while remodeling my new home a few months ago, the workers discovered a sealed door hidden beneath the panels of the wall. Odd, *non?* Which is why when the work had been completed, I instructed Harold here to remove it. And *voilà!* We discovered a spiral staircase leading down into a mysterious tunnel. I admit I have not been this excited in years."

Madame de Maitenon lowered her hand and smiled, the wrinkled edges of her eyes brightening every aspect of her oval face. "So. What number did we arrive at? We must be at least three or four townhouses in."

Charlotte's brows rose in astonishment. No. It wasn't possible. And yet . . . it had to be. This woman had actually unearthed the Sutton Tunnel. The same tunnel her great-grandfather had created as a means of visiting his mistress without the world knowing.

According to her mother, every Sutton had made use of it in some manner or another. Although her father was the one to ultimately

mend all their naughty ways. Upon marrying her
mother, he boarded up the entrance and had
workers bury it within the walls of the house—as
a noble gesture and proof that his love for her
would never require him to stray.

Charlotte released a shaky breath and tossed
aside the iron poker, sending it clattering against
the wooden floor. "I wish to see the tunnel. Might
I see it?"

Madame de Maitenon swept a hand in the direction of the corridor behind them. "*Mais oui.*
It is yours, after all."

Gathering up her skirts, Charlotte hurried in
the direction of the giant still gathering all the
splintered wood which had been scattered across
the passageway. She paused just outside the darkened entrance of the tunnel.

Moist, cold air pushed through the opening,
kissing her skin with luscious mystery. Rotting
wood and the smell of mold filled her nostrils,
hinting of secrets long buried.

A small smile tugged at her lips as she eyed the
uneven stonework that lined the short, jagged, rec-
tangular entrance. She stepped toward it. Reaching out her hand, she slid a lone finger across its
cool, stone surface. It appeared that the door had
long been removed, or perhaps had even rotted
out. For only the iron hinges remained intact.

She had always thought the Sutton Tunnel had
been nothing but a fanciful tale woven by her
mother, who had always playfully challenged her
to find it. Yet it appeared that the Sutton Tunnel
had finally found her. Long after her mother's
death.

Tears blurred Charlotte's sight. Overwhelmed, she squeezed her eyes shut, trying to prevent the drops from overflowing as renewed regret seized her. Regret for having ever trusted Chartwell.

For it wasn't until she had intercepted a pleading letter from one of her mother's servants, a letter that remained half-burnt between the coals of the hearth, that she discovered the horrid truth. That her mother hadn't been angry with her for marrying Chartwell, as she'd thought. That, in fact, her mother's silence had been caused by Chartwell himself, who thought her mother was a nuisance. This coming from a man who couldn't keep his trousers buttoned.

Though by then, it was too late. She had only been fortunate enough to see her mother one last time before she'd passed. Twelve days after her mother's death, while Charlotte remained locked in her bedchamber, grieving and unable to cope, Chartwell left for the opera. And never returned.

Well. He did. But in a pine box.

To be sure, if his disgruntled mistress hadn't up and shot him that night, Charlotte knew she herself would have. In the name of her mother.

It was moments like these that Charlotte wished she could have her mother back. To prove to her how much she loved her. How much she missed her. For there was still so much in life to discover, to cherish, and to experience, and it seemed hardly fair that she was now left all alone to do it.

"You know of this tunnel?" the French-accented voice asked from down the corridor.

Charlotte reopened her eyes, sniffed, and removed her hand from the edge of the doorway. "Yes," she murmured. "My mother shared its history with me after my father had passed due to illness. I was eleven. I never thought the tunnel actually existed."

"Ah. So you grew up in this house?"

Charlotte half nodded. "Yes."

"And what is your name, Mademoiselle? I do not believe we were ever properly introduced."

Charlotte slowly turned to the woman, her hand leaving the doorway, and met the woman's gaze from down the corridor. There was an inherent, proud strength in those blue eyes. A strength she felt oddly compelled to admire and trust. "I am Lady Chartwell. The only child of the late Lord and Lady Sutton."

Madame de Maitenon's eyes visibly widened as she hurried toward her and closed the distance between them. "You are Lady Sutton's daughter? And the widow of Chartwell, no less? I have never been one to judge based upon gossip, for there are those who gossip against me, but when I first met your husband at a gathering shortly before his death last year, strutting about like a rooster with clucking hens on every arm and every leg, I knew exactly what he was. Brusque. It isn't any wonder it all ended the way it did. And what he did to you after his death!" She tsked. "Leaving you nothing. While his family merrily tossed you from the estate without so much as a skirt. Or a *jupe,* as we French would say."

Charlotte felt her cheeks flare. It sounded even worse coming from the lips of a stranger. She did leave the estate with an entire wardrobe and close to one hundred pounds. That is, until all the legal fees started accruing. "Rumors are not always as they seem, Madame. I have done fairly well for myself. Considering." After all, she had managed to hold on to her family's London home this past year. A triumph in and of itself.

"And if you must know," Charlotte added, "I am actually awaiting a sizable settlement from the Lord Chancellor himself regarding my part of the estate. Word should be arriving from the courts any day now." She hoped.

Madame de Maitenon was quiet for a prolonged moment. She glanced at the tunnel beside them, then peered back at Harold, who was still dutifully piling splintered pieces of wood into several neat stacks.

Eventually, Madame de Maitenon turned back toward her, eyes ablaze with unusual mischief. "Aside from all the costs of the damage done to your home, how much will you take for your tunnel?"

Charlotte blinked. "Whatever do you mean?"

"The tunnel." Madame de Maitenon brushed at the sleeves of her gown, which still harbored some of the settling dust around them. "I need it. For my school."

How . . . *odd*. "For your school?"

"*Oui*. It opens in mid-May. A little later than I would have hoped, but it will still give me enough time to do all that I have planned for the Season."

Silence hung between them.

Charlotte expected the woman to further elaborate, yet clearly the woman felt as if she had said enough. "Will it be a school for children?" Charlotte prodded, hoping to the high heavens that the woman didn't intend to shuffle orphans through the tunnel for some evil purpose.

Madame de Maitenon let out a small, playful laugh. "Men can be like children. Can they not?"

Charlotte's brows came together. "*Men?* I apologize. I do not think I understand."

Madame de Maitenon sighed. "Of course you do not. No one understands. And that is the problem. No one is willing to assist an old Frenchwoman with a dream. I assure you, if I were younger it would be different. Much different."

Charlotte couldn't help but feel a twinge of empathy. For she certainly understood what it was like to have no form of aid. "What sort of assistance do you require? Could I be of any help?"

Madame de Maitenon shook her silver head while wrinkling her small nose. "Och, *non. Non.* It would not be worthy of you. You are, after all, *a lady.*"

Charlotte felt a pinch of agitation as she crossed her arms over her chest. It seemed everyone was using that excuse as of late. If being a lady was going to keep her from eating and living her life, then she'd rather be anything but. "That is for me to decide, Madame, is it not? Now if you please. I would like to know more about your school."

Madame de Maitenon paused, then relented with a dramatic sigh. "My school. *Oui.* It is—how shall I say this?—*spécial.* It will educate men in the art of love and seduction. And since its conception, I confess I have fretted and fretted over how I was going to protect the identities of my *étudi-*

ants. And *voilà*, your tunnel appears! Why, with
your house and your tunnel, I will be able to keep
the identities of my *étudiants* hidden from the
world. London shall watch me walk in and out of
my school every day, but they will never see a
single man do the same. 'Tis brilliant, *non?* For
however long it lasts."

Charlotte blinked. No wonder no one was assisting the poor woman. Because no man would
ever willingly sign up for such a thing. Not unless
he had a cocked pistol to his head. "Are you
being quite serious?"

Madame de Maitenon lowered her chin. "Do
you believe that men innately understand women
and their true desires?"

Charlotte genuinely laughed and rolled her
eyes. "I have yet to meet such a man."

Madame de Maitenon smiled triumphantly.
"You see. Which is why my school will be a success.
Now." She gestured toward the tunnel beside
them. "I am willing to offer whatever it is you want
for it. I can pay weekly or monthly. You decide."

This was rather a stunning turn of events. And
one, she confessed, she much preferred over a
trunk full of dresses. Or waiting around for the
courts to make a decision.

Charlotte eyed the woman. "What is the name
of this school?"

Madame de Maitenon held up her hands as if
displaying a large brass plaque. "I call it *Madame
Thérèse's School of Gallantry.*" She said it so proudly,
so majestically, there was no doubt the woman
believed it would be a success.

A school that would actually educate men on

the topic of a woman's pleasure? Why hadn't *she* thought of that? If only these lessons could be mandated by law. Then real progress would be made in this world. "And aside from the tunnel," Charlotte ventured, "is there anything else I could assist you with?"

The woman lowered her hands and offered a small smile. "Well. As pretty as you are, I have no doubt you could be an enticement when the men come in with their applications. *Perhaps . . .*" She shrugged her slim shoulders as if coming up with small tasks. "Perhaps you would be willing to help during the interview process? I still have not found someone for that."

"An interview process?" That sounded rather complicated. Considering what it was they were applying for.

"*Oui.* I cannot have merely anyone walking into my school. I must be selective if I am to uphold its authenticity. Even with regard to those I originally invited. You see, not everyone knows about this school. I sent off fifty-three private advertisements to a select number of titled men whom I knew would benefit from what I have to offer. Men whom I have met, heard of, or had been recommended to me as worthy of my help. So you see, these men will need a lady's finesse. A finesse in understanding what a pearl this school truly will be. Especially in the beginning. I have a good feeling you will be able to guide them most beautifully in this. After all, you have a charming, noble, and most commanding air to you."

Charlotte pulled in her chin at the thought of herself greeting titled men during their application to a school bound for scandal. "And what if someone recognizes me? Though I have no family to speak of, Chartwell kept a large circle of friends." Not to mention a large circle of enemies.

Madame de Maitenon tilted her head slightly and puckered her lips as she perused the length of Charlotte's body. "Let them recognize you. It will bring more men. And more men means more money."

Charlotte bit back a smile. She had to admit, the idea was rather intriguing. It wasn't as if she had a reputation to lose. Or anything else for that matter. Besides, she needed the money. And depending on how well the school did, perhaps she'd even be able to indulge in chocolate rolls again. And champagne.

Madame de Maitenon reached out and grasped Charlotte's shoulders, delivering more of that heavenly scent of mint. "Understand, *chérie,* that I have not even told my own granddaughter, Maybelle, about the school. It is a concept even she would have trouble accepting. Which is why if I intend to be successful in this, I will need alliances. People I can trust to do my bidding. People like you."

Charlotte glanced over at the giant, who now towered beside them. He sighed and wiped his dusty, massive hands against the expanse of his livery. She would certainly be better protected. And wouldn't need to be at the mercy of male charity. What was even more promising was that the men of London would finally receive a good spanking of an education that each and every one of them deserved.

Charlotte stepped outside the woman's grasp and stuck out her right hand, announcing in a business-minded tone, "The tunnel is at your service, Madame. As am I."

The woman grabbed Charlotte's bare hand with both of hers and shook it excitedly, a laugh bubbling from her lips. "*Magnifique!*"

Madame de Maitenon released her and swept a gloved hand toward the entrance of the tunnel. "Now allow me to show you what is on the other side. For that is where the *réel* adventure begins. Harold? Come. Lead the way."

Lesson Four

*So you think you are a knight in bright, shining
armor? Pray, humor me, and think again.
Has no one ever told you the reason why
so many knights carry such large, wooden
lances? Why, it's because they're all desperately
trying to make up for all those lost female glances.*
—The School of Gallantry

London
Early May 1830, morning

Alexander William Baxendale, the third Earl of
Hawksford, had never once lost a wager. Not in all
of his one and thirty years. And it had nothing to
do with luck, really. Luck had never existed in his
realm. Nor did he believe it existed in any realm,
despite what some people—namely Caldwell—
thought. It was simply a matter of having an
innate understanding of what was possible and
what was impossible. And anyone who thought
differently ought to be shot. Preferably in the ass.

No, he was by no means a fool. But. If there was one wager he knew he could always win, it almost invariably involved a woman. For he understood them. A bit too well.

Though only those under the age of fifty.

And Caldwell, the damn son of a bitch, had had the temerity to take advantage of that. Which is why Alexander was now in the rot he was in, being led God knows where.

"Oh, come, Hawksford." Caldwell, who sat on the opposite side of the carriage, tapped the side of Alexander's leather boot with his own. "Lady Waverly may be two and seventy and oh so proper, but that doesn't mean she isn't interested in hitching up her skirts. Or pulling down your trousers. I told you that battle-ax has been trying to get her hands on you all these years."

Alexander pinned Caldwell with a hard stare, trying not to think about what he'd endured in the name of their wager. "You still haven't elaborated as to how she got into my house. Or into my bedchamber."

Caldwell slowly grinned, his dark brown eyes practically sparkling. "Women always find a way to get what they want. The fact that Lady Waverly not only entered your house but wanted to ride you all night long proves that your viewpoint about respectable women closing their gates after fifty is absurd. Some women, much like Lady Waverly—or your mother, for that matter—flourish rather splendidly after a certain age."

"Do *not* bring my mother into this," Alexander warned, not in the least bit amused.

"Oh, stop grouching about your losses. It's

been a good year since you and I have had any fun, and I for one mean to change that." He paused, his grin somewhat fading. "In a way."

"*Fun?*" Alexander leaned far forward in his seat and poked a gloved finger toward Caldwell, missing his knee by an inch. "Whatever nonsense you have planned, remember that Caroline's coming-out depends on me avoiding gossip. I'm *trying* not to scare off any of the men who might actually take her off my hands."

Caldwell's grin now completely faded. "Does that mean you already have someone in mind for her?"

Alexander paused, noting the change in his friend's demeanor and the subject matter. "No. Not as of yet. Why?"

Caldwell cleared his throat, shrugged, and looked out the window of the carriage. "No reason. I worry, is all. You know how miserable some of these arrangements can be."

Alexander blew out an exhausted breath. "Yes. I do know. Though as of late, finding Caroline a husband is the least of my worries. I don't know how my father ever managed. Aside from my mother having lost whatever was left of her polite mind, Mary, Anne, Elizabeth, and Victoria have all up and turned into unbearable creatures, each vying for the attention that Caroline is getting. You should damn well see the lengths that Mary alone goes through. Why, just this week, she held a funeral. For a doll whose porcelain head shattered when it tumbled down the stairs. And do you know what she did? She up and invited all the neighbors and used *my* stationery to do it on. I about bloody—"

Caldwell snapped up a gloved hand and held it there. "Cease and desist, man. You are terrifying me with your stories, and I for one need a reprieve." Caldwell lowered his hand. "Now. Let us move on in our conversation."

Alexander fell back against the seat. He himself needed a reprieve from his own life. "So where are we going? You still haven't told me what the wager is costing me."

Caldwell swiped a hand over his face, pushing back his top hat slightly with the movement. "We've known each other for a long time, you and I. Fifteen years, to be exact. We've endured quite a bit, what with my father's antics before his death and *your* father's antics before his—and that, of course, doesn't include all of our antics."

Alexander eyed him. "Where are you going with this?"

Caldwell feigned a laugh as the carriage slowed, then leaned forward and peered out the window to look at the row of townhouses that were coming into view. He sighed heavily, clasped his hands together, and turned back toward him.

"Hawksford," Caldwell said in an unusually serious tone. "I am about to take the first step toward a life I know nothing of. And in doing so, I hope that I shall gain both your trust and understanding in what may seem like a dire situation."

Oh shit. What sort of trouble was the man in?

Wager or not, he should have known better than to come. He'd been hoping for time away from the madness back home, but, of course, he had forgotten that Caldwell was a different form of madness altogether.

Alexander glanced toward the carriage door, wondering if now was the time to make a run for it, then paused and blinked in recognition at the approaching townhouse beyond the glass window.

No. It couldn't be. Could it? Alexander scrambled next to the carriage window and almost knocked his nose and the brim of his hat against the glass. His eyes widened as Miss Charlotte's townhouse came into full view. Though clearly it had changed quite a bit since he'd last seen it.

It was no longer a wretched and dilapidated place in need of paint. Somehow it had been magically transformed into a pristine, white-washed little home. All of its shutters had been repainted black, rehinged, and perfectly set into place. The stone steps had been patched, swept, and washed. And a new black iron fence had been posted around it, tucking the entire house into a neat little bundle of respectability.

The polished brass numbers beside the door glinted in the afternoon sunlight, almost mocking him, and he could still hear the scintillating manner in which Miss Charlotte had breathed out "11" to him in the darkness of the hackney.

His jaw tightened as a vivid image of sultry black eyes, dark hair, and smooth, pale skin flashed within his memory. Indeed, this was her house. The same house he'd avoided riding past all these months for fear of losing all common sense and claiming her for his own mistress despite his vow to deny himself all female company until each of his sisters had been wed. Which he was seriously rethinking due to the fact that marrying them all off would take about eight years.

At least now he knew why Miss Charlotte had turned away each and every delivery he'd sent to her door. Including the first. For apparently, he wasn't the only man who *cared* about her welfare. And the very notion that there were others—namely Caldwell—who were not only seeing to her needs, but were *doing* things in return for those needs, made him want to rip apart a throat or two.

As the carriage came to a complete halt directly before 11 Berwick Street, Alexander snapped toward Caldwell and gave him an icy stare. Should he give him time to explain himself? Or simply wallop the bollocks off of him? He really couldn't decide. Yet.

Caldwell pointed at him. "Don't look at me like that. I'll have you know that this neighborhood is still very respectable." He lowered his hand and coolly went on, "Though I should probably explain a few things before we go inside."

"I'm listening."

Caldwell cleared his throat and shifted in his seat. "About a week ago, my uncle suggested I come here and meet with a renowned courtesan whom he felt could offer me a solution with regard to a problem I was having. Mind you, my uncle is madly in love with this woman and claims that no other person in all of England, or France for that matter, has more experience in matters of sex and relationships than she does. I was hesitant, but eventually met with her and found myself rather impressed by what she had to offer."

Alexander lowered his chin and continued to stare him down. The man wasn't making any sense. *At all.* From his own experience, Miss Charlotte was hardly an expert. But that was beside the point. "And what exactly does any of this have to do with me? Or the wager, for that matter?"

Caldwell leaned far forward and looked down at his gloved hands, keeping his gaze there. "I included this outing as part of my winnings knowing that most likely you wouldn't come under any other circumstance."

"Hell, this really doesn't sound promising."

Caldwell winced, "Yes, yes, I know. I . . . You see . . . she's been *assisting* me. With a particular secret I've been keeping."

Alexander's brows rose as he sat farther back against the seat of the carriage. Secrets were never a good thing. Especially if Caldwell intended to involve not only him in it but a courtesan. And not just any courtesan. But, apparently, the delectable Miss Charlotte. My, how he had misread that one. "*And?*" he impatiently prodded, sensing Caldwell would only continue speaking in these annoyingly cryptic sentences.

"*And,*" Caldwell went on, "she suggested I bring you along. Seeing how it involves you."

Alexander pulled in his chin. Oh, bloody hang it, no. Considering how Caldwell's own father, who loved both men and women alike, had died in a sexual escapade gone wrong, Caldwell's little confession about a *secret* and how it somehow involved him *and* Miss Charlotte shouldn't have surprised him. And yet it did. And how.

As silence continued to hang thick between them, fury, unlike anything he'd ever felt in his entire life, seized Alexander. He could easily accept Caldwell having a taste for all things male—though not *his* things—but he hadn't damn well saved Miss Charlotte from himself to merely pass her off to the likes of Caldwell, his uncle, and their so-called *problems*. Christ, the very thought of those two taking liberties with the poor woman made him want to up and—

Alexander jumped up from his seat, raised a clamped fist, and punched Caldwell in the jaw, snapping his blond head back. Caldwell's top hat flew off and tumbled to the side. Not feeling any better, Alexander hit him again. In the nose.

"*Oww!*" Caldwell winced as he grabbed hold of both the side of his face and his nose. He glared up at Alexander as if he meant to return the favor. "*Sod you!* What the devil did you do that for?"

Alexander towered over him and hissed out the remaining breath trapped in his lungs. "Aside from wanting to involve me in some Goddamn team sport, what sort of disgusting liberties are you and your uncle taking with this poor woman? The sort your father took with all of his flaps?"

"*What?* No! Are you daft, man?" Caldwell shoved him hard, throwing him back onto the seat. He paused, then scowled as his tongue rolled around on the inside of his cheek. "Christ, I think I lost a tooth." He searched the inside of his mouth with his tongue. "Ah, no. There it is."

A bright line of blood made its way from Cald-

well's nose down to his shaven chin. Caldwell
frowned and swiped at the streak, smearing it. He
noted the stain on the tips of his gray-gloved fingers and half nodded. "Thank you. I suppose I
deserve this. Actually, no. I know I deserve this."

The bastard was actually admitting to wrong-
doing. "So how long have you two been pumping
her? And how many others have you involved?"

Caldwell's eyes widened. "Whomever are you
referring to?" he cried in obvious bewilderment
and horror.

Oh, for God's sake! "*Her!*" Alexander violently
pointed to the townhouse beyond the carriage
window, unable to say her name.

Caldwell glanced toward the townhouse. He
paused, let out a harsh laugh, then leaned over
him, snapping back his own gloved fist. He shook
it for emphasis. "You and your fancy ideas."

He lowered his fist and shook his head in disgust, swiping at his bloody nose again. "I'll forgive you this once, Hawksford. But only because
I had it coming. Now come along. We're late."

"Late?" Alexander echoed.

"Yes. Late. Follow me." Snatching up his top
hat from off the floor, Caldwell shoved open the
door and without waiting for the steps to be unfolded jumped down and called out to his driver,
"Two hours!"

The man meant to call on Miss Charlotte for
two hours? Yes, that could only mean one thing.
And it was anything but respectable.

Alexander narrowed his gaze as Caldwell
marched up the stairs of number 11, smacked his

top hat back onto his blond head, and twisted the door bell.

The relentless bastard. He was *not* getting involved in whatever escapade the man had in mind. Although he was not about to let poor Miss Charlotte become a victim of it, either.

Alexander launched himself out of the carriage and with only a few quick strides moved up the stairs. Just as he was about to grab the back of Caldwell's coat and drag him back to the carriage where he belonged, the door swung open and the butler stepped out.

Alexander froze and momentarily wondered how elaborate a scene he wanted to make in public.

The butler blinked and stared at Caldwell for a prolonged moment. He cleared his throat. "Forgive me, Lord Caldwell, but there appears to be a bit of . . ." The butler gestured toward his own weathered and bulbous nose with his gloved finger. "Blood there."

Caldwell glared back at Alexander and yanked out a white handkerchief. He dabbed at the small line of blood, folded it back up, and stuffed it into his waistcoat pocket. "Yes. I'm afraid someone mistook me for the Marquis de Sade. Happens all the time. Even though the bastard has been dead since 1814."

Alexander rolled his eyes, knowing Caldwell was referring more to his own father than to de Sade. For as fate would have it, both deviants had died in the same exact year.

In the end, perhaps he *had* overreacted. What did he care who Miss Charlotte associated with or why? He already had more than enough females in his life to worry about without adding one more to the list. And as for Caldwell needing to disclose his *secret . . .* uh, no.

It was time to go.

Alexander stepped up onto the landing beside Caldwell and clapped him gently on the back. "So sorry. I really should not have overreacted the way I did. And though I fully support whatever path you choose, with whichever sex you choose, I am simply not that sort of a friend, and I hope you understand." He paused, quickly removed his hand, and pointed straight at the carriage behind them. "And I should go."

Caldwell jerked toward him, his expression lethally serious beneath the rim of his top hat. "Don't flatter yourself, you asshole. Even if I was that sort—*which I'm not*—you'd hardly be worth my time. Now I'm asking you to be patient with regard to this situation. I know none of this makes sense. Hell, it still doesn't make any sense to me, either. But it's already complicated enough without you turning it into bleeding Waterloo."

Alexander's brows rose. By God. What sort of trouble was the man in? Caldwell only referenced Waterloo when things were downright bad. That, coupled with the urgency in both Caldwell's tone and dark eyes, was what ultimately kept Alexander from leaving. "All right. I'll stay."

Caldwell hissed out a breath, withdrew his calling card from his breast pocket, and snapped it out toward the butler. "We've an appointment."

The portly, gray-haired man observed them rather dubiously from beneath the thick, fuzzy tufts of his brows, then reached out and took the card. After reading it, he glanced over at Alexander, then averted his gaze back to Caldwell.

The servant cleared his throat again. Only this time a bit more theatrically. "I apologize, but the appointment is set for only one. No one else, no matter their esteemed lineage, is permitted to enter at this time."

"Mr. Hudson." Caldwell stepped toward the butler. "Madame de Maitenon and I have an agreement. Surely, she must have informed you of it."

Alexander's brows came together. Madame de Maitenon? Miss Charlotte wasn't French, was she? He paused. What if Miss Charlotte no longer lived here? Actually, what if Miss Charlotte had *never* lived here? Oh hell. That would explain all the returned trunks. Aside from that corset he sent, that is. That thing somehow never did make it back.

The butler glanced over his shoulder, toward the open door behind him, then quickly turned back to them, nobly setting his plump, aged chin. "Forgive me, Lord Caldwell, but I don't recall a thing." He lowered his chin down onto his stiff collar, grouping the loose folds of skin beneath his neck all into one, and whispered, "Though a few pounds might help."

"*Pounds?*" Caldwell muttered something beneath his breath, dug into his inner coat, and withdrew his leather satchel. "Whatever happened to a man asking for a shilling?" Yanking out several coins, Caldwell tucked the satchel back into his coat pocket and held out the coins for the man. "Here. Take it, you mercenary. We'll talk about this later."

The butler paused, then brought up a gray-gloved hand and rubbed his fingers together. For more.

Caldwell grumbled, "I must be mad," then pulled out the satchel and shoved it all at the man. "Here, you bloody thimblerigger. Now let us in! Thanks to you, all of London already knows we're here."

The butler tsked. "Such language." The old man peered past them and toward the street. Seeing no one, he stuffed the leather satchel into the pocket of his dark blue livery. He then glanced expectantly at Alexander, turned up his palm, and held it out.

Since when were cards collected at the door? Alexander hesitated and eyed Caldwell.

Caldwell turned and delivered him a pointed stare.

Alexander knew that look all too well. He called it the Waterloo stare. When a British soldier desperately needed Prussian reinforcement. And he, of course, was the Prussian reinforcement.

Alexander blew out a breath, dug into his own breast pocket, and withdrew his calling card. "Exactly how much will it cost *me* to get in?"

"Not a groat." The butler plucked the card out of his hand and stepped back, opening the door all the way as he gestured for them to enter. "I was, after all, born a gentleman, with a prayer book in one hand and a drink in the other."

"Yes, and clearly the drinking hand is getting the better of you." Alexander removed his hat and stepped in first. As if being first would some-how give him a claim to the mistress of the house. That is, if she even lived here anymore.

He paused when he reached the middle of the hall foyer. The sweet smell of wine teased his heightened senses. The rich, playful scent did not match the memory of the simple penny soap he'd last breathed upon her skin. Whatever happened to Miss Charlotte? He didn't know why, but his stomach actually sank at the thought that he had somehow failed her. Had left her to a fate she did not deserve.

Caldwell paused beside him as the entrance door closed, darkening the quiet foyer. "You owe me money. Perhaps even a new nose."

"I owe you nothing. You're fortunate I'm still standing here. This is what I call a true testament to our friendship."

"Yes, and I suppose I should expect a blow to my bollocks next."

A clock chimed thrice in the distance, some-where upstairs, then clicked back into silence.

Alexander slowly turned toward the adjoining room, not knowing what to expect next. He leveled his gaze at the room.

A single piece of furniture, a gilded chair, was set in the middle of the parlor. And nothing else. There were no carpets or side tables or vases or lamps.

Instead, the fuss had been put into the expanse of the brocaded, coral silk walls. Large, gold-framed paintings of Greece, the Parthenon, vari-ous Greek temples, as well as an array of naked

Greek goddesses that ranged from Aphrodite to Athena, graced every inch of the walls.

To be sure, it was a bleeding Greek temple.

Alexander blinked as he stepped toward the room's doorway, noting some of the other contents in the room. In particular, four life-size marble statues of well-muscled, nude men—with absolutely no fig leaves covering the lower regions. All of them had been strategically placed about the parlor.

He honestly didn't know what was more astounding, the nudity or the fact that fashion accessories had been strategically placed on every one of those statues so as to better emphasize their sculpted assets.

One wore a beaver hat angled over his left eye. Another wore a silk red cravat meticulously tied mail-coach style about his neck. One had an unbuttoned evening waistcoat, displaying the well-defined muscles on his chest and stomach. And draped on the outstretched arm of the last of the four statues was an unlaced corset.

Alexander squinted at the corset. Bone rot him, it was the one thing that had never been returned. The corset he'd bought from a shop for more money than he ought to have paid. The same corset he had then meticulously folded into a trunk, along with various other dresses and banknotes in a frenzied hope of saving Miss Charlotte's virtue. What little good that did. The presence of that corset did mean one thing: That Miss Charlotte most certainly still lived here.

The butler cleared his throat from behind. "Your hat, Lord Hawksford."

Alexander turned toward the servant and hesitated. He shouldn't stay. He ought to leave. Before the last thread of reason he'd been clinging to snapped and sent him flying in a direction that he could not afford to go. And yet . . .

He genuinely wanted to see her. Wanted to know what this was all about. For he refused to believe that the woman he had met and left on that doorstep would actually resort to this sort of life. Not with the sort of vicious pride she had.

Alexander grudgingly handed over his hat and hoped he wasn't making a mistake.

The butler turned away and carefully positioned Alexander's hat onto its own red velvet cushion which lay atop a walnut hall table just outside the parlor. Right beside Caldwell's hat, which already sat on its own red velvet cushion.

Alexander's eyes suddenly widened. For there were not two, not three, but actually *four* red velvet cushions all sitting in a row. Confound it, how many other male hats had been here before his?

The very thought of it made him want to growl. No. Not growl. Roar. For it appeared that the woman preferred to sell off her body rather than accept any of his gifts.

The servant turned, then regally strode to the other side of the foyer. He removed one of five lit glass lanterns that were affixed to the left side of the corridor wall on brass hooks. With the lantern in hand, the man proceeded farther down the corridor, just past the stairs, and paused at what appeared to be a misplaced door in the wall.

The butler opened the door wide, held out the lantern for them to take, and gestured toward the darkness. "Mind the step. The passageway will lead you to the other side, where you will be appropriately greeted by Harold."

Alexander glanced over at Caldwell, who had glanced over at him. "The other side of what?"

Caldwell shrugged. "Hell if I know. Must be part of the school."

School? Alexander stepped by him and grabbed hold of his arm. "What do you mean? What school?"

Caldwell winced but didn't answer.

Alexander leaned in toward him. "Caldwell, I swear to you that if you don't tell me what this is all about, I'll rope you naked to a tree in the middle of Hyde Park and sell tickets." He delivered him a hard, pointed stare. "To love-starved women bearing horse whips."

Caldwell shuddered and pulled away. Shaking his head, he reached into his inner vest pocket and yanked out a neatly folded cream-colored parchment. "With all of your new responsibilities this past year, I knew you wouldn't come unless I manipulated our wager to my advantage."

Alexander pointed at him. "You son of a bitch. You cheated. Did you pay the woman to try to rape me, too?"

Caldwell blew out a breath. "Hawksford, I only assisted in getting her into the house. The rest she willingly did all on her own, I assure you, and for it I apologize. Now I promise I'll try to explain all of this later, but in the meantime, I beseech you to enroll. Here." He shoved the parchment at him. "I'm in the last stage of enrolling myself."

Alexander paused, sensing Caldwell's unease, then took the parchment and quickly unfolded it. He leveled the printed letters and read aloud. "*Madame Thérèse's School of Gallantry. All gentlemen welcome. Learn from the most celebrated demimondaine of France everything there is to know about . . .*"

He drew his brows together. Was he even reading any of this right? Well, yes. There it was. "*Love and seduction. Only a limited amount of applications are being accepted at 11 Berwick Street. Discretion is guaranteed and*"—He could barely finish the last word as the remnants of his patience completely dwindled—"*advised.*"

Oh, he'd bloody advise the woman, all right. Was she mad, outright inviting all of London to her door like this?

Alexander crushed the parchment in his fist at the realization that his oh so clever Miss Charlotte, who had so innocently and desperately propositioned him on the street, was now caressing the trousers off every man in London.

He didn't know why he felt so wounded. She wasn't *his* mistress, and yet for some absurd reason he felt a horrid responsibility to actually do something.

Which, of course, he wasn't going to.

"Your brain must be completely made out of cork if you think I'm going to attend such a thing. *And with you.*" Alexander shook his head and marched back toward the main entrance. "You and your bloody wagers and secrets and schools. I've had enough. I'm leaving."

Caldwell jumped in front of him to prevent him from going any farther, snatched the crumpled parchment out of his hand, and shoved it back into his inner vest pocket. "Hawksford. Please." He adjusted his coat. "Don't do this to me. It's important you stay. It'll make sense later. I swear."

With that, Caldwell hurried past, grabbed the lantern from the butler's hand, and stepped down into the darkness and disappeared. The faint golden light from his lantern flickered out into the corridor for a few moments, then faded.

How important could it be? He certainly wasn't in need of any damn lessons. And if Caldwell needed them, then hell, that was *not* his problem.

The butler continued to patiently hold open the door. "Will you be joining him, Lord Hawksford?"

Alexander shifted his jaw at the idea of coming face-to-face with Miss Charlotte again. Clearly, playing the part of a widow hadn't won her much applause, so she had moved on to far greater roles. Madame de Maitenon. A French courtesan. Indeed.

He knew the moment he'd laid eyes on the woman that she'd disturb the peace of every man. And how.

"You're damn right I'll be joining him." And with that, Alexander marched straight for the door.

Lesson Five

*Understand that men innately lack the ability
to grasp a woman's perspective. Why? Because
they are all far too occupied with trying to grasp
everything else associated with the idea of a
woman. Like breasts, derrieres, and the like.*
—The School of Gallantry

Alexander snatched one of the four remaining glass lanterns off the wall on his way over. Brushing past the butler, he slowly descended the spiraling, narrow, stone stairway. Descended down into the dank darkness that reeked of earth, dry rot, and stagnant moisture.

The door slammed shut behind him, and he knew. Knew there was no saving Caldwell from his own stupidity. Though he wasn't by any means more intelligent for following him.

At the bottom of the stairs, he stooped to avoid the low ceiling. Though not in time.

"Bleed me!" Alexander winced and rubbed

with his free hand at the dull, throbbing pain that nipped the top of his head.

Forget about being rational anymore. He was going to kill Caldwell. With his own two hands. Then bury him. Then dig him back up and kill him again. All in the name of a woman who wasn't even his and some damn secret he still knew nothing of!

Alexander paused, holding up the lantern, and blinked at the thick darkness before him, which his light refused to cut through. Where the blazes were they going? The Orient?

A faint light and the movement of a shadowed figure in the far distance caught his eye, assuring him Caldwell was in fact still determined to get to the other side. He only hoped that Miss Charlotte wasn't tying up men, emptying out their pockets, and then stacking them all here to die. Though there hadn't really been reports of large groups of wealthy men going missing.

Alexander held up the lantern toward the moss-ridden, slate walls and wrinkled his nose. "Caldwell!" His voice boomed all around him. "For God's sake, why are you doing all this? Your perspective on women isn't *this* bad!"

The light in the distance swayed then stopped. "If this is too much of an adventure for you," Caldwell's voice echoed back, "then leave! Go! I'm certain your mother could use your help setting up for tea. Or better yet . . . *a champagne party!*"

A champagne party? His mother wasn't *that* far gone. Alexander gritted his teeth and charged forward into the musty darkness, trying to keep the glass lantern steady before him. "How is your nose, Caldwell? Any better? Or shall I offer you one last complimentary blow?"

"I dare you to try to cuff me again! I bloody dare you!" There was a notable pause. "Hey, now. I actually found a door. Fancy that."

Alexander snorted. A door? To bloody where? He kept charging forward until he came upon not only Caldwell but what was indeed a rough oak door.

Caldwell, who was also stooping, glanced back at him with a quirked brow, then raised a gloved hand and rapped on the door. As if they were making a respectable visit.

Alexander paused beside him in disbelief. "Are you missing a part of your brain?" He gestured toward the abyss of the tunnel behind them with his lantern. "Doesn't this all seem rather . . . *barmy*? Even to you?"

Caldwell sniffed as he stared at the door, awaiting entrance. "You've no sense of adventure anymore. None whatsoever. The Hawksford I grew up with would have gladly knocked on this door."

Alexander scooted closer beside him and leveled his gaze at him. "Yes, and the Caldwell I grew up with wouldn't have knocked on it at all."

Caldwell glared at him, lifted a fist, and pounded on the door as if to prove otherwise, the lantern in his other hand swaying.

Alexander rolled his eyes. "Caldwell, why are you doing this to me? Is it because you don't want to enroll alone? Is that it?" Hell, he hoped it was. Because anything else would have been . . . well, disturbing.

Caldwell glanced at him and smoothed down

the side of his cloak with the hand that wasn't holding the lantern. He opened his mouth, then paused and drew his blond brows together. "Actually, it's a bit more complicated than that."

"*Obviously*. Hell, you still haven't told me what this is all about!"

"I know, I know. I . . ." He rigidly turned to him and looked him straight in the eye. "Hawksford. The truth is, I've involved myself with a woman."

Alexander paused before letting out a much-needed laugh. "Well, that's a relief."

"No, it's not!" Caldwell's voice boomed in the tunnel. "And it's not funny! Stop laughing!"

Alexander stopped laughing on command and blinked at him, noting that he was rather upset. He lowered his voice. "You, man, are beginning to worry me."

"Forgive me, I . . ." Caldwell swept his hand across his face and let it drop back to his side. "Hawksford. I've involved myself with a woman I shouldn't have. I've involved myself with . . ." Caldwell winced, as if he couldn't say any more.

"*With?*" Alexander prodded, now rolling his hand, hoping the man would just say it and spare them both.

Caldwell eyed him, then blurted out, "With an American. And needless to say, I'm having trouble coping with her heritage."

Alexander choked and almost dropped the lantern. *That* was his secret? "You're really not making any sense. At all. What the blazes does an American have to do with me?"

Caldwell groaned and threw back his head. "Someone please shoot me. Now."

A loud clank vibrated the door before them. It then creaked open. A massive, heavyset man with a mop of curly brown hair and sharp brown eyes peered down at them.

Alexander stepped back. By God. Who needed a lock? The man was his own fortress.

"Card," the man gruffly intoned.

Caldwell yanked out his calling card and handed it to the man. "You must be Harold. How are you?"

Harold glanced at the card then bowed from his place beside the door, his dark blue livery shifting against his mountainous movements. "Welcome to the other side of the school, Lord Caldwell. Congratulations on getting this far."

"Uh . . . yes. I suppose." Caldwell nodded, held up his lantern, and hurried past the man, toward the set of winding stairs just beyond.

Alexander moved for the door with every intention of keeping Caldwell within sight at all times. For he was not about to trust the man alone to Miss Charlotte. Hell, he wouldn't even trust himself alone to the woman.

Harold stepped into the small opening, blocking Alexander from going any farther, and blankly stared down at him. "There is only one appointment scheduled."

Alexander shifted, growing rather tired of his hunched position, and eyed the servant as best he could. "My good man, I can assure you, I am not here to apply. Merely to spectate." And defend whatever was left of poor Miss Charlotte's virtue.

"This is not the circus," Harold rumbled out. This time, he aggressively stepped out toward him, his massive body stooping in an effort to enter the small tunnel. "Inform Mr. Hudson on your way out that whatever he was bribed with, I shall not only remove it from his pimpish flesh, but gladly snap him into several pieces. No one betrays my Madame. *No one.*"

Miss Charlotte had gathered quite the ardent crowd, hadn't she? Alexander held up both hands and stepped back, sensing this was about to get complicated. "I assure you, I mean no harm. Especially to your . . . *Madame.* She knows me, actually. Quite well."

"*I knew it!*" Caldwell interjected, hopping up and down from behind the giant in an effort to see over his body. "I bloody knew it!"

Caldwell pointed at Alexander from around Harold. "*That's* why you up and cuffed me! Because you're involved with the woman! Unbelievable, Hawksford. *Unbelievable.*" Caldwell patted Harold's shoulder from where he stood and peered in on him. "My good fellow. Understand that this is a matter of great import. I ask that you permit Lord Hawksford entrance at once. I assure you, Madame de Maitenon has given me permission to share this appointment with him."

Alexander smiled up at the giant, reached out, and patted the thick arm before him in a friendly manner. "You see. I have permission."

Harold's gaze narrowed. He held out a large, gloved palm the size of a table. "Your card."

Alexander yanked out one of the three calling cards remaining in his pocket and set it onto his open hand. "There. My card." Anything to keep the ox happy.

Harold glanced at it then slowly stepped aside. Caldwell grinned at Alexander and then disappeared up the spiraling stairs.

"Thank you." Alexander hurried in through the door and into a small, candlelit passageway. He straightened, eager to be out of Harold's way, then pressed himself toward the nearest wall, trying to move himself around the giant. The man turned, reached out, and grabbed hold of the lantern, freeing Alexander's hands.

Edging near the spiraling stairs that led upward, he mounted them, then sprinted up the suffocating stair well. He finally stumbled out into a corridor. Of what appeared to be another house.

The wonder of Miss Charlotte never ceased to amaze him. Alexander slowly walked past a staircase that led toward the upper floor and made his way into the grand foyer, where Caldwell stood with his hands behind his back, looking about.

Alexander paused beneath a large crystal chandelier. The scent of fresh flowers permeated the air, though none were in sight.

"This way."

Harold's deep voice startled Alexander. The oversized beast mounted the red runner stairs of the mahogany staircase with unexpected grace and dignified charm.

Caldwell stepped toward Alexander, drew back a fisted hand, and punched him hard in the shoulder, sending Alexander staggering backward. "*That* is for giving me grief about Lady Waverly. Close the gates after fifty, my ass. Since when do you go about bedding women old enough to be your grandmother?" He tsked and shook his head. "For shame, Hawksford. For shame." Caldwell turned and marched up the stairs.

Alexander rubbed the top of his now sore shoulder and hurried up after Caldwell, confused. "Old enough to be my . . . Now look here, man! I don't think we're discussing the same woman."

"Oh, I think we are. You know, the French charmer with the silver hair and the nice, large breasts?"

"No, no. Who is that anyway? She wasn't French, and she most certainly wasn't old. Do you mean to tell me that some French mab now lives here? Whatever happened to the woman before her? Do you even know?"

Caldwell paused on the stairs and glanced back at him. "The woman before her? Hold now. Who is this woman you keep referring to?"

Miss Charlotte's face appeared in his mind's eye, once again, as he had last seen her in the hackney. His pulse jolted just at the thought of her. His steps slowed. "I don't think she provided me with her real name, which is just as well, but I'll never forget what she looked like. She had bundled black hair. Beautiful, dark, expressive eyes. Oval face. Perfect, pale skin. Full lips. Good, straight teeth. Sizable breasts. Slim in all the right places even without a corset. And petite. Hell, I've never met a more ravishing woman in my life."

"I gathered as much," Caldwell flung over his shoulder as he reached the landing. "I thought you'd never cease braying."

Alexander inwardly winced. He supposed he'd gone on. More than he'd meant to.

Caldwell wagged a finger at him, now trotting backward into the hallway. "With that description, I do believe you must be referring to the conductor of admissions. Lady Chartwell." He chuckled. "When did the two of you become acquainted? Before or after her husband was shot?"

Alexander almost stumbled on the last stair. The Earl of Chartwell had been Miss Charlotte's husband? The same stupid son of a bitch who'd been shot by a female in his own opera box last year before two hundred people? That couldn't be right. "I really don't think we're referring to the same lady." Alexander paused beside him. "Chartwell wasn't married."

Caldwell smirked as he followed Harold. "Of course he was married," he flung back at him. "For about six months before he was unceremoniously popped off by one of his nuns. Hell, your memory has lapsed quite miserably since the death of your father, hasn't it?"

Alexander blinked. Chartwell had been married? And to his Miss Charlotte, no less? Or, rather, *Lady* Charlotte. Alexander stood stunned for a moment longer before he was able to force himself to follow Caldwell and the servant down the corridor.

Caldwell paused before the entrance of what appeared to be a bedchamber and grinned. He mouthed "*There she is*" and then disappeared inside.

Alexander hurried in after him and found himself in a room whose walls were draped with luxurious, brocaded red velvet. Coming to a frozen halt beside Caldwell, his eyes snapped to the center of the nearly empty room. Several leather wingback chairs were set in a semicircle.

And there, sitting in a red velvet–upholstered chair behind a small, letter-writing desk was none other than Lady Charlotte. She was exquisitely dressed in black silk and satin, her full skirts perfectly arranged around the chair. Her eyes were cast downward toward a sizable stack of papers that she held in her small ungloved hands.

Alexander tensed as the temperature of his body slowly rose at the memory of her soft body pressed against his own. He could still hear her pleasured breaths in the darkness of the carriage and feel the rise and fall of her heaving chest beneath his hands.

It had all been real. *She* had been real.

Her dark, thick hair, which had been unconventionally let loose, cascaded down her slim shoulders, past her tightly corseted waist, and disappeared toward her bum, which was fitted in her seat. Without a doubt, her quiet serenity not only enhanced her beauty but personified it.

"Lord Caldwell is here," Harold offered, breaking the tense silence within the room. "It appears he brought along an acquaintance. I apologize, but he claims—"

"You needn't worry, Harold," Lady Charlotte replied, still occupied with the stack of papers before her. "Madame has already informed me about it. You may go." She took up the quill from the inkwell and scribed something.

"My humblest apologies, Lady Chartwell. I

didn't know." Harold bowed and departed, his heavy steps fading down the corridor.

Alexander blinked. So she *was* Chartwell's widow.

Lady Charlotte sighed, set the quill back into the inkwell and rose, her skirts rustling from the smooth, elegant movement of her body. She turned toward them and smiled. "Wonderful to see you again, Lord Caldwell. I—"

The moment her dark gaze met his, both her words and her smile faded. A faint but noticeable blush now crept into her cheeks as she continued to remain frozen beside her desk.

Alexander's breath hitched in his throat as they continued to intently hold one another's gaze. Just like that day in the carriage, every damn inch of him became fully aware of her astonishing beauty and presence.

Though he half expected the woman to snatch something up and throw it at his head, for he remembered how miffed she had been with him when he last saw her, she surprised him by setting her small chin and calmly stating, "Are you looking to enroll *this* man?"

"Yes." Caldwell tapped Alexander's arm with renewed urgency as his blond brows went up in what Alexander could only describe as a silent form of desperate pleading. "Humor me, Hawksford. It'll be good fun."

Yes, indeed, that it would be.

The truth was, Alexander's reformed self, who was desperately trying to set a good example for his family, insisted he leave all of this nonsense behind. Insisted that he march straight back home and get back to being a good brother and a good son. But his old self, the one he had buried and denied since the passing of his father, wanted to stay. And play.

He boldly met Lady Charlotte's gaze. She heatedly stared back. Daring him to partake in her elaborate little scheme.

It wasn't every day that a man was handed an opportunity to enroll in a school like this. With a woman like this. *Hell, it all may prove to be entertaining,* he thought. *Maybe even productive.*

Unable to resist, Alexander grinned. "I suppose it all depends. Are there any private lessons available?"

Lady Charlotte's eyes narrowed as she challenged him in turn. "Private lessons are reserved for virgins, My Lord. Are you a virgin?"

Caldwell choked back a laugh then coughed several times into his hand and turned away. He staggered toward the direction of the door.

The dunderhead was actually laughing at him. *Laughing.*

Lady Charlotte smirked, clearly pleased with herself.

Alexander lifted a brow. She had absolutely no idea whom she was dealing with, did she? "If it means acquiring lessons from you, my dear, I can be whatever you want me to be."

Caldwell guffawed. "Hawksford, you couldn't play the role of a virgin even if you *were* a virgin."

"Most amusing, Caldwell." Alexander folded his arms over his chest, turned toward the man, and tried to remain serious, even though he was anything but. "I'll have you know that I rather fancy this whole idea of enrolling. I myself have yet to figure out where certain things go and what to do with them."

Caldwell kept laughing, his voice echoing throughout the room.

Lady Charlotte eyed them, clearly not amused. "Lord Caldwell. I ask that you retire to the parlor. With Harold. I shall interview your presumptuous friend first and call upon you when we are done."

"Yes. Good. Thank you." Caldwell cleared his throat, put up a hand, and hurried out of the room.

When the room finally fell silent, Alexander crossed his arms over his chest. "Your needs, Lady Charlotte, have grown quite out of hand since we last met. Had I known I could have saved most of London's male population from a fate worse than death, I would have gladly done my part."

She set a hand on her hip. "How valiant of you to think of your brethren in their most desperate hour. As for my needs . . ." She lifted her eyes to his and arched a dark brow. "I highly doubt *you* could ever satisfy them."

With that, she turned away and moved back toward her seat. Her loose hair gently bounced against the sway of her hips, brushing the bottom of her bum most provocatively.

Alexander dropped his arms to his sides and unconsciously licked his lips, tempted to take up her challenge. His eyes remained firmly affixed to the seductive sway of her hair, her hips, and her ass. An ass he'd had the pleasure of brushing his hand up against once upon a time. An ass he now wanted to grab and make use of.

"Enjoying your view?" She paused beside her chair, purposefully keeping her backside to him. "You may want to take your time, as it will be the last view of my backside you'll ever get."

His gaze snapped up to the back of her head, where it should have been all along. She had a bit more sexual prowess to her than he remembered. And here he thought he needed to be tamed. The woman was ruthless.

She gathered up the ends of her dark hair, exposing the length of her slender neck, slim back, and a small row of black buttons that started at the top of her scooped neckline and finished off where her full skirts began.

Alexander shifted his jaw and actually felt his fingers twitch with a burning need to unbutton her gown and toss it aside right there and then. She was trying to provoke him. And what was worse, she was rather good at it. No wonder Caldwell was enrolling. Hell, *he* wanted to enroll.

She softly smiled at him from over her shoulder, then sat, tucking herself behind the writing desk. Releasing her dark, long hair behind her shoulders, she took to arranging her skirts. "Close the door, Mr. H, so that we may begin your application process."

Oh, Mr. H, was it? A complete lack of respect from the woman was not at all surprising. But to give him absolutely no name after all he had tried to do for her? Rather rude.

He stepped back toward the door and, using his

boot, slammed it shut. "I prefer Alexander if we intend to dispense with my title and all formality."

"I am not dispensing with anything. H is simply the manner in which you had signed all of your letters to me. I was beginning to wonder when you'd make an appearance. Although I believe the only thing I really owe you is that corset. Do you want it back? Is that it?"

"No, thank you," he quipped. Striding toward her, he grabbed one of the leather chairs and pulled it as close to her desk as possible. He removed his gloves and set them on her stack of papers. For good measure.

He sat and leaned back, propping his elbows on the arms of the chair, then bridged his fingertips together. "I must admit. I'm rather impressed with your progressive manner of thinking. A school for men. Brilliant. Are you paying tribute to that late husband of yours by educating men on what *not* to do?"

She sighed, then lowered her eyes and shook her head. "Please. Chartwell has been buried from mind and sight for about a year. I'd prefer to keep it that way."

He was quiet for a moment. "I apologize. I meant no ill will."

She nodded and gently pushed his gloves toward the edge of the small writing desk. She was quiet for a few moments before finally asking, "Does your wife know about your intention to apply? Or are you merely looking to surprise her with newfound talents?"

Alexander laughed and shifted in his seat. "Not to disappoint, love, but there is no wife. I am simply here to ensure Caldwell isn't swindled out of his estate. The man was born beneath an evil star and is notorious for getting into trouble."

She eyed him for a brief moment, then dragged a blank piece of parchment closer to her. "Lord Caldwell is in good hands, I assure you."

"Meaning *your* hands?" He waggled his brows, unable to resist. "If so, enroll me. At once."

She brushed at the ends of her paper, looking rather bored with their conversation. "I regret to inform you that the application process is the only time I am ever involved with the students here at the school."

"What a complete waste of your talent." Though, in truth, he was relieved to hear that she was merely a glorified secretary for this whole ridiculous operation.

Her hand stilled against the parchment, and her dark eyes suddenly met his with sharp assessment. "Do try and remember that I will be dictating the pace of this conversation. Not you. Is that understood?"

Strong-willed. Intelligent. Tough. Yet still made of enough fine porcelain to make her fragile. Indeed, she was a fascinating combination of a woman, which made him wonder how she ever ended up marrying an unscrupulous fop like Chartwell. The two hardly pieced together. "I understand. Perfectly."

"Thank you. Now. Are you genuinely interested in enrolling in the school or not?"

"Oh, I'm interested." *Interested in you, that is.* Hell, he'd enroll himself over and over again if it meant having more of these amazing one-on-one conversations. For truth be told, he'd never been so entertained. He was also fascinated as to why a woman of her status and rank would dare to conduct such a scandalous and provocative state of affairs beneath the noses of everyone in London.

He waved his hand toward her, trying to demonstrate his eagerness. "Do. Go on."

"Very well." She plucked up the quill and gently tapped the end to remove the excess ink. "Usually, our students must pass a series of vigorous tests before being allowed to even apply. The tunnel you passed through is a secret only entrusted to those who are deemed worthy to become a student. For whatever reasons, Madame de Maitenon has given you permission to accompany Lord Caldwell in the final process that will ultimately give him admittance into the school. It is my duty to interview you for consideration."

He smiled and tried not to chuckle at her serious, business-minded tone. "I certainly appreciate the opportunity."

"Allow me to explain how this interview shall proceed. I will ask you a series of questions. In turn, you will provide nothing less than honesty. If any of the answers you provide prove to be false, Madame de Maitenon will not only remove your name from the list of applicants, but will fine you a total of £250."

Alexander let out a low, exaggerated whistle. "Rather harsh."

She shrugged. "In a world governed by men, a woman has to be."

A rather warped way of thinking. What had

Chartwell done to this poor woman anyway? Left her to think that she needed to manipulate men as a means of attaining what she wanted?

Then again, who was he to gripe?

He played that game all the time. His eyes traveled down the length of her exposed neck toward her sizable breasts, which were regrettably well hidden beneath a layer of black silk. Sadly, it had been some time since he'd had any plans that involved a lovely pair of breasts. And by God, he was beginning to realize just how much he truly had missed them.

Lesson Six

*It is a known fact that men often cast aside
all reason and common sense the moment the
possibility of great sex appears. Yet what they
fail to realize is that with no reason and
no common sense present, the outcome isn't
likely to be all that pleasant.*
—*The School of Gallantry*

"Your birth name, please."

Alexander snapped his attention from Lady
Charlotte's breasts back to the paper before her,
knowing he ought to remain focused. There was
no point in giving the woman the upper hand in
a game that hadn't even started.

Attempting to appear nonchalant, he scratched
at his shaven chin. "Do you require an entire list
of titles or the most prominent?"

She brought the paper even closer toward her,
as if shielding herself. "The most prominent,
please. You'll submit the rest in written form upon
admission."

"Of course." He leaned forward and placed his hands on his knees. "That would be Alexander William Baxendale, the third Earl of Hawksford. Do you need me to spell it for you?"

"No." She gracefully scribed his full birth name and title across the top of her paper. Her eyes eventually met his again. "Let us begin. What is your age, Lord Hawksford?"

"One and thirty."

She eyed him for a moment, then wrote the number beside his name. "And are you a virgin?"

His lips quivered in an effort to remain serious. Surely their previous encounter should have adequately answered that. "No. I confess that I am not."

"No. Of course not." She tilted her head to one side and placed a small *x* beneath his name. "Were you at the age of consent during your first sexual encounter?"

He shrugged. "I really wouldn't know what the age of consent is these days. It's been a while since my first sexual encounter."

She sighed. "Twelve. The age would be twelve."

"*Twelve?*" He pulled in his chin in disbelief and snapped up straight in his chair. "Hell, my youngest sister is twelve." And Mary was in no damned state to be consenting to lecherous men. The very thought of a man having sex with his sweet though oddly morbid sister was enough to make him want to heave up his breakfast. "That seems far too bloody young. Are you certain of that?"

Her brows slightly rose. "I agree that it is far too young, but the law has been the same for quite some time, and as you know, Parliament will be Parliament. And lords, who continue to run the blasted thing, will be lords."

Alexander blew out a pained breath. It appeared he had one more thing to add to his list of endless responsibilities. Perhaps he needed to padlock each and every one of his sisters' doors and consider more reliable means of reinforcement. Like wrought-iron chastity belts.

"I am rather pleased you find the age to be abhorrent, for it truly is, but we are not here to solve the troubles of the world." The tip of her quill still hovered over the parchment. "So. Were you at the age of consent during your first sexual encounter or not?"

"Yes, yes." He waved a hand toward her paper, still feeling somewhat agitated about the whole matter. "I was one and twenty."

"One and twenty?" She paused. "Truly?"

Alexander caught the small smile on her full lips as she lowered her gaze and placed another *x* beneath his name.

As if he would admit to anyone, especially to her, that once upon a time he was a man who believed in love and happily ever afters. A man who had foolishly waited for one and twenty years for the right woman to come along, the one to whom he could hand both his heart and his virginity. Imagine his disappointment in *that*.

In the end, he learned that existing solely for pleasure was the only true way to live. For there were never any disappointments and one could easily ensure their own happily ever after one pleasure at a time. That is until reality had smacked him firmly in the head when his father died and left him with five sisters. "And how old were you, My Lady?" he demanded, genuinely interested in her reply.

Lady Charlotte glared up at him as if she meant to impale the tip of her quill deep into the confines of his beating heart. "This is *your* application process. Not mine." She dipped the quill into the inkwell once again and sighed. "Next question. Have you ever fantasized about dominating a woman?"

He slowly grinned at the thought of dominating her. "If it's reciprocal domination in the name of pleasure, then I would have to say yes. And yes again."

She placed another small *x* beneath his name. "Have you ever engaged in sex with more than one woman at a time?"

It appeared that his days of old were about to resurface. And how. He cleared his throat, wondering if she would applaud or condemn him for his next words. "Uh . . . yes. I have."

She glanced up, clearly surprised, and leveled a serious gaze at him. "Exactly how many women were involved during that particular engagement?" she asked evenly.

"Uh . . . four." He frowned, trying hard to remember if that blonde had been involved. She had to have been. She was the one who kept swearing at everyone out of pleasure. "No." He rubbed his fingers along the edge of his shaven jaw. "Actually, I believe it was five."

There was an arrested expression of disbelief

on Lady Charlotte's face. One he had never received from a woman before. In or out of bed.

And for some reason, for the first time in his life, Alexander, a born Hawksford, actually felt self-conscious. As if he needed to explain his former expeditions. "It was only once, really. And by no means did I go about initiating it. I went to this champagne party, you see. Although no one really followed any of the rules. It was brutally hot, I was stumbling about with my blindfold on, foxed out of my wits, and the next thing I knew, I was being rushed aside by a group of women. It wasn't long before I ended up with no clothing and no blindfold whatsoever. But I learned from the experience. Learned that champagne parties are not only extremely dangerous, but that I prefer devoting myself to one woman at a time. For a man can only please so many women at once with true dedication."

Which was the God-given truth.

Lady Charlotte lowered her eyes, wrote the number five just beneath his name, and circled it. Twice. "Do you sheath yourself during your escapades, My Lord? Or is there a chance you could be unclean?"

Alexander genuinely laughed in response. "A man of my experience would never engage in any escapade without sheathing himself. I *always* come prepared. Rest assured, love, I am clean. *Very* clean."

He stood and gestured toward the buttons on his trousers, trying to remain serious, though he felt anything but. "Does the school require proof?"

Her eyes coolly trailed from the trousers he

continued to point to up at his face. "Should you be accepted into the school, Harold will indeed ensure that you are clean. Complete physicals, after all, are required."

Alexander slowly sat, feeling his bollocks rapidly traveling north. Harold wasn't exactly what he'd had in mind. "*Harold?*" he couldn't help but echo.

"Yes. Harold." She dipped her quill into the glass inkwell, a small smile playing on her lips. "Next question. Have you ever engaged in sexual activities with a man?"

"What?" Alexander's brows popped up in response, his mind still not having quite gotten over the whole Harold bit. "No. Of course not."

She nodded and placed another *x* beside his name. "Have you ever considered or desired to engage in sexual activities with a man?"

"Hell, I think Caldwell may have." He laughed and then squinted at all the *x*'s she had placed beside his name. It was a downright curious way to go about documenting their conversation.

She lifted her gaze from her paper. Pinning him with a firm stare, she replied in a manner which he himself often used when speaking to his youngest sister. "I assure you your answers will not leave this paper or this room. All I ask is that you answer the question. Have you ever thought about engaging in sexual activities with a man?"

"I'm not all that worried about my answers leaving the room. Believe me, I've seen and done everything." He paused. "Well . . . except *that*."

"No is sufficient, My Lord." She placed another *x* beside his name. "There is no need to insult other people's sexual preferences. The idea behind the school is to broaden your tolerance toward all forms of sexuality. That way, there is no limit to your imagination or your form of pleasure."

Alexander stared at her. So she took buggery in stride, did she? He'd certainly always thought to each his own, but by the calm, refined look on her face, he sensed that her nonchalant approach to sexuality was in fact genuine. Which in truth astounded him. For he rarely met a woman of her rank that felt *that* comfortable with all forms of sexuality. Who wasn't a Hawksford, that is.

"Back to a few more questions," she went on. "Have you ever pleasured a woman using unconventional means?"

The heat of his body was actually becoming intolerable. For he knew he wanted to do a few unconventional things with her. Against one of the walls. He cleared his throat and smoothed the front of his waistcoat, trying to keep his lower half from becoming too involved in the conversation. "Yes. I have."

She sighed, sounding rather agitated. "Define one of those methods."

"Define one of them?" he asked in disbelief, leaning forward. He'd never really gone into detail before. Not even when discussing it with Caldwell. "You mean in detail?"

"Yes. In detail."

He swiped a hand over his face and tried to think of one of the lesser evils. He didn't want another one of those looks from her. Though he supposed that couldn't well be avoided.

Lady Charlotte lowered her eyes, pressing her lips together in a firm line, as if awaiting a response she already knew the answer to.

So. The woman thought she knew him well enough? To hell with that. He wasn't about to give her that sort of satisfaction. "Actually," he replied, trying to keep his face from betraying the fact that he wanted to laugh, "I prefer to keep things simple. In fact, I never dare wander from the prescribed position."

She eyed him suspiciously, then leaned down to her paper and marked not one, but three very large X's beneath his name, changing the pattern of all the small x's.

Hold now, that didn't seem fair. Why did she give him three large X's? He was beginning to believe she was actually looking for reasons to reject his application. He pointed toward all the marks beside his name. "Might I ask what the difference is between a large X and a small one?"

She gestured her quill to the ink marks. "They are merely for bookkeeping purposes. Nothing you need worry about."

She added another large X beside his name and met his gaze with a cool reprimand. "Now. I have one last question. One I know you will have no trouble answering. What is the purpose behind your application today? And do be specific." She lowered her gaze back to the paper, positioning her quill for the reply.

The woman wanted him to be specific, did she? And she wanted him to be honest, did she?

All right. To hell with this stupid game. He might as well get to the point.

Alexander rose and closed the small distance between him and the desk. Slowly, he placed the palms of his hands flat on the rosewood surface of the desk and leaned down toward her until their faces met at exactly the same level. The scent of soft lavender drifted around him and he shifted his jaw, vividly picturing her naked body against his.

She froze. Her eyes lifted from her paper and trailed up the length of his chest until their gazes met. Contrary to her outward appearance, the unsteady rise and fall of her breasts indicated that she was anything but calm.

"*You* are the purpose behind my application," he finally replied. "And though I've tried to rationally explain to myself that I shouldn't even be here, yet alone apply, ever since that day in the carriage, I've wanted nothing more than to engage you in all things physical."

He leaned in even farther, his eyes lowering to her mouth, imagining what he could do with just her lips alone. "Forward. Backward. Upside down. Right side up. It really doesn't matter. And think what you will of how I treated you that day, the only reason I didn't fully engage you then or in those months afterward is because I refused to take advantage of your situation. I've never paid for a frig nor will I ever. Is that specific enough for you? Or should I go on?"

She blinked, her full lips parting in obvious astonishment. The quill slipped from her fingers and on to the paper, spattering ink across the page. "I . . . that is—"

He straightened, removing his hands from the small desk and strode around it toward her, determined to quench this desire raging through him. A desire that would not permit his body or his mind to rest unless he did something about it.

She quickly stood, sending the chair tumbling backward and scrambled toward the opposite side of the desk. Away from him. Her eyes widened. "What are you doing?" she demanded, holding up a hand as if that alone would somehow stop him. "This is a business relationship!"

"Call it whatever you like. It doesn't really matter." He stepped over the toppled chair close to her and grabbed hold of her corseted waist. Though she tried to wiggle out from his grasp, he held on and dragged her toward him. He firmly pressed her warm softness against his body, which in turn only tightened the grating need within him. She ceased struggling against him.

Releasing her waist, he dug both hands deep into her soft, thick hair. He tilted her face up to him, though he was rather surprised to find that she herself was already lifting her face to his. As if she wanted this just as much as he did.

Her hands fiercely gripped the sides of his waist, their presence empowering his body's needs all the more.

"Do you have any further questions for me?" he whispered down at her.

"No." A small, shaky breath escaped her as she slowly leaned toward him and against his body.

"None." Her eyes closed and her lips slightly parted as she offered them up to him.

Alexander lowered his lips toward hers and gently breathed in the heat of her lavender-scented skin. His cock thickened and lengthened in response, pressing against his wool trousers.

It had been far too long since he had given himself over completely to the wants and needs of his body. And he was damn well tired of resisting and denying himself. He deserved this one pleasure from her. He deserved this one kiss.

He pressed his lips against hers and closed his eyes, giving in to the sensation. Forcing her velvety lips further open, he thrust his tongue urgently into the wet warmth of her mouth, savoring the taste and feel of her. Savoring this moment of utter bliss.

Her hot tongue slowly challenged his, causing his cock to thicken and harden in response. Alexander pressed her more savagely against the length of his aching body, his needy cock, wanting to be inside of her. Wanting to experience the soft wetness of her core in the same way he was experiencing the soft wetness of her mouth against his.

There was a sudden knock at the door.

Alexander's head snapped up in response, leaving his lips cool from her mouth's moisture and warmth.

Charlotte stumbled back, shoving his arms away from her body. She let out a shaky breath. "I apologize for my behavior. That was uncalled for, given the nature of our business." She eyed him. "It won't happen again."

She paused for another moment, as if allowing them both to absorb her words, then gathered up her skirts from around her feet and bustled around him. With shaky hands, she grabbed hold of her chair, setting it right side up, and called out, "Yes? Come in!" A bit too loudly.

He blew out a frustrated breath through his teeth, knowing that his opportunity with her had been lost. What was worse, he hadn't even been given the glorious opportunity of fondling her breasts.

Alexander turned toward the door and adjusted his coat in an effort to cover up his still very heavy and very hard cock.

Caldwell's blond head popped in through the opening. He eyed them somewhat anxiously. "How much longer? I've completely run out of things to say to Harold."

Of course, it would be Caldwell. Who else?

Alexander strode at Caldwell, shoved his head back out into the corridor, and slammed the door. The man never did have a good sense of timing.

"You're such a rude bastard!" Caldwell called out from the other side. "You do realize that, don't you?"

"I'm not the one harboring deep, dark secrets!" Alexander yelled back. "Now wait your Goddamn turn!"

He spun toward Charlotte and hoped that there was still some chance of salvaging the moment. Though women always regained their senses so much quicker than men.

And what was worse, their brief kiss had not alleviated a single one of his desires for her. Actually, it had only strengthened them. For he wanted more of her. Much, much more. After all, if her mouth could taste and feel that good, he could only imagine what the rest of her would be like.

She hurriedly organized her desk, setting aside parchments to one end, straightening the ink-well, and placing the quill back into it. A portion of her long, dark hair slid over her shoulder and fell onto her quick-moving hands. She shoved it out of the way, appearing annoyed.

"Thank you for your application," she hurried. "Should it be accepted, a letter will arrive at the address of the calling card you submitted. I do hope you find the rest of your day to be pleasant. Good day."

Her words sounded rehearsed, to say the least.

A twinge of disappointment reverberated through him. That was all she meant to say? After what had transpired between them? Hell, usually *he* was the one that up and gave women the hie-off. Not the other way around.

And fight it as he might, he didn't want this woman to be done with him. For yes, for the sake of all things proper he should walk away, deep inside he simply could not. Would not. He had already walked away from the woman once before, thinking it had been the right thing to do, and it had resulted in nothing but pointless torture. An agonizing mental and physical torture he had not thought possible.

"Allow me to call on you at another, more convenient time," he eventually said in a tone that was much too soft to his own ears and liking.

She leaned against the desk, the folds of her black skirt fanning forward, closed her eyes, and sighed. "I do not bed clients, My Lord. That is not the point of this school. Furthermore, it is strictly forbidden to me."

He leveled his gaze at her, sensing that she was resisting what he simply could not. "Then I ask that you revoke my application. Immediately."

She glanced toward him in disbelief and pushed herself away from the desk. Setting her hands on her hips, she turned and faced him. "This may be difficult for you to comprehend, but I am not interested in bedding you. At all."

"At all?" He stepped toward her, though he knew he really should have stepped back. "So what about our kiss? You didn't enjoy it? At all?"

She took a step back nearer the desk. "No, it isn't that. Our kiss was very . . ." She paused, her eyes visibly widening in response to what was almost an admission.

He grinned out of genuine self-satisfaction. "Very what? I'm rather curious as to what you thought of it."

A flush overtook her porcelain cheeks. "Perhaps your curiosity would be better served if I explained the reason behind my complete lack of interest."

Oo. That was certainly a good stab at his manhood. "By all means. I have all day." He lowered his chin. "And all night, if you like."

"I'm certain you do, Lord Hawksford." She huffed out a breath as if preparing herself for a speech before the House of Commons. "As you and everyone else may already know, during the height of last year's Season, I was widowed at the age of five and twenty in a very sad, very pathetic and shameful manner."

He cleared his throat. "Yes. Actually, I remember reading about it. Met him on a few occasions. Though I didn't know he was married."

"He didn't seem to know he was married, either." Charlotte laced her fingers together before her and sighed. "Shortly after his death had been so widely publicized, I was astounded to discover that in his will, I was left with nothing. Not a single farthing of annuity to support myself. It appeared he had written a letter to his solicitor, a few weeks before his own death, claiming that because I refused to perform my marital duties, I was to be removed from his will. It was as if he knew he was going to be popped off."

Alexander shook his head in disgust. To leave a woman uncared for was downright evil. "Don't allow yourself to be gulled. You have rights. Having only recently gone through my father's estate, I know for a fact that a spouse is entitled to at least a third of it."

She studied him for a brief moment, as if trying to decipher what his intentions were. "I've already hired a lawyer to contest the will. And it has cost me everything I have. Despite all of my visits to the Lord Chancellor pleading for my situation and lack of funds, I am but a name on an excruciatingly long list."

She shook her head and released a bitter laugh. "Do you realize that there are those who have waited an entire decade for their case to be heard? Unlike all the others, I have no family to financially support me whilst I await that decision. This school, that you and so many others choose to mock, is my only form of income. Which brings me to the point of this conversation. I have no intention of jeopardizing my future here at the school by involving myself with you. Is that understood?"

Alexander ran a heavy hand through his hair, feeling rather humbled by her confession. "Forgive me. I didn't know the specifics."

"Well, now you do."

He dropped his hand back to his side and didn't know what he was supposed to say. "Do you require further monetary assistance?"

"Yes. In return for a good swive, I am sure."

He let out a genuine laugh. "As I've already mentioned before, Lady Charlotte, I don't pay for my pleasure. Furthermore, your approach to all of this is rather simplistic. I have a much better idea. Why not allow me to call upon Madame de Maitenon and ask for permission to engage you? That way, you get everything. My assistance, retaining your position here at the school, and best of all, sex. With me." He grinned.

She stared at him. Then had the audacity to laugh. "After Chartwell, I can assure you, I am done tending to the needs of a man. More than done, actually." She swept a hand toward the door behind him. "If you please. I have another client, and I shan't be so rude as to keep him waiting."

Alexander's grin slowly faded. This certainly didn't bode well for him. Did it? Hell, when a beautiful woman said such horrible things, it was a man's inherent responsibility to set it right. To see to those neglected needs in a way no other man ever had. "I assure you, Chartwell does not represent the majority of the male population. I hope that you are not judging me based upon his complete inability to please you."

Her expression grew taut. "No, I am not judging you. I simply have my *own* personal needs to oversee without concerning myself with *yours*. I'm certain a worldly man such as yourself can understand."

Amen to a woman who spoke her mind.

Though he wasn't overly fond of being grouped together with Chartwell, her strong sense of bravado was maddeningly admirable. Not to mention erotic. For a woman who knew exactly what she wanted in the day, also knew what she wanted at night. "Surely your personal needs must involve an orgasm or two," he gruffly pointed out, taking another step toward her.

She gasped and dropped her hands back to her sides. "No. They do not."

"I don't believe you. Not after the way you kissed me."

"*Leave.*" She sounded fully aware that her excuses held no substance. "Before I have Harold escort you out of the school."

He held up a hand, asking for her patience. "Obviously, neither of us is looking to complicate our lives by submitting to anything serious. Which is why I suggest we keep this simple. Allow me to talk to Madame so that I may ensure that your position here is not affected. Surely a woman of her experience wouldn't want to keep two willing lovers apart. Once she agrees, you can name your rules, along with whatever it is you want or need, and I will counteroffer. That way, we both get what we want without any complications."

She tartly observed him as if she were about to smack him. "My. How quickly you thought of all that. Clearly you've done this before."

Guilty as charged.

Alexander strode steadily toward her, refusing to relinquish the possibility of having her in his bed. Once. That's all he wanted. For now.

Lady Charlotte held up a hand and started backing away. "Forcing yourself upon me will change nothing."

"I never force myself upon women. I negotiate with them." He paused before her. "Now seeing you've already had a chance to express your viewpoint, I ask that you show a bit of social grace and allow me to express mine in turn."

Her eyes widened. "You, Lord Hawksford, are relentless."

"Does that mean you are giving me permission to proceed?"

Her eyes fluttered closed as she pressed the tips of her fingers to the left side of her temple. She eventually lifted her lids and waved a hand toward him. "By all means. Proceed."

Alexander spread his legs slightly apart, positioning himself more comfortably before her. "Unlike other men, I do not serenade women with unfulfilled promises. But I do take great pride in ensuring that trust, enjoyment, respect, and pleasure are all involved in every tryst I indulge in. A rare trait in a man these days, wouldn't you agree?"

She blinked up at him. As if trying to decipher if he was being serious.

Which, of course, he was. He had always believed that communication between the sexes was vital. Otherwise it led to hysteria. And tears. Something he never enjoyed witnessing. Or being the cause of. "It's all rather simple. I stand before you a servant. A most humble servant willing to do anything to indulge in the offerings of your body."

The blank expression on her face faded as an amused smile softened her lips. She tilted her head to one side as she peered up at him. "A servant, you say?"

He captured her gaze and held it firmly, trying his best not to reach out and force his point upon her. "*Your* servant."

She leaned slightly back, as if his gaze intruded too much.

He lifted his hand and cupped her chin with it, allowing his thumb to trace the edge of her smooth jaw and cheek. He enjoyed the feel of her warm, velvet skin against his hand and sensed her leaning back toward him. As if wanting to engage and give in to his touch.

"A quick word, however," he murmured, pulling his hand away and holding up his forefinger in the air both to demonstrate his point as well as to set a clear divider between them. "I cannot offer love or marriage. This would merely be an exchange of pleasure."

She stepped back and out of his reach, reclaiming the distance between them. "You really think too highly of yourself."

He shrugged and then grinned. "I sensed that

you wouldn't truly wish to be trapped with me for a lifetime, but I wanted to be certain."

"Of course you did." The devious gleam he had the pleasure of witnessing in the depths of her eyes during the initial application process magically reappeared, tossing aside his earlier fears of complications.

She turned toward the desk, snatched up his gloves, which he'd forgotten all about, and smacked them gently against the palm of her open hand, her eyes never leaving his. "How about this, Lord Hawksford. If Madame de Maitenon accepts your application into the school, I will *personally* see to it that you're allowed to *pleasure* me. Will that suffice?"

Hardly. Picturing all those *x*'s both large and small beneath his birth name told him he had a better chance of becoming the King of England. Of course, he was never one to easily submit to defeat. He'd find a way to get himself into the school. And into her bed.

Not that he was going to tell her that.

Alexander humbly inclined his head to her. "Do try and behave yourself. It was a *pleasure*."

"You've proven to be quite entertaining, Lord Hawksford." She smiled, then graciously extended her bare ivory hand toward him. "As such, I'll give you this one last *pleasure* at no cost to you at all. Go on. You may kiss it."

The saucy little wench! He had absolutely no intention of accepting anything less than a full kiss from her lips. And eventually, he intended to collect more. Much more. Without a single bit of resistance.

He gave her a withering look of disinterest. "In all honesty, I prefer the entire soufflé."

She lowered her hand and returned his withering look. "I knew you were a glutton. Inform Lord Caldwell that I am ready to receive him. Good day and good-bye."

With that, she returned to her desk, leaving him with the stark realization that his taste for pleasure had not disappeared from his blood at all. Despite all of his efforts to *appear* proper for the sake of his family, his old self was about to reemerge in the name of the greatest conquest he had ever embarked upon.

He only hoped to God he could keep this from his family or he'd never hear the end of it. Then again, Lady Charlotte was well worth that risk. Which is why he intended to not only seize this tasty little challenge, but to do so with both hands. Not to mention the rest of his body.

Lesson Seven

*While you fret and fuss over how to prepare
for pleasure, simply remember, that the sole
point of every sexual encounter is to
measure, measure, measure.*
—*The School of Gallantry*

11 Berwick Street
Two days later

Charlotte held up Lord Hawksford's completed application and faced Madame de Maitenon once again in complete exasperation. "This is ridiculous, Madame! Considering all the men that have applied to this school, and the amount of men you are limiting us to during the first Season, why would you even bother accepting his application? The man isn't looking for an education. He's looking for entertainment."

Madame de Maitenon observed her from across the Greek-inspired parlor, remaining stoically seated upon the only piece of furniture to grace the room. "I agree that his aspirations could be somewhat corrupt, but it is imperative we involve him in the school for reasons I cannot go into. What is more, I know this young man. I once had the honor—and I do mean that—of pleasuring his father." She eyed her. "*And* his mother. Though I ask that you keep that to yourself and not tell Maybelle or anyone else." She winked mischievously and lowered her voice. "I was supposed to be in retirement, but the money was simply too good."

Stunned, Charlotte felt her cheeks flare. And she'd thought the woman was incapable of further astounding her. No wonder Lord Hawksford was naughty by nature! He'd inherited it from his parents.

What was worse, if Madame de Maitenon accepted the man's application, it was going to complicate every single aspect of her life. A harmonious, peaceful life which she'd just started to enjoy.

For Alexander William Baxendale, the third Earl of Hawksford, who had obviously bedded nearly every woman in London—if not all—would come marching straight into the school looking to collect an endless array of self-loving pleasures. She certainly recognized the devious fire that lit his eyes. He would only stop once *he* had been sated. And what was even more terrible was that she *wanted* to submit to that devious fire. As if Chartwell hadn't been enough of a lesson for her.

Beyond frustrated, Charlotte tossed the application and let it float and whirl off to the side, toward the feet of one of her Greek male statues. "I see. You pleasured the father and the mother and now you wish to pleasure the son? Is that it?"

Madame de Maitenon let out an unbridled laugh, throwing back her head as if to let it flow out all the better. She lowered her chin and shook her head. "*Non*. You misunderstand."

"Oh, do I?"

"*Mais oui*." The woman rose from her chair, her full, rose satin skirts rustling as they slid back down into place around her slippered feet. Her blue eyes were lit with an unusual amount of excitement. "You see, his father was very much like him. Wild. Forever obsessed with pleasuring not only himself, but women. He became known as the Lord of Pleasure due to his endless array of feisty dalliances. When he eventually married, some twenty years later, his lust had finally met its match. For Lady Hawksford, though much younger, was as naughty and wicked at heart as he. Theirs was not a love match. *Non*. 'Twas a *lust* match. And it is what ultimately led to their happiness."

A lust match? She'd never even heard of such a thing.

Madame de Maitenon clasped her hands together. "What a scandalous pair the two made! Lord and Lady by day. Adam and Eve by night. Each allowing the other to explore their sexuality without limitations. Unheard of in London. And yet . . . they always maintained gracious appearances for the *ton*. Which was very, very wise on their part. For they attained the best of both worlds. Their son, who was a bit of a romantic, and nothing like them, eventually followed their lead after a beautiful *femme,* seven years his senior, wounded his young heart by refusing to marry him. She claimed that he was far too young to understand the needs and pleasures of a woman and further mocked him by taking on not one, but three other lovers."

Madame shrugged. "You can say he wanted to reclaim his pride by learning everything there was to know about pleasuring a woman. And learn he did."

Madame de Maitenon turned and sashayed her way toward the statues. She lowered herself gracefully down to the application on the floor and plucked it up, rising once again.

Tilting her head, she perused Charlotte's lengthy notes regarding Lord Hawksford. Upon reaching the bottom of the parchment, she glanced up, a look of sympathy pulling her features. "Then his father died. 'Twas sad, but expected. For he was not young. Lord Hawksford naturally inherited everything, including five younger sisters and a mother. To the disappointment of every woman in London, he also retired from his pleasure-seeking days and has not entertained a single *femme* since. Or so they say."

Charlotte's eyes widened. Why did she feel as if she had stumbled upon a man that was best left alone? If she didn't know any better, she'd say the man was looking to vent all of his sexual frustrations upon her.

Madame de Maitenon knowingly smiled. "When I suggested Lord Caldwell bring him to the school, I was somewhat worried about the outcome.

Clearly, I had nothing to worry about. Though I do wonder . . . Why would Lord Hawksford enroll?" She paused, then quirked a silver brow at her. "Something must have sparked his interest. And I *know* it was not my school."

Charlotte froze, knowing full well what Madame was insinuating. It seemed downright impossible. Impossible that out of all the women in London, she, a penniless widow tossed from the ranks of society, could magically resurrect a man's need for pleasure. And that out of all the men that she could have possibly happened upon in her very last hour of need, it would have been none other than *the* Lord of Pleasure the second.

Perhaps it was time she confessed to everything. Before it became any more complicated. After all, she'd only kissed him. Surely, Madame would forgive her for that. She hoped.

"Madame." Charlotte cleared her throat, an uncomfortable heat overtaking her body. "I am actually quite certain Lord Hawksford put in his application due to my involvement in the school. He and I had actually met on a previous occasion."

"Oh?"

Oh, indeed. "'Twas brief, really. Nothing that ever led to anything. During my interview with him, however, I somehow lost sight of my duty toward the school and allowed him to kiss me."

Charlotte inwardly winced the moment her words came out and prayed that it wouldn't result in her dismissal. Prayed that Madame would understand. And show mercy.

Madame de Maitenon blinked then slowly grinned, her blue eyes practically sparkling. "The moment I first saw you with that iron poker in your hand, I *knew* you would be a valuable asset to this school. So. When will the rendezvous be? Hmm? And where?"

When? Where? Oh, for heaven's sake! "Whatever do you mean, when, where? You told me I wasn't allowed to involve myself with any of the men that applied to this school. I thought you'd be upset."

"*Upset?* Pah." She flitted the wrist of her hand back and forth. "There are always exceptions to my rules, *chérie*. Especially when pleasure is involved. Now tell Madame. What are your plans with him thus far?"

Plans? Oh, now *this* she most certainly had not expected. Though she supposed she should have. Her being the naughty, naughty thing that she was. "I don't think you understand. I refused him."

Madame de Maitenon's enthusiastic grin faded. She now lowered her chin in clear disapproval. "You refused him?"

"Yes."

"But why?"

"*Why?*" Charlotte repeated. "Aside from the fact that you told me that I needed to maintain a sense of professionalism toward all your students? Perhaps it also has to do with what my husband did to me. I'll not expose myself to harm. Which is why you cannot accept his application. You simply cannot."

A frown tugged at the woman's lips. "Why can I not accept his application? It is *my* school. I can do whatever I please."

"Yes, I know, but I told him—thinking you would surely deny his ridiculous application—that if he was accepted into the school, I would personally call on you to ask for permission to involve myself with him. Which puts me in quite the dilemma."

Madame de Maitenon's brows went up, her lips parting. She glanced at the application in her hand, then back up at Charlotte. "I see. And . . . you do not desire him?"

She rolled her eyes. "That is not the point. The man is only seeking sexual gratification."

"And that is a problem for you?"

Why was she making this into more than it was? "Yes. As a matter of fact, it is a problem for me."

"Why? Is it because you are seeking marriage from him? I thought you were done with marriage."

Charlotte placed her hands on her hips, not in the least bit amused with the direction their conversation had taken. "I *am* done with marriage. But I still have a bit of respect for myself. I'll have you know, that during our interview, Lord Hawksford admitted to bedding five women at once. *Five.* For all I know, I'd have to entertain more than just his lordship if I were to end up in his bed. And I am simply not that sort." Realizing how utterly rude that must have sounded, she quickly added, "Not to offend you, of course."

Madame de Maitenon sighed rather dramatically and shook her head, her thick silver chignon wobbling from side to side. "I assure you, Lord Hawksford, though sometimes lacking in morals, is well worth your time. He will see to your pleasure, treat you beautifully, and when you both decide to part, there will be no complications. He prides himself on satisfying a woman completely."

So that was the look he had given her. Pride. How utterly grand.

"If he wishes to pleasure you," Madame de Maitenon went on, gesturing toward her, "allow yourself the freedom to take pride in it. Especially if you secretly desire it. After everything you have been through, you deserve as much. And as long as you do not involve your heart, *chérie*, it will be like drinking endless amounts of glorious champagne, but without the headache that usually comes with it in the morning."

Charlotte felt as though her throat was constricting. The woman was mad. Stark, raving mad. What sort of advice was that to give to another woman?

As calmly as possible, for she knew if she allowed herself to give in to the hysteria of how she felt, she would be incapable of saying an intelligible word, Charlotte asked, "So you are going to accept his application? Despite my formal plea?" She hated how desperate she sounded, but the reality was, she *was* desperate. She didn't want to face that man again. For she knew full well what it would lead to. And she was ruined enough!

"Och, you do not understand, do you?" Madame de Maitenon went over to the chair placed in the middle of the room and set the application onto it before hurrying toward her with a look of genuine concern.

The woman grasped Charlotte's shoulders

with both hands. "Why is it that men are allowed to seek out pleasure from us, yet we are not allowed to seek out pleasure from them? Although society chooses to purposefully destroy our pleasures using conventional means of guilt and religion, that does not mean we should accept it. Ask yourself this. Did you deny Lord Hawksford because of the prudishness instilled upon you by society? Or did you deny him because you did not find him attractive? There is a difference."

Charlotte's chest squeezed as an odd sense of realization settled within her. The questions were simple at best. Ones she already had the answers to. But ones she had never truly taken the time to ask herself.

"I denied him due to my prudishness," she finally admitted in a broken whisper. "But fore most, Madame, I admit to fear. Surely you can understand my predicament. Chartwell took everything from me. My trust. My money. My dreams of ever having a family. And worst of all, he cost me the last moments I should have had with my mother." Charlotte fought from releasing the tears that were now beginning to burn her eyes.

"Which is why you cannot let him take anymore. Do not compare Chartwell to other men, *chérie*. It is too dangerous to your mind and to your heart. Not to mention your pleasure." Madame de Maitenon's voice was now a soft breath of a whisper. "I apologize, but I have no choice but to accept Lord Hawksford's application. It involves an agreement I made with Lord Caldwell that I am not allowed to discuss. However, if my obligation to

Lord Caldwell worries you, I can tell Lord Hawksford that there will be no rendezvous. Inform me if you feel otherwise. Now. I must bid you *adieu*. The pleasure room is in desperate need of more attention, and I have yet to find the right girls." She shook her head. "Who knew a mere attic would be so complicated?"

With that, Madame de Maitenon released her, turned and swept out of the room, heading toward the corridor and back to the school.

Still in somewhat of a semi-philosophical daze, Charlotte slowly approached one of the Greek male statues before her, the one whose muscular arm held out the corset Alexander had given her.

She fingered the smooth but stiff ends of the beautiful corset she had been unable to part with. A corset she had quietly donned on so many occasions in the confines of her bedroom. As a way of drawing him closer to her.

Despite the way her marriage had ended, she had experienced physical pleasure at the hands of her husband and knew very well what was possible between a man and a woman.

It wasn't the pleasure, however, that she had sought. All she had truly ever wanted was the kind of genuine love her parents had once known. And a family of her own.

Her mother had repeatedly warned her about Chartwell, had warned her of the rumors and his mistresses, yet his beautiful letters, the time he spent courting her, did not allow her foolish heart to see what he truly was until it was too late. And now that the man was gone, buried from both mind and sight, nothing stopped her from living the sort of life she truly wanted. And live it, she had sworn to herself, she would. In every possible way.

So why was she hesitating? She supposed deep inside she knew why. Because she liked Alexander. More than she wanted to admit. Liked his charm. His wit. Admired how protective he was during times when he could have easily taken advantage of her.

The man even conveniently came with five sisters and a mother. She could only imagine the sort of fun they always had as a family. The chatter, the laughter, and all the excitement that occurred from day to day.

She sighed wistfully. Oh, to be part of a family again. A *real* family. It was something she'd always wanted with all her heart, but something she knew she would never be part of again. Ruined as she was. It was time to admit that her dreams needed to change and reflect the true realities at hand.

Charlotte drew her hand away from the dangling corset and traced her gaze over each of her statues. Statues she had purchased as a playful nod to the School of Gallantry and a symbol of her triumph against a world of immovable, stone-hearted men.

She was no longer a naïve girl at a grave disadvantage. Unlike before, she understood the game. Understood what to expect and what not to expect from a man and could therefore orchestrate this entire situation in her favor.

So. The Lord of Pleasure wanted to indulge in the offerings of her body, did he? Damn her own curiosity, but she actually wanted to know what that would entail.

Charlotte hurried toward the parchment on the floor and snatched it up. She held it up before her, admiring Alexander's full name.

"Lord Hawksford," she formally announced, her voice echoing around her. "Pleasure me. If you can."

Lesson Eight

*Congratulations. You have officially
been accepted. The question is,
is it what you had expected?*
    —*The School of Gallantry*

"Meeeeeeooowwww."

Alexander ignored the white, fluffy feline sitting on the edge of his oak desk and opened the leather-bound book on Roman history. At last. Uninterrupted quiet time for himself. He flipped toward the section he had last been reading. On weaponry.

"Mrrrrreeeeooow." The cat reached out and batted at the book in a clear protest that he was paying attention to it and not her.

Women. Alexander eyed the cat that casually blinked back at him with large, innocent blue eyes. Fortunately, she was the only female bothering him at this particular moment. Though who knew how long that would last. He had snuck into the study two hours earlier than usual in the hope of catching up on some reading. "A little privacy, if you please?"

This time the little tease bumped her furry head against his hand. And started purring. Clearly determined.

Alexander leaned toward the cat, rubbing her affectionately behind the ears, and lowered his chin. "I'll have you know, you furry petticoat, that if it weren't for the Romans, you wouldn't even be sitting on my desk. After all, they brought all of your ancestors over. Now show them a bit of respect and stop interrupting me."

The cat blinked, then lifted her paw and started licking the length of her limb. Showing him that respect was all a matter of opinion.

"Alex? Oh, there you are! Talking to the cat again, I see." Caroline sashayed into the study, a bundle of tied correspondences tucked into her hand. "Where on earth have you been this past week? Though I confess that it was rather wonderful not having you breathing down my neck about the Season, I still missed you all the same. So. Will you be joining Mother and me for a ride today?"

"Not likely. I have far too many important matters to tend to."

"Ah, yes," Caroline drawled, eyeing him. "Like talking to the cat."

The cat snapped up her white tail, jumped off the desk, and scampered out of the room. Clearly offended.

Caroline paused at the edge of the Axminster carpet set in the middle of the room, then gracefully gathered the excess from the back of her palomino riding habit, so as not to pull up the carpet as she passed. Once fully past the carpet, she dropped her skirts behind her and continued to glide her way toward where he sat behind his desk. Her pinned and curled chestnut hair, still free of a riding hat, delicately swayed around her freckled, ivory face with each feminine step she took.

How his own sister had learned to act and walk like a woman still downright astounded him. As unruly as she'd been as a child, he would have never guessed her capable of any civil grace.

A high-pitched voice suddenly squealed from somewhere upstairs, "Alex is here! Hurry! He's here!"

There was a slamming of various doors throughout the townhouse and an echoing stampede of numerous feet.

Alexander slapped his book shut, the book he had hoped to enjoy during their morning studies, and tossed it onto the paper-strewn desk he had yet to organize. "I was hoping for a quiet and civilized day today. I've had a rather long week."

A *very* long week that had involved decanters of cognac at his club while waiting for a response from the notorious Madame de Maitenon with regard to his application. A response that had yet to come. A response, he was beginning to believe, that would never come unless he marched himself straight over to 11 Berwick Street and did something about it.

He had already put in a written offer to pay Madame de Maitenon as much as a hundred pounds per week if it meant being able to attend the school. Yes. He really was that desperate.

"There are no quiet, civilized days in this house. You know that and I know that." Caroline settled before him and set the bundle of correspondences unceremoniously onto his desk. She pointed at the pile, which had been neatly tied with a pink lace ribbon. "Upon your request. Another set of invitations. I only wish everyone would up and hang themselves. By their pennants. Yourself included."

He sighed. "Don't you ever get tired of nagging me?"

She eyed him, a glint of angry fire appearing in those blue-green eyes. "I've said it before, Alex, and I'll say it again. I hate the Season. Loathe it. Everything about it is so bloody superficial and meaningless. Lady Lansworth's gathering last night was by far the worst example of it yet. I don't want to attend another one of her horrid little parties. Do you understand me? Burn whatever she sends."

A rather strong sentiment. Though knowing Caroline, it was probably well deserved.

A stampede of feet suddenly entered the study. The rustling of skirts practically deafened him as Anne, Elizabeth, and Victoria settled in one by one right behind Caroline, their freckled cheeks flushed and their matching green-blue eyes wide with vivid excitement.

"You all know I'm not supposed to run!" Mary, the youngest, exclaimed from the doorway, her hands propped on her hips. Her golden chestnut braid was frayed and coming undone, long wisps dangling every which way. "The doctor says unnecessary exertion may very well cause my lungs to swell. And the swelling of lungs, as you may or may not know, can lead to an untimely death."

Mary demonstrated by releasing several gasping, harsh coughs that were anything but real. She tapped at her chest before heaving out an exasperated sigh. "And besides, our studies are far from done. Mrs. Peterson will be cross if she finds us down here."

"Oh, be quiet, little Miss Morbid," Anne, the second youngest, flung over her shoulder. "Mrs. Peterson is always cross, and I'll have you know that opening these letters is far more important than you and your silly theatrics."

"*Anne*," Alexander snapped, glaring at her.

Anne promptly responded by folding her slender arms over the ruffled front of her cotton blue, flower patterned dress. She puffed out an annoyed breath, deflating her freckled cheeks. "What now?"

"Reserve that tone for the cat." He leaned toward the desk. "You know full well she hasn't taken Father's death in stride as well as we have. What is more, she's little."

"*I am not little!* Most people say I can pass for fifteen." Mary marched over to his desk, kicking up the ends of her black dress with her quick movements. Although they were all officially done with mourning for their father, Mary refused to wear anything but black. "What I *have* been this past week, however, is deathly ill. But then no one really cares, do they? I could drop dead here and now and you'd all simply carry on with your day."

"You know full well she feigns illness all the time, Alex," Elizabeth joined in, passionately defending Anne. "She died twice this past week. And I for one am growing rather tired of it. What is worse, Mother finds it all endearing. Which, of course, only encourages Mary all the more. I say, instead of reprimanding the rest of us, you should be reprimanding *her.*" Elizabeth jerked her thumb in Mary's direction.

Alexander rolled his eyes, wondering if he would ever please any of them. Though in all honesty, they, much like he, knew that at the core of his soul, he was pitifully softhearted and loved each and every one of their intolerable little ways. Including Mary, who had grown a bit too obsessed with death.

He was certain it had to do with the fact that she had been unable to attend their father's burial. And though women and children of status were never publicly allowed to attend formal burials—something his other sisters and mother had preferred—Mary was still rather cross about the whole matter. And repeated visits to the grave site had done little to alleviate that. Fortunately, her obsession hadn't led to poison, knives, or caskets.

Not as of yet, anyway.

"Well, don't just sit there like an artifact in a museum." Victoria leaned forward, her thick, blond braid swaying back and forth over her shoulder as she shoved the bundle of letters at him. "Open it. We've been waiting all week for you to get around to them."

It appeared that the opening of Caroline's invitations had turned into their favorite pastime. To the horror of Caroline, no doubt.

Alexander snatched up the bundle and slowly rose, holding it high into the air for all of them to see. He tried to remain serious as he tapped at the bundle. "Unfortunately, I am still rather pre-occupied with a few matters of business, so I won't have a chance to look at any of these any-time soon. Perhaps we can resume this sometime next week?"

"*Noooo!*" they all exclaimed in genuine, high-pitched horror.

Caroline laughed and stepped around the desk toward him. She reached out and grabbed the invitations from his hand, waving them about. "Can't I just burn them? It's not as if the man I plan to marry is going to attend any of these."

Alexander stared at her. There was a man? Already? This could be good. Although knowing Caroline . . . it could also be bad. Very bad.

He yanked the invitations back out of her hands and held them away. Knowing if given the chance she would burn them. "I didn't realize you already had affections toward a particular man." He tried not to sound as though he was panicking, even though he was. "Who is he? Do I know him?"

Caroline froze then eyed him and feigned a small laugh. She stepped back and away. "As if I would ever tell you. You'd run him straight out of London."

Alexander narrowed his gaze. "If you think that *I* would run him out of London, then there must be something terribly wrong with him."

When she didn't respond, he pointed the letters at her head. In warning. "We may be Hawksfords, Caroline, but don't forget that in the end we still answer to the society around us. I involved you in the Season in order to expose you to a good match. You'd best remember that. And you'd best be careful."

Victoria leaned onto the desk toward them and tilted her dark blond head slightly. "And what exactly would she need to be careful of, Alex? Care to elaborate from an experienced male perspective?"

Anne set her hands behind her back, taking on the countenance of a professor. "Yes. Elaborate. From an experienced male perspective."

Parrots. He was bloody surrounded by parrots.

Mary's eyes widened as she suddenly glanced at everyone around her. "I know *exactly* what he's referring to. According to Mother, a man has the ability to break a woman's heart. And a broken heart, I'd imagine, would instantly kill a person."

All the girls groaned.

Alexander chuckled at Mary's attempt toward reason. "It's a bit more complicated than that. Allow me to elaborate. *From an experienced male perspective.*"

"This ought to be educational," Caroline drawled, leaning against the side of the desk.

He wasn't even going to bother with a counter-attack. "*First*"—Alexander tapped the flat edges of the invitations he held against the front of his embroidered waistcoat—"the drama commences with a glance from a man you've met in your dreams. What little you know of him, he is amiable, attractive, and, best of all, his glances are turning into stares. Ah, yes. He has officially noticed you and all of your glorious beauty. And that is exactly when your troubles begin. Your heart flutters every time he is in the room, and you begin to believe that everything about him is magical. What is more, he begins to go out of his way to make you feel good and wanted. He'll even make you believe that you can leap over the moon in a single bound. Ah, yes. But *then . . .*"

He rested his hand on his chest. "That poor little heart of yours, which he claimed to have wanted all along, is not enough. He wants more. Much more. And as besotted as you are, you resort to pathetic desperation and"—he gave Caroline a pointed stare—"start handing over everything you oughtn't."

Caroline blinked back at him. But didn't say a word.

Alexander turned in the direction of the other girls. "And what is it you get in return?" He smacked his hand hard against the top of the letters, sending a thwack of an echo throughout the study. "*Absolutely nothing!* And what is more, as women, you'll be scorned straight into the pits of hell for it. No one will talk to you or look at you ever again. You cease to exist as an entity. You become a living ghost. Which is why, as Mary so brilliantly pointed out earlier, you might as well be dead. So *that* is what I meant when I told Caroline to be careful. And you'd best be sure I intend to apply that same warning to every single one of you. Because you'll all be on the market before you know it."

All the girls stared up at him in utter silence, their expressions ranging from complete horror to fascination.

"Oh, don't listen to him." Caroline shook her head, causing her thick, chestnut curls to spring about her face. "When it comes to men, women simply have to know the rules of the game. And then beat them at it."

"The rules of the game?" He eyed her. "And exactly how do you know about these so-called *rules?*"

She crossed her arms over the breasts a brother was never supposed to notice and quirked a playful bronzed brow at him. "Aside from Mother and Father being generous with their experiences throughout the years, you can say that I've learned quite a bit from you, *O Lord of Pleasure.* You weren't always this prim and proper, you know."

The little chit! He bloody hated that name. And she knew it. "You'd best remember that no man wants to marry a tongue." Alexander reached out and aggressively tousled her perfectly curled and bundled hair, hoping to mess it up good and well.

"*Alex!*" She smacked at his hands and scrambled away, trying to pat the tops and sides of her chestnut hair back into place. "Have you no decency? I'm going for a ride with Mother in less than a half hour. It's the only social outing in London I genuinely look forward to."

He wasn't even going to *try* and reason with her. He only prayed that her manner of thinking didn't lead her seriously astray. Because Hawksfords were notorious for that. He should know.

Striding past her and the rest of the clan,

he headed to the middle of the room. He eased himself down onto his mother's favorite Axminster carpet, propped one trouser-clad leg up and the other out, and untied the lace around the large bundle of letters. Then tossed the feminine strap aside.

Within moments he was surrounded by the clapping of hands and the rush of excited voices. His sisters plopped down around him, fanning out their colorful gowns, except for Mary's black one, and arranging them about their legs.

The only soul who didn't join them on the floor was Caroline, who merely peered down at them from where she stood, looking skeptical about the whole thing, as always.

One by one, Alexander tossed the letters up in the air, letting them fall like large flakes of snow. "The first one to garner ten invitations for Caroline's coming-out wins a quid and a ride through the park. Only be sure to do your sister a favor and burn anything from Lady Lansworth."

Alexander glanced up and winked at Caroline. She grinned down at him, causing her smooth left cheek to dimple.

The ripping and rustling of paper filled the room as everyone attempted a mad scramble toward ten invitations.

"I have one for tea!" Mary cried out first, setting it hurriedly aside and grabbing hold of another one.

"And I have one for dinner!" Elizabeth, though newly fifteen and therefore typically calmer and refined, dove rather viciously for another letter and tore into it.

"Look! Look! A ball!" Anne scrambled to turn toward Caroline and waved the invitation for her to see. "Do you see? A ball!"

Caroline leaned closer to the invitation and squinted down at it. "Yes. And it's from Lady Lansworth. You'd best toss it."

Anne glared at it and tossed it over her shoulder.

"Alex?" Victoria held up a letter into the air, giving him an odd look while crinkling her freckled nose. "What is this? It says something about you being accepted into some school."

Alexander snapped straight up, his heart nearly leaping out of his nose. Mostly because his sister was holding on to a letter not meant for her innocent eyes. He scrambled toward her through the sea of letters and snatched the parchment out of her hand.

Jumping up to his feet, he moved far back out of their circle. Impossible. Bloody impossible. Madame de Maitenon hadn't even responded to any of his letters. And yet there it was addressed: *To the Right Honorable, the Earl of Hawksford.*

He snapped the parchment open and stared at the neatly scribed words he quickly recognized to be none other than Miss Charlotte's. And sure enough, just as his sister had said, it read:

My Lord,
    Many congratulations. Your application has been formally accepted and selected by Madame Thérèse's School of Gallantry. Your studies shall commence within the week. Payment is yet to be agreed upon. Do prepare to set aside early Monday, Tuesday, Wednesday, Thursday, and occasional

*Friday mornings during the remainder of the
Season. Hours of instruction will begin at seven in
the morning and end at approximately ten. These
hours will permit you the freedom to return to your
daily activities with little or no interruption. An in-
troductory letter along with detailed instructions will
follow quite shortly.*

Most sincerely,
Lady Chartwell
Conductor of Admissions

Alexander blinked in disbelief at not only having
been accepted into the school, but at what it actually meant. He grinned at the unexpected turn of
events. Imagine. Lady Charlotte was officially his.
Perhaps there was such a thing as luck after all.

Lesson Nine

Gentlemen. Never give up your God given right to pleasure. For it will only lead you astray. Aside from that, I seriously doubt that you'd even last for more than a day.
—*The School of Gallantry*

Someone within the study cleared her throat. Alexander looked up from his letter, still delightfully dazed. But his grin faded at the sight of his sisters intently staring up at him from the floor. Even Caroline was suspiciously eyeing him.

"A joke." He folded the parchment, stuffed it into his inner waistcoat pocket, and forced out a laugh, hoping it sounded genuine. "Probably Cald well." He laughed again, knowing he wasn't entirely misleading them.

Caroline suspiciously eyed him again but eventually returned to her pacing. The rest of the girls must have found him convincing enough, as well, for they all returned to their frantic hunt.

How the *hell* was he going to keep this all a

secret? He was supposed to be setting a good example for his sisters. Not to mention his mother.

Rules. He needed to establish some rules with Charlotte. It was the only way it was going to work. That is, if she would even follow them.

He lowered himself down again onto the carpet, watching his sisters as they continued to tear into invitation after invitation. He really didn't know if being admitted into the school was a blessing or a curse.

"Are we having a picnic?" their mother cheerfully chimed from the doorway. "And why in heavens wasn't I invited?"

Alexander glanced up and waved his mother into the study. "We're going through Caroline's latest set of invitations."

"How splendid! Are there any good ones?" Lady Hawksford swept into the room, dressed in a stiff, cornflower-hued riding habit.

Her golden brown hair, which showed vast gray, was neatly tucked up into a top hat that had been fashionably wrapped with a long, white silk veil that trailed behind her. Her full skirts rustled as she moved toward them, her riding boots clicking rhythmically against the wood floor. Though a widow of one and fifty, as of late she was beginning to dress and act like a woman of twenty.

Which was disturbing. Because he still had five sisters to marry off, and he didn't know if his mother had it in her to keep her bedchamber door closed long enough for all of them to find respectable husbands.

Lord Hughes had already made three calls since the opening of the Season. One call from the man meant he was hoping to get familiar. Two calls meant the man was making arrangements with his mother that involved far more than tea. And three calls meant the arrangements were done.

Lady Hawksford stood before the pile of letters scattered across the carpet, smiled, and lowered herself onto the floor next to him, arranging her riding habit around her feet. She glanced at everyone in the room then caught Alexander's gaze with those devilish green eyes that twinkled far too much for her age. "Are there any invitations from Lord Hughes? He promised to send Caroline a few during the course of the Season."

Alexander stiffened. So they *were* involved. He knew it. He bloody knew it. He'd have to talk to Caldwell about fending the bastard off. Immediately. At the very least, he wanted his family to *try* to be like everyone else. That was the whole point of even involving them in the Season and having a coming-out for Caroline.

Lady Hawksford leaned toward him and enthusiastically patted his leg. "I absolutely *adore* his parties. Everyone does."

Considering Lord Hughes had the memory of a boulder and was unpopular with the *ton* due to the company he kept, Alexander highly doubted that *everyone* adored them. "Do try and remember that Caroline is only the first of five girls we have to marry off. I'm doing my best to ensure a sense of respectability, and I ask that you do the same. After his public overture toward Caroline at the Whittle ball, I don't want him calling on this house anymore. He'll only complicate matters for us."

"Oh, don't be ridiculous, Alex," Caroline scoffed from outside their circle. "Lord Hughes has never made a public overture toward me. Why must you continue to treat him with such disrespect? Unlike us, he doesn't imprison himself in an artificial life when he steps out into public and could not care less about what the *bon ton* thinks. He involves himself with fascinating people. Do you know that he's involved with a French courtesan who plans on opening a school? A school that will educate men on the topic of women. Brilliant, if you ask me. All men ought to attend." She stared him down as if she knew something he didn't. "Yourself included."

Alexander lowered his gaze and picked up a piece of lint from the upper knee of his trousers, feeling *very* uncomfortable. For the obvious reasons. If he didn't know any better, he'd say she knew about his application to the school.

"Madame de Maitenon *is* brilliant," Lady Hawksford agreed. "As well as delightfully lovely."

Caroline stepped toward them, her face beaming with newfound excitement. "You've actually met Madame de Maitenon?"

Lady Hawksford offered a naughty little smile. "When your father and I had a fancy or two several years ago. She was wildly entertaining."

Alexander cringed. The last thing his sisters needed intimated was his mother and father's bizarre sexual escapades. "Ladies, please. Need I remind you that there are individuals here under the age of eighteen."

He flashed a quick smile over at his four youngest sisters, who had all ceased rifling through their invitations.

Alexander pointed toward the forgotten pile of letters around them. "I see a lot more invitations that need opening. There's still that quid and a ride to the park for the first one to gather ten."

Victoria smoothed out her green muslin morning gown and challenged him by arching a brow. "A quid isn't nearly enough to buy me the sort of books that I want." She then turned her gaze back to their mother. "Do go on. You were saying?"

Alexander quirked a challenging brow back at her. "Try to remember you turned sixteen last month, not forty."

Victoria glared at him. "I can assure you, Alex, that I know much more than most of the forty-year-old women in this town."

Alexander choked. "And what is *that* supposed to mean?"

Lady Hawksford held up a hand, then lowered it and sighed. "There's no need to puff out feathers, Alexander. The more my girls know about these matters, the less likely a man is going to take advantage of them. You know how they are, being one yourself. Forever trying to throw up a skirt."

Alexander felt his entire face bloom with heat as all his sisters openly smirked at him. Though, yes, he'd been born unto the wild and wicked ways of a Hawksford, and had led his life according to those ways, he was a man. It was acceptable for him. But when it came to his sisters, he simply didn't feel comfortable with the notion that respectability was but a façade one imparted for the *ton*. And that the moment no one was looking, everything and anything was permissible for them.

Sometimes, only sometimes, Alexander wondered what life would have been like if he had been born into a normal family. A family that wouldn't discuss inappropriate things in front of twelve-, thirteen-, fifteen-, sixteen-, and nineteen-year-olds.

Mary scooted closer to their mother from the opposite side and tapped her arm. "What exactly *is* a courtesan, Mother?"

He glared at his mother. *"Don't."*

"Have a bit more faith, Alex. You've become unusually uptight." Lady Hawksford patted Mary's hand and cheerfully offered, "'Tis something you never want to be, dear. That is all you need to know for now." She smiled down at her, then shifted toward Mary as if about to impart a conversation fit for tea. "Oh, and by the by. I ordered that casket for you. The one lined and ruffled with black lace and silk. It should arrive sometime in the next two weeks."

Mary clapped her hands together, a rare smile bursting forth onto her small lips. "Can I keep it in my room? *Please?*"

Alexander's heart skid from its usual rhythm. He jumped to his feet and pointed sternly at his mother. "Mother, I'll not accept you feeding into Mary's delusions like this. Hell, with all this ongoing encouragement, she's likely to start digging up bodies from the cemetery. And setting them about the house like oversized dolls!"

He paused, then eyed Mary, suddenly concerned with the notion that he might have given her an idea.

Lady Hawksford pulled in her chin, causing

the ivory veil of her riding hat to quiver. "Really, now. There's no need for dramatics. She'll outgrow it. What else would you have me do? Lock her in her room so that she may despise us all? I think not. Here in our own home, we are free to make our own rules and worry not about society. We only ever worry when we step outside that door."

To be sure, ever since his father's death, the woman had grown nothing short of intolerable. Free to make their own rules, indeed. There *weren't* any rules. And that was part of the damn problem. That was why Caroline hated the Season, why Mary wanted caskets, why Victoria, Anne, and Elizabeth acted like they were all forty, and why *he* wanted to attend a sex school and bed Lady Charlotte.

It was obvious the Hawksford household was long overdue for a solid set of rules. He was, after all, the head of the household and would be until he died. Which hopefully wouldn't be anytime soon.

"Victoria, Mary, Anne, Elizabeth." He turned to his sisters, who were all quietly and intently sitting about. They all blinked up at him, invitations still in their hands. "Return to your studies at once. Mrs. Peterson has been left waiting long enough."

"*Must we?*" the girls all whined in disappointed unison, their faces sagging.

What did a man have to do to earn some respect within his own household? "Yes, you bloody must." He pointed toward the doorway. "Off with you now. Or I'll see to it Mrs. Peterson permanently binds a quill to each of your hands."

He swiveled at Mary and narrowed his gaze. "As for you. We shall discuss this casket business later on in the afternoon. I think it high time we bring you back to the ways of the living. Now go."

"Yes, Alex," Mary muttered, lowering her eyes. She slowly rose to her feet and tossed an invitation onto the floor. She watched it float down with solemn remorse.

"Now all of you." He snapped his forefinger toward the direction of the ceiling. "Upstairs. And be quick about it."

Grumbling, one by one, all of his sisters, save Caroline, scrambled to their feet, turned, and hurried out of the room. Even Mary, who wasn't prone to running due to her *condition*, hurried out without a single complaint.

Alexander lowered his hand back to his side, feeling more at ease. As though he could breathe again. "Caroline, I need a few moments alone with Mother. If you please."

Caroline moved toward their mother, who still sat on the floor, and settled herself elegantly beside her. "If this is about Mary, I intend to stay."

Stay? Oh, no. Absolutely not. He'd already played this little game of hers many times before. And it was anything but fun. With her and Mother in the room, it always turned into a verbal war. Two against one. Meaning his mother and sister against him.

"Actually," he offered as politely as he knew how, "you look a little pale. Run off and pinch your cheeks or something. Or better yet, why not hunt down that lucky sovereign of yours. That should take an hour or two, shouldn't it?"

Caroline snapped her sharp gaze to him as the color of her cheeks heightened. "Don't be an ass *and* a bastard, Alex. I have every right to be involved in this conversation. Mary is my sister, too, and unlike the others, I cannot be ordered back to the nursery."

Alexander's lips parted in response to her boldness. She'd never sworn at him before. *Ever.* "I won't have you talking to me like that."

Lady Hawksford lifted a hand toward him from where she sat. "Help me up, dear."

"Yes. Of course." Alexander turned to his mother and helped her to her feet, waiting for her to impart some common sense into Caroline.

Lady Hawksford smoothed out her riding gown and sighed. "Alexander. Caroline is no longer a child. I ask that you stop treating her as such."

He knew it. He bloody knew they'd both start siding with one another. They always did. "Fine, fine. Let us talk about Mary instead, shall we? Am I the only one in this house that believes our family is officially mad with indecency? I ask you, who the devil goes off and buys their child a casket to play with? *Who?* She's damn well morbid enough."

Caroline rolled her eyes. "Perhaps you need to be more worried about the example *you* set. Why, not that long ago, Mother and I had to turn away yet another delusional woman who dared to call upon this home asking for the Lord of Pleasure. Lord of Pleasure, indeed. Yes, and I am the Catholic Virgin Mary."

Alexander froze, his brows coming together. "What do you mean by that?" he demanded, stepping toward her. "Do you mean to say that you're not . . ."

Caroline's face visibly flushed. She threw her hands up into the air before letting them drop in exasperation. "Oh, for heaven's sake! Do not even try to change the subject. How can you begin to judge our behavior when you yourself cannot lead this family by example? I happened to witness all of that business between you and Lady Waverly. It seems you have no qualms about frolicking with a woman who is nigh unto her deathbed, and yet you have the audacity to stand there and talk about the inappropriateness of buying a stupid casket?"

Alexander inwardly cringed though he dared not show it. This is exactly what he was afraid of. A guilty reprimand that proved him incapable of being the head of this household. "I did not bloody frolic with Lady Waverly! She ambushed me. And Caldwell helped her do it!"

She crossed her arms over her chest and studied him for a long moment. "And yet you continue to associate with him."

"If I cease associating with Caldwell," he growled, "that leaves me to only associate with *this* family. You damn well know I have no real friends outside of Caldwell, and a man needs some sort of reprieve from six overzealous women."

Caroline's lips slid into a cynical smile. "And whose fault is it that you have no other friends aside from Caldwell?"

Yes, yes. His. He knew that. But he simply didn't

relate to any of the other men. What with all their talk of marriage and children and estates. Caldwell, on the other hand, was still a rake. Albeit misguided, but still solid in his standing.

"Caroline, really," Lady Hawksford finally interjected. "It is no business of ours what friends, be they male or female, Alex chooses to associate with."

Alexander jerked toward his mother. "Pardon me while I momentarily touch upon the subject of my female friends. I have none. Truth be told, I haven't even entertained a single woman since father passed. *Why?* Because I'm *trying* to set a good, moral example for this family. Though little good it does me. If you ask me, I should be admitted into sainthood for all my continued efforts."

"Is that so?" Caroline cocked her head to one side. "And where have you been this past week? Hmm? Did you treat yourself to a brothel or two to celebrate the anniversary of your *sainthood?*"

Caroline paused and tapped a finger to her lips as if pondering something. "No. Wait. I think I know." She lowered her hand and stared at him. "You were busy *enrolling* in Madame de Maitenon's school and hoped that the rest of us savages would never find out."

Damn her, but that mouth of hers knew no bounds!

He swung toward his mother and pinned her with an accusatory gaze. "Do you see what your complete lack of discipline has created in this household? I can't even express a single opinion without it being viciously mangled and stuffed back at me."

Lady Hawksford's emerald eyes sharply met his as she set her chin. "If you feel that I am so inadequate in my duties, perhaps I should retire and allow *you* to oversee all of their activities. Especially Caroline's."

Alexander's eyes widened. Oh, no. He was *not* about to engage in endless female activities. After having escorted Caroline to the Whittle ball at the beginning of the Season, he was well and done trying to seriously coordinate anything anymore. Besides. He needed a small amount of peace and quiet. And a chance to bed Lady Charlotte. At least once!

Alexander shook his head. "No. Absolutely not. I'll see to them in other ways."

"What other ways?" Lady Hawksford presented him with a pointed stare. "You're the one that wants to marry off Caroline to a certain sort of man. If that is still your duty and your calling, then I suggest you accompany her to all those wonderful breakfasts and balls and dinner parties you've been missing out on. I certainly don't need to attend any more. I have other things I could be doing."

"*Mother!*" Caroline exclaimed. The look of horror on her face reflected his own.

Caroline turned frantically to their mother, grabbed her arm, and shook it. "You know what he's been like. And after what I went through at the Whittle ball, I am *not* stepping out into public with him ever again."

Alexander laughed. "Funny, that."

"Yes, only you seem to think so." Caroline released their mother's arm and glared at him. "Setting aside Lord *Spittle,* perhaps you should have attended Lady Newborough's dinner party. The one you insisted I attend due to *all* the nice *bon ton* that always gathers around her. Do you know that during my table conversation with Mother and one of the guests, Lord Humphrey up and stabbed a poor lady's hand with his dinner fork, thinking it was his bread, and didn't even bother to apologize! Clearly your definition of nice differs greatly from mine."

Alexander smirked, unable to resist an opportunity to prove to her that he was still very much a Hawksford. "Are you calling Lord Humphrey a prick? That's not very nice."

She narrowed her gaze. "If you'll excuse me, Alex, I have far more important matters to tend to. The chamber pot, for one. Mother, I've made my point." With that, Caroline gathered up the end of her riding gown, then turned and promenaded straight out of the room.

Alexander burst into laughter. "Did you see that look on her face? The best one yet!"

"How old are you? Six?" Lady Hawksford shook her head. "I suggest you try and spend a bit more time with this family before taking up the endeavor of trying to run it. It isn't as easy as it appears."

Alexander sighed. Maybe he did need to get more involved in their lives, instead of expecting miracles to take place on their own. It would certainly ensure a sense of stability. Maybe not for him, but certainly for them. Which is all that mattered. He'd also be able to ensure that all the caskets stayed where they belonged. In the cemetery. As for the school . . .

His stomach dropped. He knew what needed to be done, and truth be told, he hated the idea of passing on such a beautiful, beautiful opportunity.

But as Caroline had well pointed out, he couldn't demand that his sisters and mother behave a certain way if he himself couldn't behave a certain way. And if he continued on with Charlotte and the school, it would only be a matter of time before it complicated their lives.

Hell. He always thought that being a Hawksford meant the ultimate seal of freedom. But he was beginning to realize that it only applied if there weren't any women in the family that needed to be married off.

Lesson Ten

Lust can be quite a terrible predicament.
My advice is that you simply live with it. Or, if
you prefer, die from it. The choice is entirely yours.
—*The School of Gallantry*

11 Berwick Street
The following day

It was exactly four o'clock in the afternoon when Alexander was ushered into Lady Charlotte's Grecian-inspired parlor by none other than the bribe-prone Mr. Hudson. Apparently, the mercenary rotter hadn't been shucked of his position. Which meant Charlotte was either overly softhearted or downright careless about the people she involved in her life.

Not that it was any of his business from this day forth. He was here to bring things to an end between them and had strategically planned his call so that he arrived at the best time to make a respectable visit. And respectable is exactly what he had in mind. Absolutely nothing else.

He eyed the four nude male statues and paused before them, noticing that the poor chaps had been stripped of their scant belongings. He smoothed his cravat. If he wasn't careful, he'd end up just like them.

Except for the clattering of carriages and the bustle of the street outside, silence continued to hum all around him. And he didn't like it. Not one bit. For it meant he had to stand here like an idiot and listen to his own thoughts. Thoughts that included him stripping Charlotte down to only her stockings and making her kneel atop that lone chair behind him so that he could—

No. No. Absolutely none of that.

Placing his hands behind his back, Alexander started trooping back and forth, his boots echoing in the empty parlor. He had planned it all out, after all. Knew exactly what he would say and how he would say it. With reserve. With respect. And with every ounce of strength within him.

"Lady Chartwell asks that you join her upstairs," Mr. Hudson announced from the doorway.

Alexander jerked toward the pudgy butler. "What?"

"Shall I write it down for you?" Mr. Hudson said, spreading out his words.

Alexander glared at the man. The dolt was looking for a good knock. "That won't be necessary, thank you. Inform Lady Chartwell that I shall remain here. In the parlor." That way, nothing indecent would ever be permitted to occur and he could keep his visit to about ten minutes.

As opposed to the rest of the day and the entire night.

Mr. Hudson bowed and exited.

Now that that was over and done with, on to the next. Which was, the moment Lady Charlotte entered the room, he would announce that he had absolutely no intention of enrolling in the school. And that pleasuring her was simply out of the question despite the fact that he had begged, cajoled, and manipulated her into accepting him.

After all, he had to keep his sisters in mind. Without a good, solid plan, their lives could very well be ruined. And he was not about to let that happen. Not for anyone, and certainly not for baseless pleasure.

"Need I remind you, My Lord, that I shall be the one choosing the pleasures?" Charlotte teased from the doorway.

Those words rolled off her tongue like warm honey, and, God help him, all he wanted to do was lap every last bit of it up. Alexander turned toward the doorway, trying to remain determined and strong.

He blinked at what she was wearing.

"Do you like it?" She entered the parlor dressed in nothing more than a long, virginal white silk robe. A velvet red sash held the flimsy thing in place around her small, corseted waist.

It was the first time he'd ever seen her in anything but black. And she was truly a vision to behold. Like a bride on her wedding night.

"I usually don't wear anything but my mourning gowns," she went on, "but when I received word that you'd be calling on me this afternoon, I decided to wear it. Just for you."

God help him. Why was she choosing to cooperate now? Whatever happened to the I-am-quite-done-with-seeing-to-the-needs-of-a-man bit?

She closed the double doors behind her and slowly turned back toward him. Her dark eyes sparkled with an unusual amount of playfulness as she strode closer to him. As if she knew he couldn't resist.

Her adorable bare feet peered out from beneath the hem of her long robe as she continued to seductively move toward him. His gaze swept along the lengthy portion of her porcelain neck that was purposefully exposed, down to the rounds of her breasts which were fitted into a corset and outlined by the smoothness of the flowing silk. Unlike the last time, her black hair had been gathered up and pinned, bringing even more attention to everything else beneath it.

To his further astonishment, she went over to the parlor windows and proceeded to pull the curtains shut, encasing them in a gray room where only slashes of light came through.

Alexander hissed out a breath and proceeded to move backward toward the double doors. Though his feet were much too heavy to cooperate.

Charlotte turned and sashayed her way back nearer to him, pausing a mere arm's length before him. The alluring soft scent of lavender now invaded his space. He tried not to breathe.

She tilted her chin up just enough for her dark eyes to meet his and smiled rather saucily. It was a smile that could easily melt the heart of a butcher into complacency. Other than that smile, however, she offered no other form of words or action. She merely stood there, her hands on her hips. As if waiting for him to do something.

Alexander cleared his throat and did his best to appear uninterested in what she had to offer. "Lady Charlotte," he grimly began.

He willed himself to focus on the middle of her forehead, lest his resolve fail him. "I am here to apologize for my earlier crude behavior. I did not treat you with the respect you deserve and am here to withdraw from the agreement we had originally made."

Her dark brows slowly rose, crinkling the smooth forehead he was focusing on. "Oh? Is that so?"

He gave a curt nod, then met her gaze, hoping that nothing but his sense of earnestness showed. "That is exactly so."

Searching his face, she reached out a hand and slid it from his stomach, up across the expanse of his chest, toward his shoulder. His pulse leapt. And fight it as he may, his cock thickened in his trousers at the blink of an eye and demanded satisfaction.

She leaned in close. So close that the side of her robe grazed his gloved hand, which was stoically set at his side. She pressed her curvy softness against the length of his front side, promising him endless bliss.

Though he fought to maintain and steady his breathing, it was pointless. He was no longer in control of the situation. His cock throbbed to be taken into her mouth, into *her*.

"And what if I refuse to accept your withdrawal?" she whispered up at him, no doubt feeling his hard length against her own body. "What if I refuse to relinquish my pleasure?"

Alexander closed his eyes, let out a low groan, and tried to desperately keep his mind and body from swaying toward a mistake. "Charlotte, please. You must allow me to withdraw."

"*Must?*" she playfully went on. "Like you, Lord Hawksford, I am not overly fond of musts."

Touché. Touché. "Nevertheless," he breathed out, still keeping his eyes closed, trying desperately to remain focused. "We must end this. Now. There is no other way."

She paused, then slowly pulled her hand away and stepped back. "I see." Her voice grew notably distant. "You've already moved on."

The disappointment in her tone made him reopen his eyes. Her charming smile had faded. She inched back and away as if his very presence not only bewildered but disgusted her.

What truly stabbed at him in that moment, however, was the way her dark eyes accused him of being nothing more than a fancier version of Chartwell.

He stepped toward her, trying to remain calm. "Do *not* look at me like that and, in turn, insult me."

"There is no need to explain, Lord Hawksford." She stepped farther back. "After all, there is absolutely nothing between us. Nothing at all."

Absolutely nothing between them? At all?

Alexander didn't know why, but her words sounded downright harsh, even to his own ears.

Though he knew full well they hadn't known each other very long, to outright say that they were *nothing* to each other, especially after that erotic kiss, felt wrong. Mind you, he didn't know what the bloody hell they *were* to each other, but he did know it was far more than nothing.

Alexander closed the space between them, then grabbed her arm and dragged her almost violently nearer him. "We may not be involved in the traditional sense, but to say that there is absolutely nothing between us is a bloody lie. You know it and I know it. We can't even keep our hands off each other."

Her dark gaze snapped back up to his face. She momentarily wiggled the arm he held on to. "It appears *you* are the one that cannot keep your hands to yourself."

She leaned farther in toward him and glared up at him as if not aware that their lips were now close enough for them to entirely end their conversation. "So do tell, Lord Hawksford. Since we are on the subject. What exactly are we to each other?"

Alexander's jaw tensed. Holding her this close and having her ask him that question made him realize that this was all getting much too personal for his liking. And if he wasn't careful, he knew exactly where this could lead.

"I am not about to damn well prance into specifics." He tightened his hold on her shoulders, trying to prove to her that he was still unwilling to relinquish their closeness. "The fact of the matter is my withdrawal has nothing to do with another woman. Hell, the only woman I want to bed right now is you. But lust isn't something I ought to sacrifice my entire family for, is it?"

She searched his face, clearly astonished. "This is about your family?"

He released her, knowing he wouldn't be able to focus otherwise, and heaved out a sigh. "My sisters, to be exact. You see, Caroline is nineteen. The eldest. She's also the first out of all five girls to celebrate her coming-out. She would have done so last year, but we were all in mourning for my father. With him gone, all of those responsibilities have been transferred to me."

He paused. "Charlotte, my family isn't like other families of the aristocracy. We've always led a double life. One for the *ton* and one for ourselves. The *ton* has always known the Hawksfords to be a bunch of misfits, but we've never provided them with anything that would allow them to rise against us, seeing we do everything behind closed doors. Despite the many strictures of society, my mother was never one to lead the life of a traditional elite woman, and my father was a devious entity all his own. As a result of their unruly lifestyle, my sisters and I grew up a bit . . . *wild*. It wasn't until my father passed and Caroline came of age that I suddenly realized that the man she married would ultimately define her for the rest of her life. As her brother, I want to offer her the sort of stability that we never had growing up. Which means finding her a respectable match. And you . . . you'd only complicate everything I have planned. Does any of this make sense? At all?"

She nodded, then eventually whispered up at

him, "Yes. It does." She searched his face again, sadness tingeing her features, her eyes. "I know that if I had a family, I would do the same. Exactly the same."

Why the devil did she have to be so sweet? Alexander reached out and took hold of her corseted waist, savoring not only the feel of her silk robe but the fact that she actually understood. Someone in his life actually understood him. He slowly pulled her closer. "You aren't angry with me, then?"

She shook her head, her dark, pinned hair bobbing. "No. Of course not. Family should always come first. Always. And I very much admire you for it. More than you need know."

She nodded again, and to his surprise, tears glistened against those dark eyes. She pinched her lips together and hurriedly looked away. She swiped at the corner of her eyes and let out a small laugh. "I apologize. I grow emotional at the thought of family."

That was when Alexander realized something. Something that punched him in the gut so hard, he almost couldn't find the strength to breathe. For this beautiful and seemingly strong and independent woman was in fact all alone in the world. Completely and utterly alone with no family. Something he, with five sisters and a mother, took sorely for granted.

Releasing her waist, he reached up and dug his fingers into the softness and thickness of her gathered hair. "Charlotte," he whispered, leaning down closer to her face. "What happened to your family? Tell me. I want to know."

She shook her head and refused to meet his gaze. "Don't make this any more difficult than it needs to be. Please. It is best you leave. It is best for everyone."

He nodded, knowing she was right, even though for some reason he still could not entirely bring himself to let her go. To let this go. "Charlotte," he whispered again, "I don't regret meeting you. And I hope to God you don't regret meeting me. The only thing I do regret is that we hadn't met earlier. When I didn't have so many responsibilities toward others. Perhaps my approach toward this—toward us—would have been different."

Her teary gaze met his again. "Do not talk to me about what could have been. It changes nothing."

She pulled out of his grasp, placing a more notable distance between them, and stuck out a small, pale hand. She smiled up at him in an unsuccessful effort to be cheerful. "I do wish you well. Though I may not want to admit it, you've been charming and kind since first we met. Thank you. For everything."

Alexander blinked at the hand and words she offered and met her gaze. He would never come across another woman like her, would he? A woman capable of wishing him well despite the fact that he was abandoning her.

God. In that moment, he wanted her to know that despite the fact that they were going their separate ways, she had magically brought back a spark of passion and excitement into his life. A passion and excitement he hadn't felt in a very long time.

One he wanted to experience one last time before she entirely slipped from his grasp and he regretted not acting upon how he felt in that moment. "I was hoping for a different sort of good-bye," he quietly admitted.

She lowered her hand and boldly continued to hold his gaze. "What sort of good-bye?"

"The sort of good-bye we both deserve." With that, he stepped toward her and pulled her soft body close.

Lesson Eleven

*If at any point and time you were deprived of
knowing true passion, do give thyself permission
to overindulge in any given fashion.*
— *The School of Gallantry*

Everything around Alexander disappeared as
he gave in to the unfolding sensation of kissing
Charlotte one last time. Closing his eyes, he forced
her lips apart and pushed his tongue deep into
her soft, wet mouth. A mouth that tasted of warm
tea and tantalizing sugar.

She briefly stiffened against him then pressed
herself into him. Her tongue thrust against his as
she grabbed for his waist and tugged him even
more against the warmth of her body.

His gloved hands left her hair and mindlessly
skimmed the contours of her body, savoring the
softness even his gloves could not hide from him.
His fingers curved toward her backside and
cupped her ass tightly, forcing her up against him.

He released her lips and dragged his mouth

alongside the length of her smooth, bare neck, tasting and licking the heat of her skin. His hands moved from her backside to the front of her robe. There, he tugged the silk folds aside from her breasts and yanked the top portion of the garment from her shoulders, exposing the sheer chemise and tightly laced rose corset hidden beneath. The same one he'd given her. Damn, but she knew how to drive him mad with need.

She gasped and drew her head farther back as she clung to him.

He tightened his jaw, knowing that there was no way he could ever stop, and ripped the red sash from around her waist, tossing it aside. Her robe slid effortlessly from the rest of her body and cascaded down to the floor at their feet.

She stood before him, eyes closed, parts of her pinned hair escaping from their gathered hold as the rest of her hair seductively swayed against her throat and back. Her smooth cheeks were flushed, her full lips parted, and her chest rose and fell. It appeared she was just as affected by him as he was by her.

And he damn well loved knowing that.

He kneeled before her, trailing his hands down the length of her slim body. Stripping his gloves from his hands, he tossed them aside and began pushing up her sheer chemise slowly, admiring her shapely legs. Though he tried to dictate his breathing, every breath escaped more rapidly and with less reserve and control.

"Alexander," Charlotte half whispered down at him, her hands digging into his hair. She leaned almost drunkenly toward him, her grasp tightening as her fingers wove into his hair. "We . . . shouldn't."

"I know we shouldn't," he rasped, his mind focused on nothing but her. Nothing but the pleasure they both deserved. "But you need this. And I need this. Just this once. Once." He knotted the length of her chemise around his fist and yanked it straight upward, exposing the soft dark curls that hid the folds of her sex.

His cock was uncomfortably hard now, but he was determined to stay focused on her needs and her needs only. "Can you feel my desire for you?" He kissed her upper thighs, then dragged the tip of his tongue from one side of her thigh to the other.

"Yes," she whispered.

"Good. Remember it. Always." He leaned closer to her center and dipped his tongue into her folds. Dipped it right where it needed to be.

She moaned.

He licked her again then sucked at her nub, consuming the very taste of her wetness and wanting more. He opened his eyes and glanced up, wanting to see the pleasure in her face.

Her head was tilted down toward him, her long black hair encasing them like a curtain. She watched him through half-closed eyes, her kiss-reddened lips parting with each moan as she swayed against him. She widened the separation of her legs, rocking herself against him, urging him to give her more.

It was maddening to behold her need for passion. Her need to receive it. He grabbed hold of her hips to steady her and removed his lips from her folds. It was time to move her into a better position. He released her, allowing her chemise to slip back down around her legs, and leaned back.

She slowly opened her eyes.

He leaned farther back until his hands hit the soft woven rug. Laying on his back completely, he whispered, "Straddle me."

She hesitated, then stepped around him, her eyes never leaving his and extended a bare leg on each side of him. She lowered herself onto him, pushing her chemise up to her corseted waist to allow her knees to bend. She then sat on his erection and, without being told what to do, slowly rubbed against him, resting her hands on his chest.

Alexander let out a strained groan as mounting sensations from the tip of his cock ripped through the rest of his tense body. And that was just his body responding to her through all his clothing. He couldn't even begin to imagine what it would be like to thrust himself into her. "As amazing as this is, I want you to straddle me higher. Much higher."

She inched up.

"On my mouth," he urged.

She paused. "Your mouth? But don't you want me to—"

"Never mind me now. This is about *you*." He dragged his gaze to her hidden breasts and momentarily reconsidered.

"Although"—he licked his lips, wishing he could

find relief—"if you truly wish to please, pull your breasts out. So I may see them."

She bit her lower lip and slowly reached up to the dip between the top rounds of her breasts. Using her fingers to gently lift them out, she set each full breast atop the edge of the corset. Her nipples darkened as they hardened and peaked.

He swallowed and felt his cock throb in response. "You are so incredibly beautiful," he murmured up at her. He reached out and grazed his thumbs against both exposed nipples. So soft, so perfect. So like the rest of her. "Sit. On my mouth."

Carefully, she moved up, settling her hands flat on the floor, placing a knee on each side of his head, while propping the tops of her bare feet above his chest. She glanced down somewhat shyly at him then lowered herself down onto his waiting and open mouth.

Alexander grabbed hold of her corseted waist and held her in place as his tongue delved inside her. A sweet wetness coated his tongue. She was already so unbelievably wet and ready to receive him. He flicked the tip of his tongue across her nub.

She moaned and rhythmically moved against him, her breasts bobbing with each agonized moan. He flicked harder, burying the entire expanse of his mouth against her, wanting and needing her to give herself over to him completely. He suckled, causing her to buck. She grabbed hold of his hair.

"*Oh!*" she cried out, riding harder and harder against him, her grip on his hair tightening. "Yes."

He kept suckling and licking until her sweet moisture flooded his tongue and mouth. Until her nub hardened against his tongue and became more and more resistant.

She was ready for him. And he was more than ready for her. He quickly removed his mouth from the entrance of her core and slid her down the length of his chest.

"Alexander," she whispered. "I need you inside of me."

"I need to be inside you, too," he whispered back. "But I hardly came prepared. I didn't think we'd—"

She tugged at him to proceed. "I am clean, I assure you. And I trust that you are, too. Now get on with it, and do not forget to withdraw."

As if he were going to argue with her. Pressing his hands against her back, he held her tightly against his hips and rolled her onto the floor. He couldn't seem to move fast enough.

He whipped off his jacket, waistcoat, and cravat after fumbling with them a few moments longer than he would have liked. As he yanked his shirt over his head, he felt her fingers already unbuttoning his trousers and tugging them downward. He tossed aside the shirt and glanced down just as his cock heavily sprang forth, rigidly pointing toward her.

She puckered her lips seductively and slid her slender fingertips along the smooth tip, sending shattering sensations of bliss through his stomach, torso, and legs. He groaned.

Without caring about the fact that he still had his trousers about his legs and his boots on his feet, he grabbed his cock with one hand and lifted her hips with the other, and lowered himself toward her. Slowly, he found the opening to her core and gently maneuvered the tip into her wetness.

"All of it," she panted. She grabbed hold of his bare waist and thrust herself upward and into him. Hard. In one swift movement, she buried him completely inside her.

Alexander gasped in astonishment as unexpected moistness and warm tightness surrounded his entire cock. He struggled to keep himself from exploding. It had been too long. Much too long.

He lowered himself onto her and caught her mouth with his, slowly moving in and out, in and out, using his hand to position himself so that his length would rub her swollen nub every time.

Charlotte moaned into his mouth and wrapped her arms around his neck, pulling him closer. Pressing the warmth of her exposed full breasts against his skin.

Though he wanted to slow her movements as well as his own, he couldn't help but thrust himself harder and deeper. And though their lips were repeatedly jerked apart, he reclaimed her mouth every chance he got, not giving either of them a moment to breathe. Not allowing them to think about anything but this moment.

"Oh! Ohhh!" She bucked beneath him, pushing herself harder up against him and cried out against his mouth. Her wetness exploded all around his shaft, allowing him to thrust more easily, more quickly.

His breath hitched in his throat as he realized his own climax was coming. He yanked himself out and rolled onto the floor beside her. As he jerked his hand repeatedly back and forth over the head of his cock, his stomach muscles tightened, bringing on an explosion of sensations that wrapped his entire body with pulsing ecstasy. He groaned loudly as warm seed spurted out and spattered his hand with clinging moisture.

As the pace of his heart returned to normal, he blew out a long breath and rubbed the remaining seed against his chest, trying to get rid of it. He then turned toward her and grinned. Her eyes were completely closed, as if she were still absorbing all that had happened between them.

Alexander cradled her slender body into his arms. He leaned above her so as to better see her calm, beautiful face and slowly slid her breasts back into the corset, letting only the top rounds peer out.

Though her eyes were still closed, the smile on her face was priceless.

"That is what I call a good-bye," he murmured down at her.

She opened one eye and widened her smile into a full-fledged grin. "Dare I ask how you go about saying hello?"

He laughed and softly kissed the bridge of her nose. "Do you *want* to know?"

She giggled and shook her head, shifting a dark lock onto her flushed cheek and sending a few hanging wooden pins from her hair tumbling down onto the floor. "No, no." She brought a hand to her forehead and feigned distress. "I am not worthy of any more salutations."

"Wench," he growled, admiring the playful sparkle in her eyes as she dropped her hand back to her side. He brushed the dark strand of hair away from her flushed cheek and smoothed it back into the rest of her soft hair, wishing he could stay. Wishing he could linger.

"Allow me to help you back into your trousers," she whispered, her hand trailing down his bare shoulder and meandering inward toward his stomach.

His heart jumped as he grabbed for her hand and pulled it away, knowing he had already gone against every rule he had laid out for himself. "You'll never be rid of me if you do that."

"Never? Is the Lord of Pleasure bragging about his ability to entertain for weeks on end?"

The use of his former name caught him off guard. He suddenly felt uncomfortable with the notion that she knew who he had been once upon a time in the realm of scandal.

He eased off her and edged away from her side. "Is that why you permitted me to bed you?"

She hiccupped a laugh, then reached out and smacked his shoulder. "No. That is hardly the reason."

He still couldn't help but feel a crushing sense of disappointment. He didn't want her giving herself over to him because of some stupid title women gossiped about. But because of *him*. "Who told you?"

"A naughty little French bird. The same one who gallantly admitted you into the school."

Ah, yes. A woman who kept coming into all of his conversations, even though he'd never bloody even laid eyes on her. "Madame de Maitenon."

"The very one. She was rather cross with me for having turned you away. If you must know, your fancy titles could never intrigue me half as much as your promise to grant me pleasure." She smiled, her cheeks flushing all the more. "Chartwell never tried. It either happened or it didn't. And most often it didn't. Which made me wonder what all those women were really after. For it certainly wasn't what he had below the waist."

Despite her obvious amusement, Alexander could not help but remain serious. And genuinely saddened. Saddened that this amazing and beautiful woman hadn't been properly pleasured by a man.

He leaned over her once again. Their eyes met and the smile on her lips faded. They continued to stare at one another, their breaths mingling in what felt like timed and perfect harmony.

It was a moment unlike any he'd ever had the privilege of experiencing. He'd never wanted to connect with a woman after what Lady Somerset had done to him. Yet with her, he felt as if he wouldn't be able to breathe if he didn't.

Which was nonsense. He had breathed on his own accord since birth. He tightened his jaw. Clearly, it was time to return to reality. He had responsibilities to tend to. His family, namely.

He drew back, sliding his arms out from under her, and scrambled to his feet. He yanked up his trousers and buttoned them into place. Turning away, he adjusted his cock within his trousers,

which for some damn reason was growing hard
again.

He gathered his shirt, his waistcoat and cravat,
and pulled them on, scrambling to fit, yank, and
button everything back into place. He tried not
to look at her, even though he felt her eyes watching him all along. After tying his cravat, he
quickly smoothed it and checked to see if everything was where it needed to be. He blew out a
breath and turned back toward her.

Holding out a hand for her, he murmured,
"Allow me."

She shyly reached out and grasped his hand,
her soft warmth penetrating his palm. He lifted
her up onto her feet, noting how light she was.
She landed directly before him and simply stood
there, chin upward, observing him. Sections
of her dark hair were sliding down to her bare
shoulders, covering the straps of her thin chemise and curling down toward her corset.

It was enchanting to watch her hair fall down
on its own all around her beautiful face and onto
her shoulders.

"Good-bye," she murmured, lowering her eyes
to her hand, which was still firmly pressed into
his. "Alexander."

He nodded and strangely felt as if he were
about to leave a part of himself behind. Certainly,
he'd only seen her on a handful of occasions, but
it seemed that with each meeting, and with each
word, he admired and connected with her more
and more.

Which was not good.

For although she was by his standards an

incredibly beautiful woman, by society's standards she was naught but a fallen, penniless
widow working for a school that in two days'
time, with its grand opening, was going to cause
the biggest uproar London had ever seen. His involvement with her would not only affect his sisters' ability to properly marry, but could very well
destroy it. Which is why he needed to leave.
Before it became too bloody complicated.

He slid his hand from hers and took several
steps back, trying hard not to notice that she still
stood in only a chemise and corset. He turned
and walked quickly toward the closed doors, keeping his mind focused on getting out. The sooner
the better. Once he was gone, he would find a way
to completely oust her from his mind and his life.

"Alexander?" Charlotte softly called out after
him.

He paused, cringing that he still hadn't made it
out the door. Slowly he turned back at her, her
voice recapturing a large part of his resolve. "Yes?"

The top rounds of her perfect, pale, smooth
breasts came into full view as she crouched low to
retrieve his gloves from off the floor.

She swiftly straightened, her chemise settling
around her shapely legs, and held his leather
gloves in the air. "I do believe these are yours."

He nodded and made his way back, every step
feeling heavy and forced. He paused before her
and slowly slid the gloves from her hand, his eyes
holding her gaze. And damn it. All he could think
about was kissing her. Yet again.

Lesson Twelve

If you always do what is right, yes, it may save your soul. But it will also make your life uneventful, most predictable, and quite dull.
　　　　　　　　　—The School of Gallantry

"One last kiss," Alexander murmured, still lingering before her. "That is, if you don't mind."

Charlotte's pulse leapt in response to his words as he leaned in to kiss her. Though a part of her wanted to let him kiss her again, she knew it was a stupid, not to mention dangerous, proposition.

Holding up a shaky hand, she took several steps back, hoping to set enough distance between them to prevent any further selfish pursuits. "There is no need to prolong the inevitable, Alexander. You should leave."

"And I intend to." He grabbed hold of her waist, then yanked her possessively against his muscled body, leaned toward her ear, and whispered huskily down at her, "But not until I collect my last kiss."

His heated words prickled her ear and the

side of her cheek. Her breath hitched in her throat. All she wanted to do was revel in this glorious moment of being so wanted, so needed. To the end.

His large hand drifted up the laces of her exposed corset with a sly purpose, causing her senses to fade and explode all at once as he trailed around the curve of her shoulder. His warm hand cupped her neck as his green eyes met hers with firm and clear lust.

Charlotte swallowed and tried to maintain a steady mind, despite the fact that his smooth, freshly shaven face, full lips, and muscled body seemed to be closing off her ability to think, let alone breathe. It was as if he was looking to repeat their earlier good-bye.

Which is why she needed to bring this idea of a kiss to an end. He had a family to return to. And she had her own reality to return to. And he, this, was not part of her reality.

Charlotte pushed his arms away and quickly stepped back, suddenly very aware of the fact that she was still half-naked. Which probably didn't help this situation.

She glanced toward her robe pooled on the floor. Clearly, she needed to put some sort of barrier between them. She hurried over to her silk robe and sash and plucked them up. She slipped her arms through the sleeves of her robe, pulling it down and around her chemise and corset, and tied the sash snug around her waist.

She spun back to him and sighed. "Surely you don't intend to perpetuate this."

His expression stilled. Oddly, it was as if he

were looking at her for the first time in his life and he didn't know what to make of her. As he continued to stand there, his shaven jaw tightened and a taut muscle flicked in response.

"Truth be told," he finally murmured, "I wish we could perpetuate it."

She blinked at him, her pulse fluttering wildly. He said it as if he meant it.

He quickly looked away and stared off somewhere beyond the distance of her statues. "Whatever it may be worth, know that I genuinely enjoyed our time together. And I'm not even including our incredible romp."

Her cheeks stung with heat. Yes, it had been incredible, hadn't it? "You mean that?" she whispered.

He nodded, pulled out his gloves from his waistcoat pockets, and yanked them on without meeting her gaze. "Yes. I do."

Complete astonishment seized Charlotte's ability to breathe as he turned away and strode toward the closed double doors leading out. For it felt as if he were actually sharing a bit of his heart with her. Something she hadn't thought he was capable of. Mostly because he always seemed so . . . flippant.

She swallowed. This had to be the real Alexander. The one she had been waiting to meet all along. The brother to five sisters. A man who, above all, understood that duty to one's family was a duty to one's heart.

He flung the doors of the parlor wide open and stepped out into the foyer. Then turned back. "If you need anything, anything at all, do not hesitate to send word. I will see to it."

Charlotte half nodded, her heart squeezing. A woman could learn to fall in love with a man who not only saw to his family but also offered a struggling woman assistance without making it feel as such.

"Oh, and do be careful around all those students," he added. "Caldwell included. God knows why they're even here. It may very well be because of you. I know that's the only reason why I enrolled."

A smile stretched her lips, unable to form the words to thank him for being genuine. It was what she admired most about him. He was who he was, and did not try to hide it.

"Good-bye." He grabbed his top hat from off the red velvet cushion set out on the hall table, yanked it onto his head, and disappeared without even waiting for Mr. Hudson to lead him out. He slammed the front door behind him, causing the old Greek landscape portraits in the parlor to quake.

Charlotte flinched and shakily adjusted the sash around her waist. She didn't know why she felt as if an opportunity for happiness had just walked out the door. The man was naught but a rake. A scoundrel. A man incapable of understanding the true meaning of a relationship. Or love.

And yet . . . she still wanted to get to know him because she knew full well she would never meet another man like him. A man capable of stirring her deepest passions, her deepest hopes, and the grandest of dreams.

Charlotte placed a shaky hand against her lips, which still burned from his kiss, and turned away. Why was it she always leapt heart first instead of headfirst? Why?

Lesson Thirteen

Lust is a path men will always walk on.
                    —The School of Gallantry

11 Berwick Street
Several days later, shortly before seven o'clock
in the morning

Mr. Hudson peered out from behind the door. His gray brows rose in clear acknowledgment.

Alexander grinned and sheepishly admitted, "I am here for class."

Although he had tried to stay away—hell, how he had tried—he found that he simply could not. He simply hadn't been able to sleep, eat, or even think rationally since leaving Charlotte. For every day he had spent away from her, he worried. Worried that she would continue to have to battle the Court of Chancery on her own. Worried that while she waited for her settlement, men like Caldwell, and God knew who else, would be marching in and out of her house eyeing her and waiting for the perfect opportunity to do . . . more.

Which is why he had not only sent two of his solicitors straight over to the Lord Chancellor demanding her case be given priority, but was now standing at her door using the School of Gallantry and his accepted application as a pathetic excuse to see her one last time.

The butler stepped back, pulling the door farther open. "Good morning, Lord Hawksford, and welcome to your first day of class."

"Thank you. Good morning." Alexander removed his hat and ventured inside, glancing toward the empty parlor. He peered up the length of the stairs, hoping that he would be able to at least catch a glimpse of Charlotte. "Is, uh . . . Lady Chartwell at home?" he dared to ask.

Mr. Hudson snatched up the only remaining lantern hanging from the hook on the wall and walked over to the door leading to the tunnel. He unceremoniously yanked it open. "No. She is not."

Alexander made his way over to the man. "What do you mean she is not at home? It's not even seven o'clock in the morning. Do you mean to tell me that she is unavailable, as in, unwilling to see anyone? Or do you mean that she is not at home?"

Mr. Hudson held out the lantern and eyed him. "Any more information pertaining to Lady Chartwell, My Lord, will require a form of payment."

The devil had clearly seized this man's priorities ages ago. Anger rippled through Alexander as he stepped toward the man. "You ought to take better care of ensuring the safety of your mistress, old man." He soundly hit the man's chest with the rim of his hat. "Or you'll have *me* to contend with."

Mr. Hudson's eyes widened. He leaned back and glanced up toward the ceiling, the aging skin on his round chin quivering. He lowered his eyes back to Alexander, appearing unusually serious. "I may be a good many things, that I know, but I would never stoop to lowborn treachery against a lady who's given this old man his pride back. What is more, Harold would be the first to toss me into the Thames with a boulder attached to my neck."

"Harold will be the least of your troubles, I assure you." Alexander stepped back and adjusted his cloak around his shoulders. "Are you not paid well enough? Is that it?"

Mr. Hudson sighed. "No one could ever pay me well enough, My Lord. What with me having seventeen grandchildren and all. Most of them girls."

And he thought *his* house was full. "The devil, you say." No wonder Mr. Hudson was forever trying to pry money out of Charlotte's visitors.

Upon his life, the man needed some form of assistance. He himself knew what five girls were costing him. He could only imagine what adding twelve more to the bill would be like.

Alexander shoved his top hat beneath one arm, then reached in and yanked out the small leather satchel from inside his inner jacket. He held it out. "Here. This is for your grandchildren. Vow to watch over Lady Charlotte while I am not about, and I will see to it you get an additional five pounds per week. I'm not overly fond of the idea of all these men coming to her door. She requires more protection than she is receiving."

The butler hesitated.

"See to it." Alexander rattled the satchel at him. "You owe me nothing but her safety."

Mr. Hudson handed over the lantern to him, then slowly took the satchel from his hand. He humbly bowed. "Payment is hardly necessary when in the presence of Lady Chartwell."

The man was absolutely spot-on about that. Alexander leaned toward him, shifting the top hat beneath his left arm, and raised the lantern in his other hand to illuminate the man's face. "So is she at home or not?" he drawled.

The butler paused and whispered, "She always sleeps past one, My Lord. She's an owl. Of the worst sort."

Alexander pictured Charlotte tucked into the linen of her bed, daylight fanning across her sleepy face, and couldn't help but grin. Seeing it was far from one, the slumbering beauty wasn't going to make an appearance for several more hours.

Which meant he could either go home or . . . go to class. He supposed attending class was far better than listening to his sisters and his mother.

Alexander gestured with the lantern toward the open door leading into the tunnel. "I take it Harold will be friendlier this time around?"

"Much friendlier. He'll even offer to take your hat and cloak on the other side. Though you'd best hurry. Everyone has already arrived, and Madame will be arriving shortly herself."

"Good. Thank you." He swiftly turned, then

paused and turned back. "Should Lady Charlotte rise before class ends, inform her that I wish to see her."

Mr. Hudson brought the heels of his boots together. "I will, My Lord."

"Thank you."

"And thank you."

Lesson Fourteen

Learning the true nature of others can be quite horrid and daunting. As a gentleman, you must learn to remain calm. Or at least pretend to be.
— *The School of Gallantry*

Alexander paused outside the room Harold had led him to—the same room where Charlotte had interviewed his misguided soul not even two weeks earlier—and leaned toward the entrance-way just enough to peer inside.

Caldwell, who was all dressed up in full morning attire, was propped against one of the four leather wingback chairs, discussing something with the other two seated men.

The red velvet upholstered chair behind the small writing desk, where Charlotte had once sat, stood empty. Waiting to be filled by the notorious Madame de Maitenon.

He still didn't know why he'd ultimately decided to attend. Curiosity, perhaps. Or maybe he was trying to prove to himself that a man, no matter his history or long list of experiences, still had room to learn.

Caldwell paused midway through his conversation and turned. He grinned. "Hawksford! There you are! Hell, I thought you weren't coming."

Alexander slid in through the doorway and adjusted his morning coat. The only way to survive this with any form of dignity was to simply make do and adhere to the belief that he, a man who had once been dubbed the Lord of Pleasure, still had room to learn a thing or two about women. Or one woman, anyway: Charlotte.

Striding in, Alexander headed toward the two men who had already risen to their booted feet.

"This is Banfield," Caldwell supplied, gesturing to the gentleman on his right. "He and I have become rather quick friends."

Lord Banfield swiped away a long strand of sun-tinted, brown hair from the side of his face, forcing it back into his outdated queue. He smiled, though Alexander sensed it was forced, and extended his hand, stepping around his chair and toward him.

"Hawksford," Alexander quickly obliged, shaking the man's hand. "How do you do?"

Lord Banfield retrieved his hand and stepped back, now appearing rather amused. "With you here, I suppose I shouldn't feel quite the dolt."

Alexander let out a less than enthused laugh, sensing such quips were but the beginning of what he had to contend with, and turned his attention to the other man, who had already stepped up to him.

The man solemnly held out a heavily scarred hand. "Brayton. How do you do?"

"Well enough. Thank you." Alexander accepted his grip, noting the long, jagged scar that ran from the left side of the man's ear to the bottom front of his square jaw. He met the man's cool, blue eyes. "If you don't mind my saying, that's a rather wicked scar you have there."

Lord Brayton gave a curt nod and took back his hand. "I've learned to never trust a woman with a knife."

Alexander let out a much needed laugh and countered the man's quip with a lopsided grin. "Fortunately for you, she stayed above the waist."

Brayton stared at him for a weighty moment, not in the least bit amused, then turned and took his seat, extending his legs.

Alexander's grin faded. Had he misunderstood the whole woman-and-knife bit? Hell, and he thought *his* social skills were in need of good polishing. He cleared his throat and eyed Caldwell, wondering what he thought of the man.

Caldwell shrugged.

"*Bonjour!* Might we begin?"

Alexander jerked toward the sultry French-accented voice and was surprised to find a slim but well-endowed, silver-haired woman. Primly dressed, she wore a pale pink printed muslin gown with puffed sleeves. Despite her elegant and matron-like appearance, her pale hand held a tightly coiled, black leather horse whip.

She breezed across the room, wafting a soft scent of mint in their direction, and paused beside the red velvet chair. Her blue eyes scanned

all of their faces as her full lips curved into a playful smile. She set the whip onto the desk and
gracefully seated herself with a self-assured sigh.

She gestured toward their chairs. "Be seated. I
am very pleased you are all here."

Alexander quickly sat in the chair closest to the
door. Should the woman decide to put the whip
into use. He shifted in his seat and wondered if
he was the only one who felt uncomfortable with
the idea of an older woman toting a horse whip.

"I am Madame de Maitenon. By the end of this
Season, I expect to see notable results from all of
you. Results that will be evident in the lives you
are leading. And though I would be most honored to have all of you reenroll with each Season,
I have organized the lesson plans in a way that requires you to attend only one Season's worth of
classes."

She laced her fingers on the desk before her.
Her hands unnervingly close to the whip. As if she
meant to snatch it up at any moment. "Though
you are all here due to various reasons that shall
for the most part remain undisclosed, in accor-
dance to some of your wishes, I can assure you,
each will equally benefit."

Madame de Maitenon stood, pushing back her
chair, and snatched up the whip. With a snap of
her wrist, the braided leather horse whip unrav-
eled and thudded against the wooden floorboards.

Alexander instinctively bristled in response as
he watched her slender fingers tighten around the
handle. He didn't even need to look over at the
others to know exactly what they were thinking. A

lesson in flagellation, perhaps? To each his own, but pain was not his idea of pleasure.

"For some"—Madame de Maitenon strolled around her desk, the whip dragging behind her morning gown, and headed toward them— "pleasure knows no bounds. It is a way of life they weave not only into their own daily lives, but the lives of others. They are what I would call the gifted few."

She paused directly before Alexander and met his gaze head on. "You are all here because you have come to the profound realization that you are not among those men. Your pleasures have turned into a form of punishment. And it has caused you to do things you normally would not do."

Sensing she was challenging him, Alexander leaned forward in his seat. "Such as?"

Madame de Maitenon swung the whip aggressively at his leg, missing it by a mere inch. "Such as enrolling in my school."

Alexander glanced down at the tasseled edge of the braided whip that now tamely rested beside his boot. He looked up at her and smirked. "I assure you, Madame, it will take more than the crack of a whip to educate a man on the topic of pleasure."

She tugged the end of the whip back toward her and slowly raveled the whip into a circular coil around her hand. "So true. So true." With that, she held out the whip. "Take it, Lord Hawksford. You have earned the lead in my first lesson."

All three of the other men turned in their seats and eyed him.

Alexander grinned at all the unnecessary attention

and rose. He took the whip into his right hand, then stepped back and released its length, allowing the end to thud to the floor. Unable to resist, he gestured toward the whip and quipped, "So I take it length *does* matter?"

Caldwell burst into laughter, as Banfield chuckled behind his hand. Brayton, on the other hand, remained his grave, stoic self. Clearly not amused.

Madame de Maitenon turned to the men and clapped her hands in reprimand. She turned and pointed at Alexander. "Now. Extend the whip in Lord Caldwell's direction."

Alexander feigned a small laugh and shifted from boot to boot, the leather whip suddenly heavy in his right hand. "You want me to whip the man? What for?"

Caldwell scrambled to his feet. "Madame. This is not what I had in mind."

Madame de Maitenon snapped up a hand. Then pointed at Caldwell. "Sit. You came to me for assistance, and I intend to give it."

Caldwell paused, not appearing in the least bit convinced, then flopped back down into his chair.

Alexander glanced over at Caldwell, then back at Madame de Maitenon, sensing something was seriously amiss.

"You are all here to learn," Madame finally went on. "And learn you shall. Though first, I will require respect. My experience outweighs all of yours by almost two decades. I have bedded well over one hundred men, all of them privileged such as yourselves."

"You've also bedded a few women from what I hear," Alexander added, knowing full well the woman had entertained both his father *and* his mother.

Madame de Maitenon waved him off with a hand, jangling the ruby bracelets on her wrists. "*Oui*. And all of them were far more knowledgeable about my needs than most men. For the art of pleasure involves more than just that stick between your legs. Most women's delicate little pearls cannot even be reached by those sticks, no matter how long or how large. Which leaves a woman quite wanting."

Alexander bit back a smile. "And your point, Madame?"

She smiled. "My experience is what will eventually lead you all to a form of enlightenment. A means of not only seeing to your own pleasure but, more importantly, to that of your lady. Now. What is about to happen here today shall not be breathed or whispered of outside of this school. I pride myself on giving privacy and ask that you in turn give privacy to those around you. Is that understood?"

There was a moment of silence, then a unanimous though still somewhat uncertain "*Yes*" by all of them.

Alexander blinked, wondering which direction this lesson was about to take.

"Let us begin." Madame de Maitenon turned toward Alexander and arched a silver brow. "Extend the whip toward Lord Caldwell. Though try to keep it above the waist."

Alexander paused, the room growing awkwardly silent. He pointed to the whip in his hand.

"I really don't see what this has to do with plea-suring a woman."

Madame de Maitenon sighed, then swept a hand toward Caldwell. "Is that a woman, Lord Hawksford?"

Alexander laughed. "Uh . . . no. I hope not. Though he did mention having a secret."

She rolled her eyes. "I am attempting to demon-strate the power a man holds whenever interacting with others." She paused and fully turned to him. "What sort of man are you, Lord Hawksford? Can a man or a woman trust you to remain calm when a dire situation arises? Even whilst you hold a whip in your hand?"

Alexander glared at her. What sort of nonsense was this? "I know myself well enough to say that I would never whip anyone. No matter how dire the situation."

"Let us hope so." She glanced toward Lord Caldwell expectantly. As if waiting for him to say something.

Alexander followed her gaze and met Cald-well's all-too-serious gaze from across the short distance of the room.

A sense of dread slowly came over Alexander. This was about his secret. Alexander tightened his hold on the whip but vowed to remain stead-fast and calm. No matter what. "Whatever you have to say, Caldwell," he finally offered in a non-chalant tone, "I vow to remain calm."

Caldwell nodded, then stood and firmly an-nounced, "I deflowered Caroline, and I hope that in time you'll forgive me."

Lesson Fifteen

Shall I name all the ways a woman can
complicate a man's life? Or how it all applies
the other way around? No, I suppose there is
no need to begin. Otherwise school shall forever be
in session and we will all be in dire need of gin.
—*The School of Gallantry*

Lord Banfield and Lord Brayton scooted their seats away from Caldwell's chair.

Alexander stood in a daze, feeling as though he'd been slammed into the side of a brick building. With his head. His arm tensed as anger seized not only his brain but his very heart. He instinctively drew back the whip. "You did *what*?"

Caldwell winced but did not move. "I bedded Caroline."

No. No. Alexander refused to believe that Caldwell, his one true friend since he was sixteen, would do such a thing to him. To Caroline.

Caldwell coolly and calmly added, "I did not know it was her, Hawksford."

Oh, as if *that* made sense! "*What the devil do you mean you didn't know?*" Alexander roared, feeling the veins in his very throat swelling. He raised the whip higher, ready to use it to its full extent, when Lord Brayton jumped up from his seat and stalked toward him.

Alexander hissed out a breath, knowing full well what the man was after, and tossed the whip to his feet. Clearly, he didn't know himself as well as he thought he did. He'd actually almost whipped Caldwell. "I need a moment alone with him."

"*Non.*" Madame de Maitenon waved at him to proceed. "We stay."

Alexander turned completely toward the woman in disbelief. "My *life* is not a theatrical you can pay admission for."

She nodded. "*Oui.* But you are very angry right now. And as such cannot be trusted to do the right thing. Which is why we will all stay." Madame de Maitenon lifted her hand and snapped her fingers at Lord Brayton. "Pick up the whip. He cannot be trusted."

Lord Brayton nodded and strode nearer Alexander, following her command.

So. They all wanted a lesson, did they? All right. He'd give them a Goddamn lesson.

As Brayton leaned over to pick up the whip, Alexander firmly smashed his boot onto it, and glared down at the man. "It stays. Now move away."

Brayton peered up at him from over the wide shoulder of his morning coat with dark, menacing eyes. The jagged scar that ran from his ear to the bottom front of his jaw appeared eerily more pronounced. Without changing his bent position, Brayton swept a muscled arm out and cracked the backside of Alexander's knee.

Alexander stumbled backward, his knee bending against his will.

Lord Brayton snapped the whip up from the floor and rose to his full height of over six feet. "Take a breath, Hawksford," he said in a low, cool tone.

Alexander regained his balance and stepped toward him, meeting both his height and his gaze. Gritting his teeth, Alexander snapped his right fist back and rigidly held it in the air beside his own head, inwardly fighting his urge to let it fly. "*You* take a breath, you tosspot! What if this was *your* sister?"

Lord Brayton quirked a dark brow at him as he wound the whip several times around his scarred hand. "I don't have a sister. Now as I said before, take a breath. The rage will pass. In time." He turned, leaving Alexander's fist to continue to hang there, and strode casually back to his seat.

What the hell was the man talking about? His rage had yet to crest!

Alexander snapped his shaky hand back down to his side. He glanced across the room at Lord Banfield, who had long since risen from his chair. The man stood silently watching him with wary brown eyes.

"*Merci,*" Madame de Maitenon called out to Brayton. "I knew your skills would prove useful."

Skills? Alexander jerked his gaze back over to Lord Brayton, who lingered off to the side, suddenly realizing that the scar on the side of his face was anything but accidental.

The room fell completely silent.

Alexander savagely sucked in air through his nostrils and let it out through his mouth. "You told me that you had involved yourself with an American," he eventually said in a voice that was deceptively calm. Unlike how he felt.

"I lied." Caldwell paused, then added, "*Obviously*. But I did mean it when I said I was having trouble accepting her heritage."

"Jesus Christ, Caldwell, what the hell were you thinking?" he cried out in complete exasperation, not knowing what more he was supposed to say or do. "Caroline is intelligent and . . . and *sweet* . . . and you are . . . *anything but!* How could you even think to . . . I . . ."

He couldn't even find the words anymore. They were all fluttering away into the abyss of reality. The reality that Caroline, his innocent, beautiful, brilliant little sister, was no longer . . . *God!*

This was his own fault. He hadn't warned her enough. Hadn't protected her enough.

Caldwell raked his hands through his blond hair. "Upon my life, Hawksford, if I had known I . . . I wouldn't have." He dropped his hands, sending unruly hair down across his forehead. "You know I wouldn't have."

Alexander felt his nostrils flare as he sucked in another deep breath. "And yet you did."

Caldwell spastically swiped a hand over his face and started pacing, reflecting the rising restlessness that Alexander himself felt. "Yes. I did.

Hawksford. I wanted to tell you the moment it happened. But how does one go about telling one's childhood friend that he compromised his nineteen-year-old sister at the peak of her first Season?"

Alexander's stomach turned. Nausea seized him. He stalked toward Caldwell, feeling the room around him swaying and buckling. "When were you alone with her?" he demanded, his throat tightening and hindering his ability to breathe. "Did you scale up through the window and into my house? Is that it? Did you cause that diversion with Lady Waverly so that you could run yourself over into Caroline's bedchamber and have your way with her? Is that it?"

"No, of course not! Hell, I—" Caldwell glanced at the others in the room, then back at him. "I think we've said more than enough before this crowd. Don't you?"

"Oh, flog yourself already!" Alexander paused before him and frantically waved at those around them. "Do you think it matters what we say before them? It isn't any damn worse than what you've already done! I want an answer, and I want it now. When were the two of you alone? *When*?"

Caldwell hissed out a breath. "At the champagne party your mother hosted with my uncle."

Alexander's eyes widened. "*What*?"

"My blindfold went on, as customary," Caldwell rambled on, clasping a hand to the back of his neck. "Hell, you know what it involves, that's when you and all those women . . ." He paused, noting the look on Alexander's face, cleared his throat, and dropped his hand back to his side.

"Anyway, your sister claimed me, led me into a room, and I initiated physical contact. Without knowing it was her. The thing is, she knew damn well who I was. So we . . . you know . . . and then I upset her because . . . well, never mind that. And that's when I stripped off the blindfold and . . . *hell*. You know?"

A champagne party. What the devil had Caroline been doing at a champagne party to begin with? His mother. Of course. Of course!

Alexander grabbed hold of Caldwell's shoulder and squeezed it hard, digging the tips of his fingers into the flesh beneath Caldwell's jacket.

Caldwell winced but otherwise remained motionless.

"God save me from murdering someone," Alexander growled out. "How do I know she hasn't done this before?"

Caldwell now stared him down with a fierceness Alexander had never witnessed. "I can assure you, Hawksford, as experienced as she might have seemed to me with the blindfold on, Caroline was in fact . . ." He paused, clearly unable to finish.

"*A virgin,*" Madame de Maitenon supplied.

"Yes, thank you, Madame," Caldwell bit out over his shoulder. "Thank you."

Alexander released him and swiped his hand over his face, wishing this devil of a nightmare would disappear. "Is she with child? Do you even know?"

"No. She shouldn't be. I didn't . . ." Caldwell winced, unwilling to further elaborate.

The other two men in the room coughed and sniggered.

Alexander feigned a laugh, even though what he really wanted to do was smash a fist into Caldwell's face and take it through his skull.

"I was completely ridden with guilt." Caldwell let out a less than enthused laugh. "Completely. My uncle insisted that I seek out assistance so as to bring this matter to your attention in a civilized manner. He recommended going to someone who understood these sort of situations. And so here we are."

"Yes. Here we are. All so civilized. All standing in a school that educates men on the topic of love and seduction." Alexander pointed savagely back toward Madame de Maitenon, who stood behind them. "Thanks to you, Caldwell, our lives are now being orchestrated by the bloody French!"

Madame de Maitenon tsked. "Do not blame me for any of this."

Alexander fisted his hands in a strained effort to remain calm. He needed to remain calm or he'd do something irrational. Something illegal. Something he was going to be hanged for. "Your uncle is the last person you ought to take advice from," he bit out. "He barely remembers the day of the week."

Caldwell swiped a hand across his face again. "Yes, I know, I know. But he's the only family I have. I was desperate. And it made sense to me at the time! Hawksford. I do intend to marry her."

"You damn well *better* marry her, you bastard!" He paused. Although . . . Caldwell wasn't exactly the type of man capable of leading his sister down the right path. *Obviously.* "Despite your so-called offer, I cannot help but fear the sort of a husband you'll make. What with your background, your father, and all."

Caldwell shifted his jaw and stepped toward him. "It was always my intent to be a good husband."

"Is that so?" Alexander gave him a pointed stare. "And what would you even know about being a good husband? You aren't even capable of being a good friend!"

"Now that's not bloody fair!" Caldwell pointed at him rigidly, getting up close and into his face. "I may have been born onto a bleedin' Marquis de Sade, but I am still capable of decency!"

Alexander shoved him back. Hard. Wishing Caldwell would keep his distance before he thrashed him simply to make himself feel better. "Are you including *this* in your definition of decency?"

Caldwell sighed. "Hawksford. For God's sake, I . . . Aside from trying to be responsible, that night with Caroline was . . . well . . . incredible. I cannot deny what occurred between us." He paused, then dug into his waistcoat pocket. He withdrew a gold sovereign and held it up. "Do you even know what this is? Have you seen it before?"

Alexander blinked at the coin for an abashed moment, slowly recognizing it. "Caroline's lucky sovereign." The one she always carried about with her.

"*My* lucky sovereign, Hawksford," Caldwell sternly corrected him. "I once gave this to your sister with a promise. A promise I intend to keep."

Caldwell glanced at the coin and shoved it back into his pocket. "I suppose all you need know is that despite everything, I have always thought Caroline to be incredibly beautiful. But with her being your sister and a Hawksford, I never . . ." He cleared his throat. "I suppose I've said more than enough."

Alexander swallowed in response to Caldwell's sincere and unexpected confession. If he didn't know any better, he'd say Caldwell was in love with Caroline. Damn, but this was disturbing. Not to mention beyond his comprehension. "Are you telling me that . . . you're in love with her?"

Caldwell froze. Then stared at him as if he were mad. "Well, no. I mean . . . well, I may be, but—"

"*May be?*" Alexander shouted. "What do you mean you may be? You either are or you aren't, Goddamn you! Don't you even know?"

"For God's sake, man! I've never *been* in love!" Caldwell argued back in equal frustration. "In lust, *yes*, but never in love. And this . . ." He violently shook his head. "I don't know what it is. I don't know."

'Twas a sad, sad day in London when an ambitious man such as Caldwell appeared to be confused out of his bloody mind.

Hell. Love. Did the notion really exist? Could two people actually find a happily ever after? Or was lust simply getting the best of all of them and a select few were trying to alter the rules in the hope of making it appear more hopeful than it really was?

In the end, he knew Caldwell was a good man. An insane man who never did things the way they needed to be done, but he was still a good man.

Reliable. At times. Had a title. Had vast wealth. Though not much of anything else.

And if Caroline was pregnant, which he would rather assume she was, they needed to get married. Immediately. For he refused to have his sister made into an outcast. She needed to be protected from the masses before she suffered for it. For the rest of her life.

Not wanting to think about it anymore lest his head explode from the agony of it all, he said, "I shall obtain a special license from the Archbishop."

Caldwell stepped toward him, his face brightening. "You will?"

Alexander poked him in the chest, hitting the buttons on his waistcoat. "In the meantime, you will make everyone in London believe, including myself, that this is a match based on all things civil. And above all, you will make her happy. For if she is not happy"—Alexander pointed to himself and narrowed his gaze—"then *I* am not happy. Is that understood?"

Caldwell tugged his coat into place. "I can make her happy. I know I can."

Alexander gave a curt nod, not wanting to talk about it anymore. "Good."

"Good?" Caldwell grinned. "Really?"

He glared at him. "Not another word. Lest I change my mind." If his sister was with child, that meant he was soon going to be an uncle. Which, although that may have been rather nice under different circumstances, only meant *more* responsibilities. He hoped to God it wasn't another female. He'd been outnumbered for far too long.

"So is this particular lesson over?" Madame de Maitenon finally asked from behind. "Or do you both require more time?"

Alexander turned toward the woman who, blast her, had not only turned him into a lesson but had also turned him into a brother-in-law to his own friend. "Next time, Madame, I ask that you deliver such news in a letter."

She waved him off as if he was being childish. "I mean to personally assist each and every one of you."

"I never asked for assistance," he replied sharply.

"Most men never do." Madame de Maitenon leaned closer to him, her crisp blue eyes narrowing. "Which is why they always end up making life so miserable for themselves and everyone else around them. They think they can solve everything on their own. But what you, Lord Hawksford, and every man needs to remember, is that even the King of England requires assistance from his subjects in order to retain his throne. We French know that story all too well."

Stepping back, she swept a commanding gaze across all four of them. "Do you know that thirty men had originally applied to my school? Thirty. And out of all those men, I chose *you* to be the first in this endeavor. Why? Because I believed you were all capable of more. Do not disappoint me. I expect all of you"—she turned and pointed at Alexander—"including you, Lord Hawksford, to attend every class I give up until the end of the Season. You cannot learn anything about yourselves or about women if you are not willing to put in an effort. Should you choose not to attend, for whatever reason, I promise you will regret that decision."

May the devil seize them all. That sounded like a threat. Yes, well, he had absolutely no intention of attending anymore of these stupid classes. "I regret to inform you, Madame, that this will be my last class."

"We shall see." She clapped her hands at them and went back to her desk. "Now. Sit. All of you. We only have one hour remaining."

Too exhausted to even bother marching out the door, Alexander headed for his seat and plopped himself down into it. What the hell was he going to do? How was he going to tell his own sister that he knew she'd been compromised? How was he going to ever look at his sister again, knowing that she'd . . .

God. He didn't want to admit it, but Madame de Maitenon was actually right. A man *did* need help from time to time. Though what he specifically needed right now was female help. And needless to say, his mother was the last person he wanted to talk to about this.

The only reliable and steady-minded person he could even think of was Charlotte. Though he couldn't exactly have her over for tea to discuss this, could he?

"Lord Hawksford?" Madame de Maitenon sounded agitated.

Alexander stiffened and glanced up. "What now?"

She leaned into her desk toward him. "Have you been listening to the lecture?"

It was like being back at Eton. Only worse. Because this particular class was being conducted by a woman who reasoned men were incapable of thought. "I'm afraid not."

She sighed. "You will stay after class. The rest of you, *adieu*. It has been a pleasure. Until tomorrow, *oui?*"

Oh, bloody come now! Hadn't he been through enough in one day? He leered at Caldwell, Brayton, and Banfield as they all headed out the door. Traitors. How dare they abandon him to the French like this?

Caldwell did appear to have some humanity left within him. For he paused, turned back, and opened his mouth to speak.

Alexander snapped up a hand to prevent him from doing so. "No. Not a word. I need time."

Caldwell solemnly nodded, then turned and disappeared out the door.

Madame de Maitenon sighed again. Only a bit more dramatically. "It appears that you do not wish to be part of my school, Lord Hawksford."

"As of now, that is an understatement. I confess that this was by far the most elaborate scheme I've ever been a part of."

"Ah, but you learned something. You learned that you do not know yourself as well as you think you do. For you, Lord Hawksford, have played far too many roles in your life, and now it is beginning to unravel. Aside from Lord Caldwell bringing you here, supposedly against your will, were you also not the one to pen several passionate letters pleading to me for admission into this school?"

She had to remind him of that. "A mistake on my part."

"Ah. I see. A mistake." She rose from her seat and rounded her desk, making her way to his chair. She eventually paused before him and tilted her silver-coiffed head. "Lady Chartwell is a very beautiful woman, *non?*"

Alexander looked away, feeling uncomfortable about the way she continued to eye him. "Yes. Yes, she is."

"But of course she is," she purred. "And that is why you are here." Madame de Maitenon leaned toward him, reached out her ungloved hand, and pushed aside his hair from his forehead in a gentle, feathery manner.

He clenched his jaw, bridling his urge to shove away her hand.

"Though it may not seem so, Lady Chartwell is quite vulnerable and still coping with the tragedies that have befallen her." She lowered her voice to a hush and continued to play with his hair, her fingers occasionally grazing his forehead. "I hope that with your vast amount of experience you know what it is you are doing. For she is not like you or me. She has romantic dreams. Romantic dreams that even Chartwell was incapable of destroying. I suggest you be kind and make your attentions brief. For the longer you stay, the more complicated it will become." She drew away her hand and straightened. "For her, that is."

Alexander felt as if his gut were being held in a vise. He hated to admit it, but the woman was right. Charlotte was not like any of his other conquests. She had a genuine, gentle soul. And a whip of a mind. And aside from her incredible beauty, that is exactly what drew him to her. And why he wanted to stay. To bask in what she was. If even for a small while.

He stood and intentionally towered over the woman. "I am well aware of the complications. I simply refuse to abandon her knowing she is financially unsound and in your hands. I've already sent my lawyers over to the Court of Chancery to assist in this. Though I ask that you keep that to yourself. I've learned firsthand that Charlotte is not one to easily accept assistance."

Madame de Maitenon's silver brows rose in response. She stepped back. "*Mon Dieu*. Is it possible that my Charlotte has brought in your sails?" She tsked. "How will you ever fare at sea without them?"

He leveled his gaze at her. "I wasn't aware we knew each other that well, Madame."

"I know you much better than you think." She shrugged, however, as if none of it mattered. "I suppose there is only one way we can go about this. As of today, Lord Hawksford, you are no longer permitted to return to my classroom. You are . . . as you English say, *banned*."

That was by far the best news he'd heard all day. "Glad to hear it."

She held up a hand so as to keep him from further interruption. "I do intend to still charge you that one hundred pounds per week for the rest of the Season. For wasting my time. For unlike you, Lord Caldwell and the others are genuinely intrigued by what I have to offer."

"*One hundred pounds per week?*" he demanded. "Do you plan to sink me, woman? Hell, I have five sisters to marry off. *Five.*"

"*Oui.* I can count in both English and French. And *you* should have thought about that before you decided to enroll. Remember that there are men here who are genuinely looking to become more." She gave him a once-over. "Unlike you."

Madame de Maitenon turned away and waved him off. "You may go, Lord Hawksford. Our business here is done. I expect all payments to be made by the end of every week."

All payments by the end of every . . .

Too furious to impart any more words, Alexander jerked toward the door and stalked out. He wasn't even going to bother arguing with a damn Frenchwoman who was clearly out of her mind.

Lesson Sixteen

*No. Not all men are created equal. For there are
those that possess qualities that go beyond the
wildest expectations of a woman's dreams.*
                                   —The School of Gallantry

Four days later, evening

Charlotte sat perched on the edge of her bed
and stared at the sealed parchment in her hand.
The one she hadn't been able to open since its ar-
rival early that afternoon. The letter *H* had been
perfectly pressed and centered into the round red
wax seal. She had hoped Alexander would write. At
the very least.

After Mr. Hudson had informed her that
Alexander had attended the first day of school and
had even asked for her, she had been not only
shocked, but thrilled. For she had been certain
their association was over. And yet clearly it was not.
Although he hadn't made an appearance back at
the school since.

What could this attempt to contact her mean?

Charlotte nervously turned it over in her hand. She had to know what it said. She simply had to. Drawing in a deep breath, she cracked open the seal and fumbled to pull the parchment apart. She carefully evened the creases and let the breath she'd been holding out.

Alexander's crisp, handwritten words appeared along with the opening *My Dearest Charlotte.*

Her heart fluttered. His dearest? Lord, she was too easily excited as of late. She quickly read on.

My circumstances have changed quite considerably since we last met. Hence this letter. I am in need of your advice. I will gladly explain myself in more detail should you agree to see me. If I do not receive word from you declining this invitation this evening, an unmarked carriage will arrive at your door at midnight tonight. A reliable source assures me that you are a night owl and that the hour would better suit you. I thank you in advance for your time and consideration.

Your Humble Servant Always,
Hawksford

Her cheeks burned. What a terrible, terrible gossip Mr. Hudson was! If it weren't for the fact that he had so many grandchildren dependent on him for wages, she would have tossed him out ages ago.

Charlotte sighed and set her finger firmly upon Alexander's name. If only she could place a finger so easily upon the man's heart. She knew he had one. He simply guarded it with a vicious intent in the same manner she did her own.

What sort of advice could the man possibly need? Biting her lip, she folded the letter, trying to calm the rapid pace of her heart. She supposed she would find out soon enough. Tonight.

At exactly midnight, an unmarked carriage strapped to four black horses arrived at her door. Charlotte let out a shaky breath as Mr. Hudson opened the door. She gathered up her bombazine gown and slowly stepped out into the cool, foggy darkness.

She glanced around, feeling as if she were about to engage in highway robbery.

The footman hopped down from behind the carriage, opened the door, and hurriedly folded out the steps for her. He then snapped straight and held out his gloved hand for her.

She nodded her thanks to the young man and with his help climbed inside the carriage that was dimly lit with a lone lantern hanging from the red brocaded ceiling. She eyed the empty seats.

Lovely. An unmarked carriage and no suitor. She officially fit the role of a wanton.

Charlotte sighed and sat on the leather-cushioned seat as the footman folded the steps back into place and slammed the door. The carriage lurched forward and clattered off. She eyed the small brocaded curtains that had been pulled shut over all the windows. Did he not want her to know where she was going? Or did he not want anyone to know that she was inside?

Time passed and the carriage still clattered on and on and on. She tapped her feet. Growing bored with tapping, she turned to twirling the fabric of her gown around her forefinger over and over and over.

She eyed the curtains and quickly pulled one side back. She peered out, but nothing but darkness swayed beyond the glass window. Well. That was helpful.

She fell back against the seat, letting the curtain settle into place. Oh, for heaven's sake, when would it ever end? She couldn't take much more of this torture!

The carriage slowed, then swayed to a halt.

Oh. Well. Good.

The crunching of gravel beneath a steady pace of boots and a low exchange of male voices floated toward her.

She froze. Her bonnet. She still had her bonnet on.

Charlotte hurriedly untied the ribbon from beneath her chin, knowing she looked better without it, and cast it aside. Patting her coiffed hair, she arranged her gown daintily around her, trying to calm the rapid beating of her heart.

The carriage door opened. The footman stoically unfolded the steps and held out his gloved hand.

Grabbing up her bonnet, she took his hand and stepped down. She glanced around at the unusual amount of trees towering in the shadows. Warm, glowing lights shone up ahead through the glass panes of a lone home. It appeared to be some sort of cottage. Somewhere on the outskirts of London.

Drat him. She had managed to become his naughty little secret, after all.

"My Lady." The footman strode around her and quickly led the way down a narrow path to a front door whose small, stone archway was covered with ivy.

The man opened the door and ushered her inside. Before her, a small, narrow wooden staircase led to the second floor. Though she could see several portraits scattered across the uneven timbered walls, the lighting was so dim, she couldn't make out any other surroundings.

"To your right, My Lady." A servant stepped forward and led her into a small, elegant room, immersing her in polished wood and burgundy brocade. He then closed the single door. She was now completely trapped in his realm. A sensuous realm scented with raw, rough leather and that familiar zest of freshly sliced lemon.

The evening shadows and warm candlelight played and flickered with one another across the space of the quiet room decorated with simple country-landscape paintings.

Charlotte tightened her hold on her bonnet as a movement from the far corner of the room caught her eye. She turned just in time to see Alexander rise from one of the upholstered chairs.

His green eyes met hers from across the candlelit room and his firm mouth curved into a tired little smile. As if he lacked the strength to do it.

Which was so unlike him.

Something was terribly wrong. As a matter of fact, it appeared everything about him was out of place and wrong. Only the black and gray pinstriped attire he wore appeared to be tidy. Unlike the rest of him.

His bronzed hair was wild and unkempt, falling onto his forehead and into his eyes. His strong jaw was heavily shadowed with dark golden facial hair, making him appear rough and rugged. And what was perhaps even more unnerving about him in that moment was that he continued to say absolutely nothing. He simply stood there and looked at her with the softest gaze she had ever received from any man.

"You came." He said it as if she had bestowed him with the greatest of gifts.

She tried not to linger on the softness of his tone or what it could mean. She was actually more concerned about the state he appeared to be in. "Is something wrong?" she quietly asked. "You seem . . . not yourself."

He let out a gruff laugh and gestured toward his face and hair. "I apologize. I haven't had time for more than the basics." He cleared his throat. "Thank you for coming. I apologize for the ride, but I thought it best we meet here."

She nodded and glanced about the small parlor. "Do you come here often?"

"No. But my father did whenever he wanted to be alone. He bought it from a struggling merchant some twenty years ago. It's not quite the country, though not quite the city, as he always liked to say."

"'Tis charming."

"Yes." He nodded. "It is."

Silence hung between them once again.

They stared at each other in awkward silence. For what seemed like an eternity.

He eventually let out an exhausted breath. "Please. Sit." He pointed to the chair beside his. "I was hoping we could talk. About my sister."

Charlotte blinked. *His sister*? Why on earth would the man bring her all the way out here merely to talk about his sister?

Something had to be wrong. Very wrong. She hurried over to the seat he had offered and, gathering up the sides of her gown, seated herself. She awkwardly turned toward him, not knowing if she should ask him or simply let him speak on his own.

He sat and placed his large hands on his knees, leaning forward. He glanced at her, then looked away. Gazing at the curtain-drawn windows across the room. "Caroline's Season is officially over," he muttered. "Done."

Over? Done? Lord, the Season had barely commenced. Charlotte's brows rose as she studied the profile of his body and face. She almost dreaded to ask why. Was it because of her? Of them? "Whatever do you mean? What has happened?"

"My mother permitted Caroline to attend a champagne party. And there . . ." He closed his eyes and slowly shook his head. "Charlotte. She may very well be with child."

Her heart dropped, and she lowered her gaze to her hands. Oh, dear God. "I . . . is she all right?" She glanced up again. "She wasn't . . ."

"No. No. She was willing." He feigned a laugh. "A bit *too* willing, from what I understand."

Though she'd never been to a champagne

party, she knew full well the sort of people that frequented them. Chartwell having been one of those types. "Dare I ask what breed of man she succumbed to?" she ventured.

He grumbled something.

She leaned toward him. "Pardon?"

He turned to her. "Actually, you know this particular breed of a man."

"I do?" She hesitated, dread seeping into her voice over the travesty of his situation. "Who is it?"

He shifted his jaw, then bit out, "Caldwell."

Her eyes widened in astonishment. "*Lord Caldwell?*"

"Yes. The very same. It seems he and Madame came to some sort of agreement prior to his enrollment. He didn't know how to go about telling me that he had deflowered my sister. So they turned me into a lesson."

She eyed him. "Madame mentioned the agreement, but she never shared any of the specifics." She shook her head in disgust, remembering her interview with Caldwell. The bastard. "Do you know what Caldwell told me during his application process?"

Alexander paused. "Do I want to know?"

"He claimed he was intent on seducing some American. You know, that one girl who caused an uproar by wearing trousers and pistols in public?" She shook her head again. "I don't know why I ever chose to believe him. I suppose it's because no story seems too far-fetched to me anymore."

Alexander swiped a hand over his face and swore under his breath. "I don't want to talk about him anymore. I really don't. Charlotte. I'm trying to ensure that none of my other sisters find out about what could potentially lead to a very ugly situation. Which is rather ironic, because all along I'd been worried about how *I* was going to affect them."

His brows came together as he leaned farther forward and looked down at the floor beneath his boots. "I know it is presumptuous of me to sit here and ask for advice, but I have no one else to turn to. No one else I can trust."

She bit her lower lip, trying to pinch some sort of real sensation back into her body. The great Earl of Hawksford, the Lord of Pleasure himself, was asking for advice? She didn't know whether she should be honored by the request or frightened out of her mind.

"I cannot even trust my own mother. Hell, she is the very reason Caroline is in the situation she's in."

Charlotte fought back the urge to reach out and rub his back. As a means of offering him some sort of support and comfort. But she knew better. Knew that with all that had already transpired between them, touching him was the last thing she should do. He was coming to her as a friend. Something no man had ever done before.

She slowly wrapped the ribbon of her bonnet around her wrist and eyed him. "What makes you think that I have any sound advice to give? Given my current occupation and experience with men."

He glanced over at her and straightened in his seat, shifting toward her. His unshaven face was now but a mere foot away from hers, his heat reaching out toward her. "You have a way about you, Charlotte. You show strength in your convictions. A strength that even I myself have trouble adhering to. I don't want to push Caroline away and make this situation even worse. How can I talk to her about this?"

She nervously poked at the ribbon wrapped around her wrist, fully aware that he was indeed seeking advice from her. "Talk to her in the same manner in which you are talking to me right now. Be reasonable and patient and listen to what she has to say."

"But how do I go about saying it?" He squared his shoulders. "Do I walk into the parlor, sit her down for tea, smile, and say, '*So I hear you frigged Caldwell. Would you care to tell me all about it?*'"

Charlotte released a small laugh and shook her head. "Heaven forbid you do. I suggest you arrange an outing for the two of you. Perhaps a picnic in the park. Something that will prevent a scene."

"She does like picnics."

"There. You see? Make her feel comfortable and safe in her environment. Remind her that you are her brother and that she can trust you."

He hesitated, a slight look of horror on his face as if contemplating the fatal moment. At last, he sighed. "I can try."

She smiled assuredly. "That is all you can do."

"God. Charlotte . . ." Alexander scrambled out of his chair, grabbed both arms of the chair, and leaned forward, sealing her into place.

She froze, painfully aware of how close his face was to hers. Close enough for him to kiss her. She knew, however, that thinking about it at a time like this was most selfish on her part. He needed a friend right now. Not a lover.

He urgently searched her face. "She'll hate me for what I've done. But I had to do it. I simply had to."

Charlotte paused. "What on earth have you done?"

He slowly kneeled, sinking to the floor, still holding on to the arms of her chair. He looked away. "I've applied for a special license for her and Caldwell. Without telling her about it."

Oh, well, now *that* was indeed a dilemma. The poor girl goes and makes a mistake, and she's imprisoned to a man for the rest of her life.

Charlotte lowered her chin, showing him her clear disapproval. "Why wouldn't you talk to your own sister about it before making such a life-altering decision for her?"

He hit his hands against the arm of the chair. Twice. "Because she has a tendency to want to do things *her* way. And when it comes to this, there simply is no other choice. She *has* to marry him. She simply has to."

"*Has to?*" Charlotte sighed. "There are always choices, Alexander. You simply snatched away her ability to make one. And seeing you fear her reaction, you clearly understand that quite well."

His features tensed. He eventually nodded and murmured, "You're right. I simply . . . I still see that scrawny, annoying girl who used to ask me why we have ten fingers and ten toes instead of eight fingers and eight toes. Even back then, she never liked any of my answers. She always told me I ought to find better resources."

His sister sounded like quite the rebel. Much like her brother. Charlotte reached out and placed a hand on the rough edge of his cheek, wishing she could make his troubles disappear.

He stiffened, his green eyes meeting hers.

She lowered her hand, sensing that her touch had irked him. "Your intentions are well placed. At least have faith in that."

He lowered his chin slightly, and she heard the arms of the chair creak from beneath the applied pressure of his hands. "As of late, I have very little faith in any of my intentions."

"I have faith in your intentions." Charlotte reached out again and traced the outline of his husky profile with her forefinger. Starting from his stubbled chin, she moved her finger up to his soft lips, over his smooth nose, then up across his forehead. "You're a good man, Alexander. Misguided at times. But you're a good man. Believe that. I know I do."

He didn't move. He didn't even blink. He simply remained frozen. As if there was something improper about her presence, about her touch. About that moment.

She slowly took back her hand again. "Forgive me. I don't mean to keep touching you."

He blinked, his green eyes taking on the hazy, heavy look of a late summer sky night. "You can touch me," he murmured.

Her pulse leapt in response to his soft words. What a never-ending mystery he was. He seemed capable of giving so much and yet so little. She reached out and played with the silk of his embroidered gray waistcoat, wishing there was a way she could dig out the man hidden beneath.

He reached up and gently brushed the side of her cheek, taking on a much too serious appearance. "Might I ask you something?"

Charlotte leaned the side of her face into the warmth of his palm. "Of course. Ask me anything."

"Why do you still mourn for Chartwell? Hasn't your time of mourning for him passed?"

She lowered her gaze, suddenly unable to look at him. "I have never truly mourned for him," she finally whispered. "I actually am mourning for my mother."

"Forgive me." His fingers brushed the side of her face as he tilted his head slightly to one side. "You must have loved her very much."

Charlotte blinked away tears that threatened to tumble forth. And for the first time in a long while, she felt as if she would fall apart if she didn't share what had been trapped within her all this time. This sense of not being able to forgive herself.

She removed his hand from her face, brought it to her lap, and squeezed it. "Yes. She was an amazing woman." Her voice sounded exhausted. Even to her own ears.

Charlotte lifted her hand and pointed to her lower lip with the tip of her finger. "She had this scar. Right here. She claimed she had received it in her younger days as a fish. When my father reeled her in with his hook."

Alexander grinned. "Clever."

She nodded and gave him a small smile. "Yes.

She was born with natural wit. What is more, she was forever looking for an opportunity to make me laugh. Which is what I truly miss most."

Her smile faded. "When I met Chartwell during my first Season, I was smitten. He was so charming and handsome. My mother told me right away, 'Charlotte, do not involve yourself with him. Your heart will only be torn asunder.' Indeed, she saw him for what he truly was. Yet I doubted her. I thought I loved him. Thought I knew him. I sought him out wherever I could. When he eventually proposed and ardently outlined how well suited we were for one another, never once did he include the notion of love in his proposal. Fool that I was, I accepted his proposal for I believed that once we were married, he'd eventually come to love me as much as I loved him. My mother grudgingly agreed to the marriage, mostly because she knew it was what I wanted, and our finances allowed for it, but told me I would live to regret it."

Charlotte shook her head. "After I married him, my mother would only see me if I called alone. I couldn't understand it. I was simply too naïve. Whenever I professed my love to him, he merely nodded. Or changed the subject. Each day, I waited for his words of love, but they never came. When my mother ceased asking that I call upon her, I thought it was because she was still angry with me. My only hope was that in time I could show her how happy I was."

She paused. "Then one afternoon, not even a week into the Season, I came home early from an appointment with my modiste and found

Chartwell entertaining a woman. Though not in his bedchamber. But in mine."

The disgust and anger within her swelled as images of him and that large-breasted brunette flashed through her mind. "What was worse, he wasn't in the least bit apologetic. He told me repeatedly that *I* was being irrational about the whole matter, that it was perfectly acceptable for a married man to keep a mistress." She feigned a laugh. "Acceptable. And then you know what he did? He asked me to leave. As if *I* were the one to have done something wrong."

She was quiet for a moment, still in disbelief of the direction her life had taken. "I was so ashamed. What was worse, I had no one to talk to. Respectable women simply aren't allowed to discuss these things amongst themselves. I desperately wanted to tell my mother about what had happened, but I was so ashamed. So the silence between us grew."

She drew in a shaky breath and let it out. "Then one night, I found a half-burned letter in the hearth of Chartwell's study. A letter from my mother's servant. Begging that I see her. That she had suffered from a form of apoplexy and was fading. That is when I knew Chartwell had been destroying her letters all along, and in turn had been destroying me. He wanted to punish me for not accepting his indiscretions." A tear finally slid down her cheek. "I never understood how he could be so cruel."

Still kneeling before her, Alexander raised his hand and brushed away the tear with his thumb.

He shifted his jaw, then hoarsely whispered, "He deserved what he got."

Charlotte smiled with trembling lips.

Seeing the compassion and tenderness in his eyes made her feel as if a new beginning was possible. And it was a wonderful, warm feeling, to say the least. For when she thought about everything she had been through with Chartwell and her mother, a deep anger and regret always flared within her.

But now, with Alexander touching her like this, looking at her like this, with so much understanding in his eyes, a shielding calm came over her, and for the first time since her mother's death, she believed she could survive. And not only survive, but become more because of it. So much more.

Lesson Seventeen

Men can be so annoyingly sensitive
when it comes to the subject of their pride.
Sadly, it is a trait they are born with.
And sadly, it is a trait they will die with.
— *The School of Gallantry*

Charlotte pressed Alexander's hand to her cheek more firmly with her own, wishing to God she could hold on to this moment, this feeling, namely *him*, forever.

Silence hummed in the room around them.

Alexander pulled his hand away, then suddenly leaned in and brought his mouth down to hers.

The timing of his kiss was perfect. She accepted his lips with a genuine need she had never felt in her entire life. His hot tongue pushed open her mouth.

Although his kiss was loving, soft, and slow, Charlotte wanted so much more. She wanted a true night of passion. One she would carry with her for the rest of her days, no matter what happened between them from this night forth.

She tore away from their deep kiss, grabbed hold of his jacket, and pushed it back from his broad shoulders and off his arms, letting it slip to the floor. "I want you," she whispered, grabbing hold of the buttons on his waistcoat and undoing them as fast as her fingers would allow. "Before we say good-bye."

Alexander let out a gruff laugh and grabbed at her hands, trying to still them. "Charlotte. As amazing as your offer is, I cannot take advantage of you anymore. Aside from advice, I admit to bringing you here for one other reason. I wanted to personally assure you that although we are going our separate ways, I've ensured that you'll never have to depend on anyone again. Not Madame de Maitenon, not the school, not anyone. In two weeks, you will receive papers from the Lord Chancellor. Sign them, deliver them, and your part of the estate will be returned to you without delay. Without further waiting or court proceedings."

Her eyes widened. Impossible.

He paused, his eyes soft. "I hope that I haven't overstepped my bounds. I simply wanted to ensure you were cared for."

She blinked, almost refusing to believe him. For what she had been unable to accomplish in a year, he had accomplished in less than a few weeks. And what was more, he did it without her having to ask him to do it.

"Oh, Alexander," she breathed, her heart squeezing at the beautiful gesture. "I . . . thank you."

"You are most welcome."

Overwhelmed, Charlotte leaned toward him, wanting to show him more than ever how she desperately needed and wanted him. And it didn't matter that she was going to have to let him go. All that mattered was this moment. Here. Now. "Make love to me," she whispered. "This one last time."

He blew out a heavy breath and squeezed her hands tightly with his own. "It is late, Charlotte. You have an hour's worth of travel ahead of you."

Her brows came together, not quite understanding his intentions. Didn't he want and need her, knowing that most likely they would never see each other again?

She slipped her hands away from his and met his gaze. Leaning toward him, she slowly unbuttoned his waistcoat. "I want this. Don't you?"

Alexander grabbed her hands again, stilling them with his own against the last button of his waistcoat. His breathing was notably heavier, his chest rising and falling in deep rhythms. "You deserve more than this. You deserve more than what I have to offer."

Charlotte freed her hands from his again in disbelief. She stared at him. Hard. Something was different. Something she couldn't quite explain.

"Is something wrong?" she prodded.

"I . . ." He paused, then dramatically quirked a bronzed brow as if to prove otherwise. "No. Why?"

She lowered her chin, showing him that she was on to him. "Because the Alexander I know would have thrown up my skirt over an hour ago."

He let out a laugh and groaned, tilting his

bronzed head slightly back. "Yes, yes. I know, I know. Charlotte. I merely want to do what is right by you."

She blinked. "What is right by me? And what do you think that is? Denying me my last pleasure? This is our last chance to be together, and I'll not live with regret. I'm done living with regret." She stared him down, a sense of naughty urgency driving her. "Now I am ordering you to frig me. Senseless."

Alexander's eyes widened and his lips parted in clear astonishment. "Charlotte!" It sounded like a reprimand.

She rolled her eyes, irked by his exaggerated seriousness. Where was the carefree man who had so arrogantly boasted of his prowess? Who was this man anyway? "I am not asking you to marry me and in turn destroy your family. I am merely asking for a night of passion. Isn't that all you wanted from me all along? A good frig? What makes this moment any different from the rest?"

He exhaled loudly through his nostrils. Then half nodded. Ever so slowly, he rose to his feet until he towered over her, parading his full height of over six feet. He stared down at her, his green eyes harboring a sharp, wild light she'd never witnessed before.

Silently watching her, he stripped off his waistcoat and whipped it to the floor. His jaw tightened as he yanked off his lopsided cravat and collar and tossed them aside.

Charlotte's heart thundered as she stared up at him, frozen and confused. He was furious with her. Both his stance and his eyes shouted it, and yet for some reason he continued to undress with obvious determination.

His fingers undid the three small buttons around his throat, exposing the open slit of the shirt that ended at his midchest. He gathered up the bottom of his shirt and ripped it up past his broad chest and shifting shoulders and up over his head. He lashed the shirt aside, his well-defined arms, chiseled stomach, and broad chest tightening and shifting from the violent motion.

He stepped toward her, blocking her completely into the space of the chair. "If it is the Lord of Pleasure that you seek, Charlotte," he said in a raw, harsh tone, "then it is the Lord of Pleasure you shall get."

With that, he grabbed her by the waist, yanked her up and spun her around, redirecting her back into the chair. Without even giving her a chance to properly grab hold of the chair, his grip tightened on her skirts.

Her heart skittered as she heard cloth ripping from her waist. He jerked her backward several times, making her gasp in an odd combination of fear and excitement. He finished tearing off the last of her skirts and sent them in a rustling whoosh down to the floor.

Her eyes widened as she glanced down. He had separated her dress in half. In mere seconds.

He leaned toward her, the heat of his body encasing her exposed chemise and lower half. "I hope you brought spare clothing," he growled into her ear. "Or you'll be traveling naked back to London. Now hold on to the chair and don't let go."

Charlotte instinctively tightened her hold on the arms of the wooden chair as her lips parted to say something. For she wanted him with all of her heart, yes, but not at the expense of his pride. "Alexander, I didn't—"

He violently ripped the rest of her clothing from the upper portion of her body, scattering small onyx buttons everywhere, and shoved it down the length of her arms. He yanked the silk material off completely from her wrists and hands, causing her to scramble to try to hold on to the chair.

His hands slowly slid from her shoulders down the length of her arms and curved toward the inside of her waist, sending fluttering sensations across her entire body, making her very aware of the fact that she only wore a pair of pantaloons, a chemise, and a corset.

He leaned in, his warm breath heating the side of her bare neck, and suckled at her skin. Her entire body pulsed with roaring heat as he sucked harder, looking to intentionally leave his mark.

As provocative as it was, it was also a touch frightening. Because it was very, very obvious that he had absolutely no intention of making love to her. Oh, no. He planned on frigging her. The very thing she'd asked for.

Alexander shoved up her chemise, then grabbed hold of the open flaps of material belonging to her pantaloons right between her thighs. She stiffened as he jerked the seams viciously apart. The pantaloons now loosely clung to her hips by mere threads, exposing her naked backside to him.

He nudged her legs apart with his knee, and she felt his hands unbutton his trousers. He released himself, and she felt his stiff, heavy cock fall onto her backside.

"Alexander," she whispered, wanting him to know that she was sorry for making him feel as if he meant nothing more to her than this. "Forgive me. I—"

His hand slid between her thighs and found that blissful area that always brought paradise. He rubbed it hard, sending a jolt of unexpected pleasure up the length of her core, then moved his finger and slid it deep into her. "Enjoy it," he said softly.

Unable to focus, Charlotte reluctantly released a small moan.

His finger slid in and out, in and out, causing her world to whirl with a rising, pent-up pressure she wanted to release.

"Do you know what the best part about fucking is?" He rubbed faster, causing her to gasp. Causing her to grow so wet, she could feel his finger slipping. "No matter who you are, you can always momentarily find utter bliss."

He removed his finger and positioned himself behind her, spreading her bum tautly apart. She breathed in and out, gasping, unable to catch her breath, unable to say anything anymore. Even in response to his words.

"We all want utter bliss, don't we?" he whispered. "We simply all define it differently." With a single violent thrust, he buried his thick cock deep inside her.

They both cried out at the same time.

He reached down around her, toward her lower front, and fingered her, forcing her to climb much quicker to her pleasure than she wanted to. She panted and pushed back against his shaft, which completely filled her, then moved forward again toward his fingers, which promised just as much. Between the two, she was utterly blind with pleasure.

She desperately tightened her hold on the chair as he repeatedly slammed into her, forcing her to take in more of the unspeakable pleasure that was swiftly cresting within her. All the while, he never stopped fingering her. His ability to focus on both, when she could barely stand, yet alone hold on to the chair, awed her.

She gasped repeatedly as he pushed out every breath from her with each forceful, slamming thrust. Each breath she took brought her closer and closer to that moment she wanted so much. That moment of complete bliss.

She cried out as her core tightened. Her entire body followed, releasing every flying sensation in her being, pushing her to the most amazing peak she'd ever experienced in her entire life. Her arms weakened, and she felt herself wanting to fall into the chair.

Alexander savagely held her in place as he continued to drive repeatedly into her wetness.

"Did you find it?" he hoarsely demanded between each thrust. "Did you?"

"Yes!" she cried out, almost in a sob. "Yes!"

"Good . . ." The hand that had been fingering her slid up and out and grabbed hold of her waist. He slipped his cock out. Using his other hand, he hurriedly finished pleasuring himself, making a point to keep her in place to the end.

The back of his hand jerked and slapped against her bollocks as his breaths grew all the more ragged and guttural. His hand jerked faster and faster, his hold on her waist growing tighter as he ground his body against her backside.

Her heart skipped as his large hand, which viciously held and jerked his rigid cock, repeatedly grazed her skin with a heat that slowly burned from the unrelenting contact.

He groaned aloud as his body stiffened behind hers. A sticky warmth spurted across her backside. He groaned again, wrapping his hot, sticky hands around her body, and pulled her backside flat against the length of his sweat-ridden large, muscled body. He shuddered as his shaft spurted the last of his warm seed.

They both stood there, their breaths heavy, their bodies still naked, silence and night still all around them.

Alexander slowly pulled her chemise down and around her torn pantaloons. And stepped away. As if only now realizing what they had done.

Charlotte turned, her arms and body shaky, and fell back into the chair with a thud, knowing she shouldn't even try to stand. Her gaze floated past Alexander's naked body and met his gaze.

He stared down at her for a long moment, his unshaven face flushed, his green eyes hauntingly serious. He then turned away and grabbed up his trousers that were laying crumpled nearby. "I didn't want it to end like this," he finally murmured. Without so much as looking at her, he pulled his trousers on and yanked them up. "Allow me to find some clothes for you. So that you may leave."

He walked past, buttoning the flap of his trousers into place. The soft glow of the candlelight bronzed the broad back of his skin in the most beautiful way. He disappeared into the darkness beyond the small parlor.

It was all too much.

Charlotte closed her eyes and placed a shaky hand to her mouth, stifling an aching sob. It was well and over. She had completely and utterly destroyed whatever had been left between them. Without meaning to. Fool that she was, she had been much too focused on her own needs and her own pleasure to realize she should have been focusing on what truly mattered most to her and her heart—*him.*

She had seen it all in his eyes. The betrayal of what she'd done. She hadn't asked for Alexander. She had asked for the Lord of Pleasure. As no doubt so many others had asked for. And now? Now she wished she could have her Alexander back.

She reopened her eyes and lowered her hand, knowing she couldn't possibly face him after what she'd done. She hurried over to where her shredded clothes lay, gathered them to her chest, and hurried out of the room. Spotting a cloak hanging from one of the hooks in the corridor, she snatched it up and wrapped it tightly around herself. She flung open the door and disappeared into the night. Where she well and truly belonged.

Lesson Eighteen

If you suffer and long at the mere thought of her,
I assure you, whether you approve of it or not,
love has officially made its appearance.
> —*The School of Gallantry*

She had left. Without even saying good-bye.

Alexander sat cross-legged on the wooden floorboards, half dressed in only his riding boots and trousers. He stared at the chair beside him. The chair he would forever associate with Charlotte. And though he tried, God how he tried, he could do nothing but simmer in the reality of how it had ended between them.

It was over. He had seen to it.

He clenched his jaw, then raised his foot and kicked the chair as far away as he could, sending it skidding and then tumbling to the floor. He had tried to do the right thing.

He wanted to prove to her, and to himself, that he respected her, cared for her, and that if it weren't for the future happiness of his sisters, he might have even married her. Though clearly, in her eyes, he was naught but a frig. A stupid, worthless frig. Nothing more than what the rest of the women viewed him as. The Lord of Pleasure. And it was by far the worst moment of his life.

Most of the candles in the room had long extinguished themselves, leaving him to sit in almost complete darkness. Only two flickering candles remained, fighting to give him the light he needed. Though he knew, like himself, they wouldn't last for much longer. It was time to return to London. Away from here.

The clattering of carriage wheels crunching against the gravel pierced the silence. He slowly turned his head and gazed in the direction of the windows but otherwise did not move. His mind and body were still too numb to try and respond.

Hurried steps outside came rushing toward the house, and moments later the front door in the entryway creaked open. Then slowly closed.

Alexander shifted toward the open door and squinted at the darkness. A shadowy, slim figure in a gown rustled by, heels clicking hurriedly past him, heading for the stairs leading to the second floor.

He caught his breath, inwardly hoping she'd come back. Back to tell him that she wanted *him*, Alexander, all along. "Charlotte?" he called out.

The clicking came to a halt. The steps came one slow heel at a time back in his direction. The shadowy figure drew closer into the doorway, bringing the person into full view. A petite woman with long chestnut curls and a pale, stricken face stood in the open doorway of the parlor.

His eyes widened as he choked on his own astonishment. Bloody hell, it was Caroline! What the devil was she doing all the way out here? And at such an unearthly hour?

He jumped up to his booted feet. "Caroline! What are you doing here?"

Her eyes flickered across the length of his bare chest. She cringed and snapped up a gloved hand to shield her eyes. "Why are you prancing about half-naked? I realize it's the country, but *really*."

Alexander snatched up the shirt from his pile of clothes and yanked it hurriedly over his head. As if his night hadn't already taken a turn for the worse. He supposed he might as well finish it.

He stalked toward her, stuffing the ends of his loose shirt into the depths of his trousers. "My chest should be the least of your worries."

Caroline dropped her hand to her side and glared at him. "What is that supposed to mean?"

He stopped before Caroline and bit back from altogether shouting at her for the agony she'd put him through this past week. "I can overlook the bloody hour, but why the devil would you come all the way out here? And alone? 'Tis anything but safe."

"I brought two footmen and a driver. I always come out here whenever I need time to myself." She eyed him. "What about you? Why are you here? Dare I even ask?"

"*Me?*" He shrugged, caging his fury as best he could. "I needed quality air, is all. Can't trust anyone these days."

"You are being annoyingly cryptic." She

paused, then rose on the tips of her slippered toes and tried to glance around him and into the room. "Is someone here?"

He stepped aside and showed her the empty room, trying to keep his voice steady. "As you can see, no." He didn't even want to think about Charlotte right now. Or he'd completely lose the last of his patience and sanity.

Caroline dropped back onto her heels but didn't say anything.

He pinned her with a firm stare. "I know about Caldwell. He told me."

"*He told you?*" Caroline scrambled back into the darkened hallway and raised a gloved hand to her mouth.

"Yes. And he also told me that Mother and Lord Hughes were in on it."

"Actually," she said through her cupped hand, "Mother wasn't in on it."

Alexander leveled his gaze at her. "What do you mean?"

She lowered her hand back to her side and shook her head, sending sections of her long, loose curls bouncing about her face. "She knew that my going to a champagne party would upset you. But I went all the same. I . . . never mind why. When she saw me grouped with all the women, she quietly left. I didn't know until afterward that she had seen me." She sighed. "In the end, she wanted me to follow my heart. She wrote Lord Hughes a letter about it, seeing that he had invited me, and asked for further assistance. It only got more complicated from there."

"*Lord Hughes invited you?*" he choked out, stepping toward her.

Caroline held up both hands in an effort to calm him. "Alex, please. Don't blame him. He was only trying to help."

"*Help?* Oh, he *helped.* He *helped* debauch you. That no good son of a bitch! That fucking bastard! I'm going to kill him. I'll kill him!"

She rolled her eyes. "Alex, please. My bedding Caldwell was inevitable."

He choked. "Christ have mercy, do not say things like that so matter-of-factly." He violently raked both hands through his hair and huffed out a huge breath. This entire night was nothing short of a godforsaken nightmare! The only good thing to have come out of this was that his mother wasn't the hellfire he had thought her to be.

"Alex. Try to forgive me. I . . . I was caught up in a moment. I know that now. I thought . . ." She pinched her lips together and lowered her gaze down to her hands, which now played with the folds of her dark burgundy gown. "Never mind what I thought. 'Twas foolish."

At least she realized *that* much.

Alexander stepped closer to her and cupped her chin with his hand. He lifted it and forced her to look up at him. "Why? Why did you do it? Tell me."

Her green-blue eyes searched his face, and after a moment, she muttered, "Because I've loved him ever since I can remember."

She loved him? She loved Caldwell? Alexander slowly released her chin in disbelief, though, oddly, a huge part of him felt relieved. Relieved knowing that her marriage to Caldwell wasn't going to be a form of punishment. Because punishing her was the last thing she deserved or needed.

Caroline sighed miserably. "Not that it matters. He and I are completely ill-suited. What he wants out of a woman is not what I have to give. It's best I simply move on."

"Move on?" he demanded. "Wait, wait. What? Did something happen?"

"It's complicated."

"Yes, well, it's not complicated anymore."

Caroline blinked up at him. "What do you mean?"

"Caldwell has asked for your hand in marriage."

Caroline froze as if he had told her quite the opposite. A raging blush rose to her face. "Why would he do that?"

"Well . . ." This was certainly awkward. He didn't think he'd have to explain the obvious. "Because it's the right thing to do. The *only* thing to do."

Caroline stepped back and away from him. "So he doesn't *want* to marry me. He merely feels *obligated* to marry me. Is that what you are saying?"

She appeared to be spitting angry at him. As if he had created this mess. "Caroline, *I* should be the one to be upset here. You have no idea— *and I mean, no idea*—the lengths that Caldwell went through in order to tell me what happened. After everything I witnessed, I think he may very well be in love with you."

"*May?*" she yelled up at him, now clenching her fists at her sides as if refraining from pounding them against his chest. "No. Do forgive me, Brother dear, but *may* is not good enough. It *may* be good enough for you, it *may* be good enough for him, but it is *not* good enough for me." She paused and glared at him as if a hoard of daggers would not be enough for what she had in mind. "You threatened him into marrying me. Didn't you?"

Alexander let out an unbridled laugh, trying to release the pent-up emotions within him. "As angry as I was, I didn't need to threaten him into marrying you. Caldwell is his own man and, in the end, knows when to do the right thing. And marrying you is the right thing. Forget about your stupid need for romance, Caroline, and use your common sense. You'll grow to love each other. As all couples do."

She kept on shaking her head, as if that was the only thing she knew how to do. "No. I won't have him. Not like this."

This is exactly why he had enlisted Charlotte in the first place. Because women were ever-changing weather patterns he simply could not read despite all his years under the sun.

Alexander waved his hand at her in complete frustration, his patience gone. "Caroline, when Father passed, I was given full responsibility for not only your well-being but also your future. And your future will be Caldwell. I have already applied for a special license. You and he will be wed in five weeks' time. Or next week. The choice is yours."

"*Next week?*" she shouted up at him in clear disbelief, her eyes widening. "Oh, like *that* won't ruin me?"

"Then in five weeks' time. It really doesn't matter. You'll have him for the rest of your life, either way."

"But he doesn't even love me! You can't throw me into a loveless marriage. You simply can't!"

"*You* made the decision when you damn well flipped up your skirts!" he shouted back, venting every last bit of his fury. "Don't you understand what you've done, Caroline? You're ruined! Completely and utterly ruined! And unless you marry him, not only will *you* be at the mercy of the *ton*, but so will all of our sisters. Have you ever stopped to think about them during your self-indulgent lust parade? Even once? You'll render all of their opportunities useless! Useless!" There! He'd finally said every last thing he ever wanted to say to her.

"Damn you, Alex! Don't you think that I know that? Don't you think I . . ." Caroline whirled away from him and swung a gloved fist through the air. As if she were hitting someone who wasn't there.

She muttered something beneath her breath, shook her head, then lowered her hands slowly and primly back to her sides. After a few more moments of silence, she calmly turned back to him, bearing a mask of new, deceptive calm. "You're right. It's the right thing to do. For our family. For our sisters."

Thank God she understood that much. "Good. You're heading back to London with me. We're not staying here."

She crossed her arms over her chest. "I suppose you expect me to still love you after all this."

"Damn right I do. Just as I'm expected to love you. We are and always will be family. And as such, we have no choice but to remain steadfast." Or something like that.

Lesson Nineteen

*There are times you will be forced
to face your deepest fears. Do not
disappoint me and let it end in tears.*
— *The School of Gallantry*

*11 Berwick Street
Two weeks and two days later, early morning*

A knock on the door startled Charlotte straight
out of a deep slumber. She blinked and stared up
at the brocaded canopy of her bed. A familiar
ache rose within her chest. An ache that never
seemed to go away. She had been dreaming of
him again. Of his full smile. His green eyes. His
warmth. The cruel reality was that she would only
ever see him in her thoughts and in her dreams.

She blinked again and slowly turned her head
toward her closed bedchamber door.

There was another, more urgent knock. "My
Lady?" the chambermaid called out from the
other side.

"Is it already past one?" she called back.

Drat. Why did she still feel so horridly tired? She knew she shouldn't have stayed up past three, but once she had commenced organizing the pleasure room as per Madame de Maitenon's request, she had become blissfully occupied— not to mention slightly horrified—with a world other than Alexander.

A world of every imaginable contraption designated for the art of pleasure. Horse whips, shackles, chains, gloves, feathers, fur mitts, fur rugs, paddles, canes, candles, and . . . yes. Even leather dildos. Boxes and boxes of them.

Charlotte scrambled out of bed and slipped her feet into a waiting pair of silk slippers.

The chambermaid opened the door partway and peered in, a worried expression upon her young, round face. "It be early, My Lady, I know. 'Tis only eight, but Harold desperately needs you. Actually, we all need you."

"Why? What is it?" Charlotte grabbed her brocaded robe off the chair and pulled it about herself. She tied the sash around her waist and headed toward the dresser, where a basin of fresh water waited. "Allow me twenty minutes."

The chambermaid was quiet for a brief moment, then frantically burst out, "But it may already be too late!"

"Too late? What—"

"Madame is missing! All the men have been waiting in the classroom for over an hour, and both Mr. Hudson and Harold have already checked the correspondences four times. There is no word from her, My Lady. None at all."

A sense of dread pooled in Charlotte's stomach. Madame de Maitenon would never miss class. And she was always punctual. Always. At the very least, the woman would have sent word if she intended to be late. Why, just the other day Madame had been prattling on how only death alone would ever keep her from performing her duties at the school.

Charlotte paused as her breath hitched in her throat. Oh dear God. What if something horrible had happened? What if . . .

Charlotte spun back toward the chambermaid. "Have Harold come up to my room at once! You'll assist dressing me while I speak to him. In the meantime, tell Mr. Hudson to call for a hackney and have it ready within fifteen minutes."

The chambermaid blinked, as if unable to comprehend all the orders.

"At once!" Charlotte snapped.

The chambermaid disappeared, her running steps echoing down the length of the corridor.

Charlotte clasped her hands and lifted her eyes heavenward. "Mother," she whispered. "Father. Please keep her from harm."

She dropped her hands and willed herself to stay focused. Though she damn well wanted to, she couldn't run out into the streets in a mere robe. She'd cause a riot. And that would hardly help Madame right now.

Charlotte ran toward her dresser and flung the lacquered wood doors open. Her collection of bombazine gowns glowered at her, whispering that she could be wearing them for much, much longer.

"Cease worrying, Charlotte," she told herself as calmly as she could. "It will be fine. You will see." She had to keep assuring herself of that. Or she wouldn't survive. She yanked out a gown and hurried over to the bed, tossing it onto the crumpled linen.

Hurried steps echoed back down the corridor. Within moments, the door was thrown wide open.

She turned.

Harold towered in the doorway, his large brown eyes reflecting the concern and worry that gripped her own mind and heart.

The chambermaid hurried in and rushed toward the other dresser at the far end of the room, grabbing for everything Charlotte would need.

"What were her plans for yesterday?" Charlotte demanded of Harold. "Do you even know? Did she tell you?"

Harold shook his head, causing his mop of brown curls to shift against his large forehead. "I'm not supposed to be privy to anything outside of what goes on in the school. Madame says I'm too obsessed with her as it is and that knowing personal things about her life wouldn't be at all proper."

Lovely. Information that was anything but helpful. All she knew now was that poor Harold was madly in love with Madame. Just as she'd suspected.

The chambermaid scurried to Charlotte's side and started untying her sash and pulling her robe apart from her body.

Harold gasped, shielding his eyes.

"Oh, Harold, really." She frantically waved at him. "Turn around if it bothers you. There's no time for decency."

"Yes, My Lady." With his eyes still covered, he swung around, setting his massive back to her.

She scrambled out of her cotton nightgown and into her chemise. "Do you know anything about where she might be?"

He lowered his hands, shook his head again, and still kept his back to her. "No. Which is why I worry. What with all the threats we've had, I . . ."

Her stomach clenched. "*Threats?*" she demanded, stepping toward him. She was forcefully yanked back by the chambermaid, who was still attempting to properly dress her. "What threats? I was never informed of any threats."

Harold slapped both large hands onto his head, resting them there for a moment, before hissing out a sigh and dropping them back down. "Damn. I wasn't supposed to say that. Madame didn't want you to worry. It was only a few letters here and there from some religious lot. They threatened to set fire to the school. So that we may all properly burn in hell, where we belong."

"I assure you, it is *they* who shall burn if they so much as touch Madame. For heaven's sake, Harold, where else could she be? We must try to be rational and not jump to any conclusions." She paused for a moment. "Is there somewhere else she would need to be? Try to think."

"I . . . don't know. With her granddaughter?" Harold offered with obvious uncertainty.

The chambermaid fitted the corset around Charlotte and commenced lacing her into it, yanking at her torso. Charlotte turned and grabbed hold of the bedpost to steady herself as the maid continued yanking at the laces. "Yes. Good. You're right," she insisted from over her shoulder, back at him. "That forwarding address she gave me, you know the one where I always send all of her letters that I get for the school? Is that where Madame resides along with her granddaughter?"

"Yes," Harold said.

Well, at least he knew that much. "Good. I will go immediately. Someone has to know where she is. Her granddaughter, her servants. Someone. If she isn't at home and no one there knows a thing about her whereabouts, then I'm going straight to an investigator. In the meantime, Harold, I want you to send all the students home. Though whatever you do, don't alarm them. Madame would never forgive us. Inform them to await word as to whether class will resume on the morrow. In the meantime, wait for her in the classroom. She may eventually return."

After twisting the doorbell of Madame de Maitenon's residence twice and still receiving no answer, Charlotte used the knocker. Several times.

She leaned back and eyed the curtained windows above, trying to quell the growing hysteria within her.

To her surprise, the door before her slowly opened. A tall, balding man dressed in gray livery eyed her.

Charlotte stepped toward the butler, refraining

from grabbing the man's lapels and shaking him. "Is Madame de Maitenon at home? I am Lady Chartwell. The conductor of admissions for her school. Please. I must know of her whereabouts. She was not in class today and sent no word as to where she would be."

The butler leaned out the door, then offered in a hushed tone, "Madame is here. But she is not taking any visitors."

Relief soared through her, exhausting her into a sense of calmness. She glanced upward, toward the dull, gray sky that did not reflect the summer, and quietly thanked her mother. She was safe.

She sighed. "Forgive me, sir, I did not bring any of my cards." She didn't have any cards printed, as she never made outings, but that was beside the point. "Could you please be so kind as to announce to Madame that I am here? I'm certain she'll see me. We are friends."

The butler grimaced and glanced at the street, clearly aware that the longer she continued to stand on the doorstep, the ruder he appeared. He opened the door and ushered her quickly inside.

Closing the door after her, he scooted her into the corner beside the door, in the direction of the hat rack.

"What in—"

"*Shhh.*" He glanced toward the stairwell behind him, then whispered down at her, "I apologize, but I am disobeying strict orders by even speaking to you. Madame's granddaughter is not allowing anyone to call on her. Especially those from the school."

Her granddaughter? Maybelle? What? Was she holding her grandmother against her will? None of this made any sense.

"I don't care what her granddaughter says," Charlotte snapped, trying her best to confine her growing agitation. "All of her students were left waiting for over an hour, and none of us received any word as to why. I am rightfully concerned and demand to see Madame. *Now.*"

The butler impatiently tapped a gloved finger to his lips in a desperate effort to quiet her. "Madame collapsed at a soirée last night. The doctors believe she suffered from apoplexy, but that is all I am allowed to say. I'll inform Madame of your visit when she is well enough, but right now, she needs her rest."

He quickly strode toward the door, then yanked it open and waited with his hand outstretched pointing to the street outside.

Charlotte swallowed, unable to comprehend the horrible words he had just spoken. After all, her own mother had died from the very same thing. When Charlotte had been able to finally rush to her side, her mother could not even hold her hand, let alone speak. She had become naught but a shell of the woman she once knew and loved. For the apoplexy had ravaged her. Completely.

Charlotte fisted her hands until they throbbed with the same thundering pulse that matched her heart. Madame de Maitenon was going to leave her, after all. How eerily fitting that it would end this way.

"I . . . *please,*" she urgently whispered, trying to

keep her voice steady. "I need to see her. If even for a moment. It would mean so much to me. I'd never be able to forgive myself if something were to happen to her."

The butler hurried over to her, grabbed her gloved hand, and patted it affectionately as he forcefully led her out through the front door. "Madame is much stronger than that, My Lady. All she truly needs is rest. She will send word when she is ready to see you."

He feebly smiled, then retreated and gently shut the door, leaving her alone on the doorstep.

Charlotte turned and watched as people and carriages bustled by before her. Everything blurred as tears flooded her eyes. Yes. Her mother had been strong, too. And yet, she had died.

Feeling as though the world were visually slowing, Charlotte grasped the iron railing. One heavy step at a time, she made her way down the set of stairs and onto the pavement. Ignoring the hackney awaiting her, she turned in the opposite direction and walked. She needed time to mourn for Madame in her own way. The only way she knew how. By breaking every single conventional rule.

Lesson Twenty

One cannot fight what is meant to be.
It would be like forcing the English to
survive without their sugar and their tea.
—*The School of Gallantry*

Hyde Park, Rotten Row
hours later

Alexander tightened his gloved hold on the leather reins of his horse and veered closer toward Caroline, who quietly rode on her own horse beside him. Like him, she hadn't breathed a single word since they had left the townhouse for their morning ride. Truth be told, he didn't know who was more miserable. Caroline or him.

"Good morning, Lord Hawksford! So lovely to see you out and about." An older lady, whose name he knew but which eluded him at the moment, waved her lilac silk handkerchief in his direction from her polished barouche as they caught up to his moving horse. A young girl stiffly sat beside the woman, adorned in a bright pink embroidered muslin morning gown with full upper sleeves and ruffles. The girl's oversized matching pleated bonnet framed a long and miserable plain face and blond curls.

"This is my beautiful and only daughter, Lady Cornelia." The older lady gestured with the handkerchief toward the young girl. "'Tis her first Season. And it has been a good one, at that. So many offers."

How he bloody wished the *ton* would simply all hang themselves. By their pennants, as Caroline had once so brilliantly stated. It was due to these sorts that he was mindlessly miserable and would continue to be miserable for at least another eight years. Until all his sisters had been married off.

Alexander gave a curt nod in the direction of the young Lady Cornelia, whose cheeks were now almost the exact color of her gown. And though the girl desperately tried to smile up at him from beneath the shade of her bonnet, it appeared as if she were painfully straining into a chamber pot.

Yes, well, and on that note . . .

"It was a pleasure. Good day to you both." He then nudged his heels into the sides of his horse, to quicken the horse's stride, and moved on. As far away from their barouche as possible and into the crowd of other moving horses and carriages.

Caroline urged her horse forward to keep up with him, the long white silk veil that was attached to her black top hat flapping out behind her. She glanced over at him. "Why, Brother dearest," she teased, lowering her voice, "I do believe you just let your future wife ride away. Society certainly doesn't get any more nice and respectable than that."

He grunted. "I'm not in the mood to entertain marriage-minded petticoats."

She sighed. "You've been in a foul mood ever since that night in the cottage. And what is worse, you barely say anything anymore. You're not still angry with me, are you?"

"No. Of course not." He simply didn't feel like talking. For he feared he'd eventually end up on the subject of the one person he didn't want to think about: Charlotte.

His sister was quiet for a long moment, the thudding hooves of both their horses and all the others filling the air around them. She sighed. "Mary hates all the new gowns you're forcing her to wear. Last week, she officially stopped eating to prove that point and intends to start planning her own funeral."

Leave it to Mary to resort to morbid tantrums. "I doubt she'll resort to starvation. She hasn't missed a meal, or a second helping, since she was six."

Caroline muttered something then finally veered her horse dangerously close to his. She leaned toward him from her sidesaddle position and quietly hissed out, "Alex, how can you force Mary to be something ashe isn't? Or turn me into something I am not? I understand the need for appearances and respect them, believe me I do, but our home is the one place where we can be ourselves. The only place."

He stared straight ahead of them, glancing at the scattering of trees lining the road where various people stood off to the side watching them pass. "I thought the purpose of this ride was to take in air. Not words."

Although he tried to remain indifferent to Caroline's statement, helplessness choked him. It was the very same helplessness he felt every time he thought about Charlotte.

"I don't like the person you've become," Caroline went on, lowering her voice just enough to appease him. "None of us do. And I know for a fact that Father would have never approved. It appears you are one of them now. Censoring everything and everyone around you for your own purposes." Caroline veered her horse back to its respectable distance and said nothing more.

Alexander shifted his jaw. For the truth was, they were born unto the ultimate privilege with the ultimate form of responsibility. There were consequences for not following the rules. As Caroline was seeing firsthand. And by not establishing some of those rules inside the house, one could not readily establish the discipline needed to survive outside of the house.

They quietly continued on the designated dirt path, the clattering of hooves, the endless din of male and female voices, and the chirping of birds whirling all around them. All of it meaningless.

"What on earth is that woman doing?" Caroline shifted on her horse, staring out somewhere down the road. "Fresh from the country, you suppose? Or is she riding on an invisible horse?"

"An invisible . . . what?"

A shout and the whinny of several horses on the riding path before them summoned his focus. Up ahead, through the throng of endless carriages and people on their horses, he glimpsed a woman marching along the edge of the carriage path, ignoring the shouts flung at her and the passing horses and barouches that veered to get around her.

Although the woman's back faced him and she wore a bonnet that covered her hair, her fitted bombazine gown, her slender physique, and petite height told him without question who it was.

Charlotte.

Alexander yanked his horse to a complete halt in utter disbelief. His stomach flipped. By God. What the devil was she doing? Aside from causing an uproar for walking on the path the *ton* very much preferred to designate for themselves, she was likely to get herself trampled.

And though his pride urged him to simply let her march straight into the Thames for all he cared, a much larger part of him roared at him to do something. Immediately.

"Follow me," Alexander snapped at Caroline, affixing his top hat more firmly onto his head. "And be sure to keep up."

Caroline squinted at him. "Keep up? What—"

Without further explanation, he nudged his heels into his horse and steered himself straight between two carriages. He galloped forward, moving swiftly left and right between tight spaces. All the while, his eyes were trained on Charlotte as she continued to march down the side of Rotten Row.

Why was it that no matter how bloody hard he

tried to remove her from his thoughts and from his life, she always managed to reappear?

Glancing over his shoulder, he rushed his horse into a small space alongside the road before another set of carriages and horses came upon him. He gritted his teeth and urged his horse in Charlotte's direction. Her slender back was still to him, her skirts dragging behind her on the path.

Alexander looked behind him again to ensure there were no oncoming carriages. He galloped forward. When she was a mere few feet away, he slowed his horse down to a walk. Then pulled up right alongside her.

Charlotte marched steadily on as if he and his horse weren't even there. And oddly enough, she was muttering something to herself.

He leaned down toward her and brought his horse to a complete stop. "Charlotte. What are you doing?"

She jerked to a halt, snapping her head up at him. Her dark eyes, which were shaded by the wide brim of her bonnet, snapped up to his face. She stared up at him, clearly stunned. Her pale face now flooded with a burst of color.

Her full lips parted into a hesitant smile. "Alexander," she whispered up at him in disbelief. "How . . . what are you . . ."

Seeing her beautiful face again not only made him realize how much he had truly missed her, but also how much he had suffered since he had last seen her. And he couldn't help but wonder: Had she even thought about him? At all? Had she missed him? At all?

She set her chin. "I apologize, Lord Hawksford,"

she firmly announced, "but fury compels me on. I bid you a good-day."

She turned away, gathered up her skirts from around her feet, and started marching down Rotten Row again. But at a much more pronounced pace.

What the devil was she even talking about? *He* was the one who had the right to be compelled by fury. Not her!

"Charlotte!" He moved his horse after her, bringing himself alongside her once again. "You aren't supposed to be on this path. You do know that, don't you?"

She marched on, steadily staring straight ahead. "I know full well that I am not supposed to be on it. Which is exactly *why* I am on it. What I have come to understand in these past few hours is that there is absolutely no point in following the rules anymore. We all die in the end anyway."

And he thought *he'd* been a loose fish since they'd gone their separate ways. Alexander straightened in his saddle and scanned their surroundings both in front of them and in back of them.

Men and women were craning their necks to look at him and Charlotte as they all clattered by. Some slowed their carriages or their horses so as to get a better view, raising eyebrows and lowering chins.

He might as well wave, for he was officially embroiled in a full-fledged scandal. Which meant, hell, he might as well finish it off with complete panache and put himself out of his own misery.

Alexander tightened his reins and galloped

forward, then settled his horse at a slow trot beside her. He leaned down toward her again. "Charlotte. I'm going to dismount. The moment I do, I want you to take my horse and ride it back to wherever you are going. Do you understand?"

"Please stop talking to me. You're making a scene."

"*I'm* making a scene?" he growled out. "I'm not the one pretending to be a horse."

Caroline drew her steed alongside him, slowing her pace, and eyed him. "Alex?" She glanced at all the passing spectators who were gawking, then mockingly raised both brows and lowered her chin in his direction. "You do realize that engaging an unchaperoned lady in public, and on the Row, of all things, is not something respectable men do, yes?"

If helping a woman and keeping her from harm was not respectable, then damn them all, he supposed he was going to burn in hell for it and have to let his sisters rely on their substantial fortunes rather than a pristine reputation. For he'd had enough!

If Charlotte wasn't going to cooperate on her own volition, he was going to damn well *make* her.

After jerking his horse to a complete halt, he threw his leg over the other side and hopped down, landing firmly on the ground with a thud. Striding toward Charlotte, he reached out, grabbed her from behind by her corseted waist, and scooped her up into his arms. Charlotte let out a shocked yelp as he hooked her knees around one of his arms, careful not to expose her legs for everyone to see, and forced the rest of her body against his chest.

Alexander turned and marched them back to his horse, ignoring the fact that people around them were gasping and murmuring at their expense.

Charlotte frantically looked around them, her bonnet bumping his chin repeatedly. "Alexander!" She grabbed hold of his jacket and waistcoat and yanked on it. Repeatedly. "What are you . . . Are you crazed?"

"Yes. And I have you to thank for it. Though take heart, as it appears we are equally matched."

He stopped right beside his horse, plopping her back down onto her feet, and glared down at her. The building frustration he felt within him constricted his chest.

"We'll discuss this later," he gritted out, grabbing hold of her waist in order to hoist her up onto the horse.

She shoved his hands away and quickly maneuvered around him. "Oh, no. I am not joining *this* parade."

"My apologies, but you've already joined it." He grabbed her waist again, yanked her back toward himself, and popped her up into the air and into the saddle, settling her sideways. He arranged her skirts around her legs, then rounded the horse and pointed at Caroline. "Take her straight to the house. Serve her tea and let her rest until I return. Above all, do not let her out of your sight, and do not let her leave the house until then."

Caroline turned her horse closer to him. "What about you?"

He put up a gloved hand. "I'll walk. It will draw less attention."

"Less? Is there such a thing?" Caroline grinned. "I can hardly wait to read all the details in the rags. Do you suppose they'll sketch a picture of me upon my horse?"

"I hope not." He waved them off. "Go. Take her."

Charlotte glanced down at him, then tightened her hold on the reins and moved the horse onward.

Alexander stepped off the road, watching as his sister and Charlotte journeyed through the crowds. He blew out an exhausted breath, then turned and marched across the grass.

A group of young men beneath one of the trees hooted and clapped in his direction.

"I say, that'd be the way to do it!" one yelled.

"Can I have a horse the next time you're out?" another shouted out, laughing.

Alexander shifted his jaw and headed through the grass of Hyde Park toward a path that he knew would eventually lead him home. It was obvious that there was only one respectable thing left for him to do: marry Charlotte. And the sooner, the better.

Lesson Twenty-One

Do not accept anything less for yourself,
other than everything for yourself.
                    —*The School of Gallantry*

Charlotte leaned toward the small table before her, which was laden with fruit and pastries, and grasped the yellow and blue porcelain teacup. She willed herself to keep the delicate cup steady, despite the trembling in her hand, and brought its steaming warmth to her lips. She swallowed it, savoring its soothing flavor. It gurgled loudly in her empty stomach.

She lowered the cup to her lap and nervously glanced up at the five young females who all quietly sat in a row on the long sofa across from her. Grinning. As if she were the Queen of England making a personal visit.

Though they all sat at different heights, and wore varying brightly colored morning gowns, some having large, silk bows in their golden hair, they all had the same mischievous blue-green eyes, small, sharp noses, ivory freckled faces, and heart-shaped lips. The elegant lady, whom she now knew to be Caroline, sat on the far end of the sofa, still dressed in her riding habit, black hat, and veil. Her grin had to be the widest. No doubt about it.

Fortunately for her, Alexander's mother was out on a call, or this would have turned into quite the experience.

"So who died?" the youngest of the girls finally blurted out from where she sat tucked between all of them.

"*Mary!*" her sisters exclaimed, some reaching out to smack her white-frocked knees, their grins all replaced by looks of horror.

"Don't you dare scare her off," the one who introduced herself as Anne hissed, leaning forward. "Need I remind you, little Miss Morbid, that she is the first female Alex has ever formally allowed into the house since Father's passing? This may very well be *it.*"

Charlotte let out a nervous laugh, tightening her hold on her teacup. *It.* Yes. Right.

She met Mary's thoughtful gaze from where she sat and eventually offered, "'Twas my mother who passed. Although it is long after my time for mourning, she was very special to me. So I honor her as best I know how. By continuing to wear bombazine."

Mary rubbed her small hands against her ivory cotton morning gown and nodded. "My father was very special to me, too. Of course, no one here really understands that. They all like to call me little Miss Morbid."

Charlotte bit back a smile. "I'm certain they understand more than they let on. We all simply grieve differently. I know when my mother finished formally mourning for my father, she continued to grieve for him by wearing lavender gowns. Because he had always loved the color on her."

Mary was quiet for a moment. "Father didn't have a favorite color. I don't think."

The room fell silent.

Once again, the girls returned their attention to Charlotte. And smiled. Though with a tinge of melancholy and longing.

Sadly, Charlotte knew that particular look all too well. She lifted the teacup back to her lips and gulped the already cool tea, praying that Alexander would return. She didn't know how much longer she could sit here feeling like a window display.

Anne sighed, plucked up a pastry from off the serving tray before her, and bit into it. "So," she said in between several thoughtful chews. "Do you and Alex already have plans to marry? Or is this just the beginning of your courtship?"

Mary paused, then furrowed her thin brows at Anne. She leaned far forward upon the sofa and looked down the row of girls on both sides of her. "Now how is that any more appropriate than *my* last question?"

Charlotte let out a laugh, trying not to spill her tea, and set her cup onto the matching porcelain plate before her. If there was any doubt that these girls were related to Alexander, it had long fled.

"Your brother and I are friends," Charlotte finally offered, not really able to think of anything else to say. "That is all. Good friends."

Mary pinned her with a more than dubious stare. "Good friends? Yes, and *I* am a Catholic virgin."

"*Mary!*" everyone exclaimed all at once again.

Caroline removed her riding hat after a few violent tugs and tossed it toward her sister. "Why must you always repeat everything you hear? Really, now!"

A bubble of laughter erupted from Charlotte's lips at the absurdity of the entire situation. She then burst into uncontrollable laughter. And laughed and laughed, despite the fact that her corset was beginning to make it difficult for her to breathe. She simply couldn't help it. What was more, it was an unexpected, glorious moment of release.

The girls on the sofa across from her started laughing, too. Clearly entertained by the fact that she was.

Hearing all of their jovial giggles mixed together with her own was utterly intoxicating. It reminded her of the days when she and her mother would laugh until they'd be begging the lady's maid to unlace their corsets.

"*Have you all gone mad?*" a male voice boomed from the doorway.

Charlotte choked back her laughter, bringing it to a gasping halt at the sudden realization that Alexander was back. Obviously, her visit was officially over. She snapped her gaze toward the doorway of the parlor, silence now painfully humming against her ears.

Alexander towered in the doorway, still fully dressed in his well-fitted riding clothes, looking about as furious as he'd been when he rode up to her in Hyde Park. His sharp features and shaven jaw were rigidly set. His green eyes narrowed as he scanned everyone in the room, his impatience practically pulsing out toward them.

He eventually stripped his top hat from his head, scattering his bronzed hair across his forehead, and pointed with it at his sisters. "Upstairs, if you please."

One by one, the young girls each popped up, curtsied at Charlotte with a quick spread of their colorful skirts, then scattered out of the room.

Caroline snatched up her riding hat from the sofa and rose in an elegant, trained manner. She smiled, her left cheek dimpling. "I'm certain we'll be seeing more of you, Lady Chartwell." She winked. "Much, much more."

With that, she gathered up the train from her riding gown and breezed out of the room with the grace of a queen.

Heaven forbid all of his sisters thought she was going to be a permanent fixture in the household. She was about as permanent in Alexander's life as a petal was on a wilting flower.

The silence within the room returned. Alexander continued to stand in the doorway, glowering at her.

Charlotte bit her lip and slowly rose, sensing that it was best she leave.

"Stay seated." Though it wasn't entirely a command, it wasn't in the least bit friendly, either.

Charlotte sat back down, trying not to panic at the stark realization that he was not only angry at her for what had happened, but probably also angry that she was in his house. In his parlor. Chatting and laughing with his sisters. When all he had ever meant to do with her was keep her tucked away in the back pocket of his life. For no one else to see or know about.

Alexander set his mouth into a tight, firm line and flung his top hat at the curtained windows. Charlotte winced as it tumbled then rolled back and forth toward one of the corners.

She eyed him, waiting for whatever it was he wanted to say. Or do. He deserved to be angry. She should have listened to him when he asked her to leave the road. But sheer determination to march away her woes and in turn prove to him that she didn't need him or anyone else, had gotten the best of her.

He purposefully strode into the room, his eyes never once leaving her, and headed straight for her. "Do you have a pact with the devil to destroy the last of my sanity?" he shouted, waving his gloved hand about in the air. "Is that it? Bloody hell, Charlotte, everyone in London knows that particular road through Hyde Park isn't meant for pedestrians! And it *especially* isn't meant for unescorted women. Widowed or not!"

Charlotte flinched at every shout that lashed at her ears as equally as it lashed at her heart. In some way, she deserved it. But regardless, she refused to be treated this way. Especially by him.

She scrambled up to her feet, fisting both hands at her sides. "Why are you yelling at me? You were the one that made a scene of it! I was walking, mind you. *Walking*. And last I knew, walking was anything but illegal. Even for a woman! I ask you, why couldn't you ride by? Why?"

Alexander halted before her, his height and his muscled, domineering presence forcing her to look up into his eyes.

His nostrils flared as he continued to glare down at her. His wide chest rose and fell with each breath he heavily took through his nose, the brass buttons on his waistcoat shifting in response. "Because you were in clear distress, and the very sight of you on that road displeased me. Now. On my way back, I thought about this entire situation, and based upon the gravity of what this may do to not only you but my entire family, we will marry. The sooner, the better."

Her eyes widened, and her stomach fluttered at the unexpected words. They truly should have been the most joyous, most beautiful words to have ever fallen upon her ears. And yet his tone, his stance, and the wild blaze in his eyes withered them to absolute nothingness.

She shook her head, somewhat in disbelief that she was about to refuse him. Refuse an opportunity that she would have earlier seized not only with both hands, but also with both feet. "No. I'll not marry you."

He blinked, the anger in his taut face slightly dissipating. "I don't think you have much of a choice."

She glared at him and fought from flaring her own nostrils. "My reputation isn't for you to save, Alexander. Not that it *can* be saved. It was ruined well enough long before you ever came into my life."

His anger returned. "You *will* marry me."

She mocked a laugh. "I am not some servant you can order about. No means no."

His eyes narrowed. "I see. I was good enough for a frig, but not good enough for marriage. I suppose I should have known you had only one true calling."

Her eyes widened as she stepped back. By God. He hated her. He truly hated her after what she had said and done that night. It reeked and dripped into every single one of his words. And knowing that convinced her all the more of her decision. No matter how much her heart wanted him, she simply would not have him. Not like this. She had already once married thinking she could change a man. She was not about to make that same mistake twice.

She swallowed, willing herself to look at him. "Forgive me for what I made you feel that night. I was selfishly focused upon my own pleasure, knowing that I would never see you again. 'Twas never my intention to hurt you, Alexander, and I hope that one day you will forgive me for it. Madame shared with me the sort of hurt you'd been through. But I will not let you continue down this path of righteousness and in turn abuse me. Do you honestly think that our marriage will erase what happened today? Do you?"

She waved a hand toward their surroundings. "Nothing will ever erase the way these people feel or think about respectability, Alexander. It is ingrained in them like the root of a tree, and no matter how hard you try to meet their favor by watering their roots, the only thing you'll ever unearth is misery. For that is what the *ton* ultimately feeds off. The misery of those who happen to stumble. The only reason you are even asking me to marry you is because you're still seeking the *ton*'s approval for the sake of your sisters. And though I fully understand your concern for them, I'll not marry into that. I simply will not."

He sucked in a harsh breath and let it out, the warm husky scent of his breath grazing her forehead. "So what will you marry into? Tell me."

She snapped her gaze back to meet his heated, intense eyes. "If I have to tell you that," she coolly replied, "then we need not speak of this again."

With that, she walked around him and headed straight toward the doorway, focusing on every step. She paused, realizing she hadn't told him about Madame de Maitenon. He would find out, yes, but she wanted him to hear it from her. So that he knew exactly what she'd been through today.

She turned.

He hadn't even moved. Hadn't even put any effort into turning around to look at her.

Which she was glad for. For it would make it easier for her to share what had happened. "Do you wish to know why I was on that road today?" she asked in a low, steady voice. "Because I was mourning the loss of Madame de Maitenon in the only manner I knew how. By breaking respectable rules."

Alexander slowly turned toward her, his brows drawn together. "She passed?" he demanded in disbelief.

"No." She tried to keep her voice from quivering, but it was no use. "Not yet. But she may. She didn't come to class today, Alexander. So I went to her home, frantic, only to discover that she'd suffered a form of apoplexy last night. And what is worse, her granddaughter won't allow anyone to see her. Although I know Madame needs her rest, I cannot ease my mind or heart until I know that she will be well. In some way, I cannot help but feel betrayed by a woman I haven't even met."

"Oh God. Charlotte." He stepped toward her, his voice drenched in sympathy. "Why didn't you tell me?"

She held up a shaky hand, refusing to accept any of it. She didn't want sympathy from him. "I just did." She set her chin, vowing to remain strong, at least until she returned to the school. "I've been away for far too long and don't intend to disappoint Madame. At least not in the manner I have disappointed you. I've had nothing but the utmost respect for you until you proposed to me today. For even after Chartwell, I firmly believe marriage is worth far more than what you make it to be."

She then walked out, ready to start anew. Without him. For she refused to accept anything less than what she deserved from this day forth. She would not live in some dark corner of his life, tucked away from his heart or his world. She wanted all of Alexander's heart. Not a mere, useless sliver of it. She had settled once and she was not settling ever again.

Lesson Twenty-Two

Men seem to think that flowers are enough to
express the way they feel and the way they think.
But if that much were true, a woman would
have absolutely no need for a man at all. She
would marry her garden, make love to the
longest, thickest stem she could possibly find,
and plant an array of new flowers whenever
they wilted or died. Which is why you must take
this advice, gentlemen. Instead of giving her
more flowers, simply look to give more of yourself.
—The School of Gallantry

11 Berwick Street
Two days later, evening

After letters that yielded no response, Alexander knew that either his words weren't enough or
he wasn't enough. Which was why he was here. To
find out which of the two it really was before he
lost the last of his rational mind. He only prayed it
wasn't the latter. For the reality was, scandal or not,

he wanted her. Wanted her more than anything he'd ever wanted in his life. And it took seeing her on the side of that road, at the mercy of everyone around them, for him to fully realize it.

And when she had confessed how sorry she was about that night, his stomach had nearly dropped to the floor. For in the end, she understood how she had made him feel and had not only acknowledged it, but apologized for it.

With a dozen red roses in hand, Alexander climbed up the night-cloaked stairs leading to Charlotte's house and twisted the bell beside the door. He dug out a five-pound note and nervously cleared his throat.

The door eventually opened, and warm golden candlelight filtered out toward him.

Mr. Hudson stoically stepped out.

Alexander grinned down at the man, then tucked the money he held into the pocket of the man's livery. "For your grandchildren." Alexander then raised the flowers he held. "And these here are not for you, but rather for the beautiful Lady Chartwell."

Mr. Hudson sniffed, clearly not amused, then stiffly dug out the five-pound note with the tips of his gloved fingers. He held it back out for him as if it were a bit of gravy-soaked bread pulled from the depths of a heap of rubbish. "Forgive me, Lord Hawksford, but I am merely ensuring her safety by not admitting you. Especially after calling hours."

Alexander lowered the roses and tried to hide his disappointment. "She won't see me? At all?"

Mr. Hudson set his chin down onto his high

collar and pinned Alexander with as deadly a stare as the old man knew how. "No. But even if she wanted to, I most certainly would never allow it."

The butler stepped toward him and tucked the five-pound note into the top of Alexander's waistcoat. He tsked and stepped back, shaking his gray head. "'Tis the worst sin in the world to make a woman cry, My Lord. The very worst."

Alexander felt his stomach, his heart, and his soul crush together in a single drop down to his very feet. He had made Charlotte cry?

"All of her servants, myself included, have had quite enough of you." Mr. Hudson turned, rudely giving him his back, and stepped into the house, fanning the door toward him.

No! Alexander shoved his shoulder and body into the remaining open space of the door and pushed at it, crushing his roses against his arm and chest in the effort. The door bumped his top hat from his head and sent it rolling down the front stairs.

"I must see her," he growled out, forcing the door farther open with his weight. He'd been needlessly rude, and his proposal had been outright cold and damn blunt. So unworthy of what she deserved. "Allow me to apologize to her! She deserves an apology!"

Mr. Hudson grunted as he desperately tried to force the door back against him. "*Kindly . . . move . . . away . . . from . . . the door!*"

"*No! Now . . . kindly . . . let . . . me . . . in!*" he yelled, adjusting his grip on the edge of the door and pushing it more forcefully. The muscles in his arms and legs quaked as they continued to meet great resistance. Shit! For an old man, Hudson had the hold of an elephant! He gritted his teeth. Why the blazes couldn't he—

The door suddenly fell wide open and Alexander stumbled inside, sending him and his flowers down onto the floor in a flurry of rose petals. Alexander scrambled up to his feet and swiped his shambled roses back up.

At last! What was Charlotte feeding the old man anyway? He straightened, then froze as Harold stepped toward him, his massive frame blocking his view of the candlelit hall.

Hell, *now* he knew why he couldn't get the door open.

Alexander blew out a breath and stepped closer to Harold, knowing that he might very well be taking his life into his hands. Despite his own noteworthy build, he had no doubt Harold could pop him in two and ferret him away to a nice little resting place in the tunnel. "Harold, you seem like the reasonable sort. Let me talk to her."

Harold crossed his mutton arms, bumping Alexander's chest purposefully in the process. "Before Madame's apoplexy, she informed me that you were no longer a student and therefore no longer welcome. And that was *before* you did what you did to Lady Chartwell. I suggest you leave. Before I hammer your head into the floor like a nail."

What the devil had Charlotte been telling her servants anyway? There appeared to be only one way to go about this.

"Obviously, I am not welcome here. Good night." Alexander spaced his words evenly in an effort to remain calm, his hold tightening on the stems of the roses. The thorns bit through the leather of his glove. He turned, pretending to head toward the door that Mr. Hudson had promptly reopened. After taking several more firm steps, he quickly swung around and bolted around Harold and straight for the stairs.

"You son of a bitch!" Harold's large hand grabbed him by the back of his jacket and yanked him violently back.

"Release him, Harold." Charlotte's exhausted voice echoed from somewhere up above. "Whatever are you doing, Alexander?"

Harold grudgingly released his coat, but not before giving him a good, solid push.

Alexander glared back at the ox, then tugged down his waistcoat and jacket in a dignified manner with the one hand that wasn't holding the roses and looked up toward Charlotte, who stood at the top of the stairs.

His breath quickened as his eyes met hers.

She was dressed in a simple brocaded, green robe and matching slippers. The white cotton of her nightgown peered out at the bottom edges of her robe, and her dark hair was bundled up into a silk white cap, as if she was preparing for bed.

He held up the roses in his hand. "I brought these for you."

"Oh?" She tartly observed him. "They look mangled."

He paused and surveyed the flowers in his hand. The red petals on several of the roses were missing, and those that did have petals were drooping miserably, and those that weren't drooping had broken stems that were causing them to fall off to the side.

They were downright pathetic. And looked exactly how he felt at that moment. "Forgive them," he murmured, not knowing what else to say. "I assure you, they were not like this when I first came to the door. I simply came to apologize."

He glanced up at her from the distance she continued to keep between them. "Charlotte. Since my father's death, I felt inclined to take on a certain role for my family, only to find myself struggling between who I am and who society expects me to be. It's no excuse, I know, but my overall behavior toward you, toward everyone this past year, has been a result of my frustrations in trying to define the role I must play."

He quickly got down onto his right knee and held out the flowers as best he could. "Charlotte. I am asking you to be my wife. Not because of what happened that day, or because I am trying to uphold a reputation, but because you want to be my wife. And because I want you to be my wife, too." He paused and waited for her response.

Charlotte sighed dramatically, came down the length of the stairs, stepped toward him, and snatched the flowers out of his hand, causing petals to fly everywhere. She then marched back up the stairs. "It will take more than flowers to convince me that you are sincere," she called out from over her shoulder. "Now, whatever you do, don't call on me or write any more of those pathetic letters describing my fair beauty. Any man can do as much." She then disappeared into the darkness of the hallway somewhere upstairs.

Alexander jumped to his feet. "But if you won't see me or read any of my letters," he yelled up impatiently after her, "how else am I to bloody prove myself?"

After a few moments of silence, Charlotte reappeared with his mangled flowers still in hand. She met his gaze and then said to him in a low, mysterious tone, "I am certain that the man I fell in love with will find a way. Good night, Alexander. And thank you for the beautiful flowers." With that, she disappeared again into the darkness of the hallway.

Alexander stood there for a stunned moment, suddenly feeling unusually light-headed and, simply put . . . not like a man should. Because he suddenly wanted to skip. Like a little girl.

By God. How could he not have seen it? How could he not have known? The utter fool that he was, he'd actually been blind, thinking *he* was the only one harboring all of these feelings. He'd wallowed in so much self-pity, he'd fooled himself into believing that no one, especially her, could ever love him for more than the pleasures he had to give. Amazing.

Alexander grinned, feeling as though he could strap the world onto his back, and spun toward Harold and Mr. Hudson, who were both staring at him.

Alexander hit his chest soundly. "You heard her. She loves me."

"Yes, women sometimes say those types of things to those they feel sorriest for," Hudson supplied. "Now out with you." He jabbed his thumb toward the door.

Alexander laughed, held up a finger, and

wagged it at them as he strode past. "No, no. She loves me. And as such, you both better damn well believe you haven't seen the last of Lord Hawksford."

"Harold will be ardently awaiting your return," Mr. Hudson said satirically.

Full of renewed hope and energy, Alexander hopped down onto the doorstep outside and into the darkness of the night, still grinning like an idiot. Even as the door slammed shut behind him.

So. She didn't want flowers. Jewels were definitely too superficial. Sex was obviously out of the question, and he'd already taken care of the Court of Chancery for her. What more was a man to do?

This was indeed a dilemma. But one he intended to overcome. He quickly made his way down the steps, then looked up toward the top windows of the house. Toward whichever window was hers. Though they were all closed and there was not a single light to be seen in their glass, he could sense she was watching him.

He grinned and turned, about to head back to his waiting carriage, when he noticed his top hat lying sideways on the pavement before him. He snatched it up and dusted it off. Tapping it onto his head, he finally allowed reality to seep in. Exactly how did a man prove his worth to a woman who wouldn't see him or accept gifts?

Damn, but he was going to need a miracle. Although one had clearly already happened. Charlotte loved him. She actually loved him.

Lesson Twenty-Three

*If you try to lead your life according
to your heart, I promise it will give you
strength to attain a new start.*
— *The School of Gallantry*

If there was one thing Alexander knew, it was
this: it was going to take a bloody miracle to get
Charlotte back. After all, what more did he have
to do to prove his love?

He'd already composed three sonnets and sent
them over along with a year's supply of chocolate
rolls and champagne. Hell, he'd even arranged
for the King's own choir to sing outside her door.
And yet, she continued to refuse him. Continued
to deny him permission even to call on her.

Though he had never been one to believe that a
man had the innate ability to create a miracle, he
had no choice *but* to believe. What else was there
left to do?

Now, as with all great miracles, one had to relentlessly work toward it. One devoted prayer at

a time. Or as in his case . . . one devoted bribe
at a time.

So first, and immediately, he wrote identical
letters to all the students of the school. Banfield,
Brayton, and yes, even Caldwell.

He explained to them not only the tragedy
that had befallen Madame de Maitenon, but that
as her students they all had a duty to send an obscene amount of flowers and an obscene amount
of letters to the address he was enclosing. An address he had received from his own mother, who
from past dalliances with Madame de Maitenon
knew exactly where she lived. Whoever knew his
mother's own indiscretions would prove to be
helpful in his time of need.

Sending a ridiculous amount of flowers and
letters to her door was not only the right thing to
do, but the only thing to do. For it would show
Madame de Maitenon that she did in fact matter
to her students. It would also prove to her damn
snot of a granddaughter that Madame de Maitenon mattered more to them than she would
ever know. And that none of them were about to
relinquish their grasp on the naughty woman.

In return for following his requests, Alexander
promised each and every one of them any favor in
return. Well . . . except for Caldwell. Caldwell
damn well owed him whatever he asked for, considering he'd spared both his life and his bollocks.
And he intended to collect on it every step of the
way.

Once his letters had all been hand delivered by
his own servants, Alexander sent an additional
twenty pounds' worth of orchids and roses to the

woman's door. For good measure. He hoped the entire household grew deliriously giddy from the perfume he was going to create.

And that was but the beginning. Caldwell and Lord Hughes, who were both in deep debt to him because of Caroline, marked another part of his plan by securing and arranging certain invitations.

He had even arranged for a midnight visit with Madame de Maitenon to see to yet another part of his plan, courtesy of the same balding butler, Mr. Clive Adams, who had earlier denied Charlotte entrance. For he and Mr. Adams shared a little secret.

Once upon a time, Mr. Clive Adams liked to dress in female clothing. Actually, the man *still* liked to dress in female clothing. And not just any female clothing. Madame de Maitenon's clothing, to be exact.

Of course, it took a little over twenty pounds in investigative fees and three people to watch both the front and back door of Madame de Maitenon's townhouse twenty-four hours of the day for an entire week to divulge that bit of scrumptious news.

It appeared Mr. Adams rather fancied making midnight outings in Madame de Maitenon's best evening gowns. Other than that, however, the man had proven to be a very pleasant and understanding man who simply did not want his fancy, little midnight outings made known.

Oh, yes. Charlotte may not have told him what it would take to get her to marry him, but she was about to discover that escaping Alexander Baxendale was simply not an option. He would force her to breathe the same air as he, and take pleasure in it. He would force her to live in the same space as he, and take pleasure in it. He would force her to engage in the same activities as he, and take pleasure in it until she finally gasped with the realization that she needed him and loved him as much as he needed and loved her.

Then she, he, and all of his sisters—and, yes, even his blasted mother—would *all* live excessively and happily ever after. The way a Hawksford damn well should.

Madame de Maitenon's butler glanced over his shoulder, down the long corridor behind them, then turned back to Alexander and whispered, "She is waiting, Lord Hawksford." He gestured stiffly toward the closed door. "In there."

Alexander nodded his thanks to the balding man, who insisted on keeping watch in case the granddaughter decided to make an appearance. He slipped into Madame de Maitenon's room and closed the door behind him, stripping his hat from his head. Lilac perfume permeated the warm air of the candlelit bedchamber.

"Lord Hawksford," Madame de Maitenon's playful, accented voice cut into the silence of the room. "What have I done to deserve this glorious honor?" She smiled coyly. "Aside from nearly dying."

Alexander hesitated, then made his way toward the large mahogany bed where Madame de Maitenon lay resting atop a mountain of linens and pillows. Despite the merry tone of her voice, it was obvious she had been affected by the stroke. Her usually bright features appeared pale and sickly, and her silver hair, which she always kept bundled up and away, cascaded around her face and shoulders in unkempt waves.

He paused beside her bed, and, although he knew Madame de Maitenon would not have wanted him to pity her, he couldn't help himself. "How are you feeling, Madame?"

She shrugged and sat farther up against her pillows. "As a woman my age should, I suppose." She patted the space beside her. "Sit. Tell me why you are here."

He nodded and sat down on the edge of her bed, setting his top hat beside him. "Lady Charlotte worries a great deal about you, Madame."

Madame de Maitenon shook her head. "I do not think she worries as much as she first did. She and I have exchanged many letters since that day, and in each letter I receive from her, she assures me she worries less. All she asks is that I keep writing. And so I do. She is remarkable considering all that she continues to do for me. She forwards all my correspondence from the school, ensures Harold is not lonely, and sees to it that my little desk in the classroom does not acquire dust. I hate dust. It makes everything feel so unused and unloved."

Alexander leaned toward her. "Have you allowed her to call upon you yet? Last I saw her, she was upset about not being allowed to do so."

She sighed. In the way only a Frenchwoman could. "I am not allowed to have visitors. Maybelle is very insistent that I rest. Though very sweet, she is also very fierce at heart and just as persuasive.

Like me. What is more, I do not think it wise Lady Chartwell see me like this. She will see me in due time. When I am more presentable. Now." She reached out and patted his gloved hand, a flirtatious smile curving her lips. "What are you really here for, Lord Hawksford? Hmm? I know it is not for this bit of gossip about my health."

Alexander leaned back, shifting on the edge of the bed, and inwardly chanted that, yes, even the King of England needed assistance at times. "I am asking for permission to attend your school." He paused. "When and if it reopens."

Her brows rose. "Oh? What for?" She paused, as if answering the question for herself, then shifted toward him. She smiled. "Ah. Lady Charlotte has seized the ship and removed the sails, has she?"

Alexander let out an amused chuckle. "Yes, she has indeed. What is worse, she isn't allowing the captain to board." He cleared his throat. "It is my intention to marry her, Madame. The sooner, the better."

"Marriage is one thing, Lord Hawksford, but love is quite another. Do you love her?"

"Yes. I do." Although it didn't seem real and probably wouldn't feel real until she was officially his.

"*Bien.*" She patted his hand again, only with a bit more affection. "Knowing that, I will assist. Between you, your five sisters, and your mother, I know that she will be very happy." She eyed him for a moment. "The only condition I will set, however, is that you attend class for the rest of the Season. I am not interested in going through the complications of placing another student. Agreed?"

He grinned. "Agreed."

"Your return will come at a good time. I have finally found all of the girls for the pleasure room and have even added an unexpected new student." She beamed. "My granddaughter will also be teaching until I am able to make a complete recovery."

"Your granddaughter?" he drawled. "You mean the same one that I'm bloody trying to avoid? The same one who turned Charlotte away from the door and disapproved of your school from the very beginning?"

"The very same." She winked up at him. "You will find Maybelle to be quite entertaining. I ask that you arrive at the school next week, Monday. Though earlier than the usual seven o'clock. About six-thirty. I want all the men to arrive before my granddaughter does so that no introductions are missed. Oh. And bring your nightshirt."

He quirked a brow. "My nightshirt? Whatever for?"

"Maybelle will be hosting a lecture and will be offering valuable advice on bedside manners."

Alexander choked on a laugh. Hell, a man couldn't pay enough for the sort of entertainment she was offering. Although, he intended to personally ensure that Maybelle de Maitenon's first day at school was as memorable for her as his had been for him. As a gallant nod toward the unnecessary suffering Charlotte had endured that day when she'd been turned away from

Madame's door. "I will gladly bring my nightshirt in for observation."

"*Bien.* In turn, I will ensure everything is in place for you to attend. So that you will be able to board your ship, put up all your glorious sails, and head out to sea. Where you belong."

"I do have one more thing to ask of you. If I may."

"There is more?"

He grinned, reached into his inner waistcoat pocket, and withdrew the next step in his plan. He stood and set the sealed invitation onto the side table next to her bed. "I am not putting much value on its outcome, which is why I am reenrolling in your school, but I ask that you have her attend all the same."

"Oh-ho. What delicious adventure do you have planned for my Charlotte?"

Alexander reached down and tapped his gloved forefinger against the invitation. "Nothing elaborate. It's for the Rutherford ball. It's a bit short notice, but given the duke's reputation, I thought it might be fun. Have Charlotte attend. Tell her that she'll be meeting a new, prospective student and have her wait beneath a portrait or a mirror in the ballroom so that I may easily find her. If you do all this, I vow to pay forth not one but two hundred pounds per week up until the end of the Season."

Madame de Maitenon stared at him for a prolonged moment. She rolled onto her side, toward him. "The Rutherford ball? How small and quaint London can be."

Hardly small and hardly quaint. But who was he

to argue with a woman recovering from apoplexy? He sat beside her again. "Might I also ask that you have Charlotte dress appropriately?"

She bowed her silver head to him. "I shall *personally* see to it that she attends on behalf of the school and dresses accordingly. Thank you, Lord Hawksford, for your generous donation of two hundred pounds per week to the school. It will be put to good use, I assure you."

"You are most welcome." He patted her hand. "I should probably take my leave. I've intruded upon you long enough."

"*Non.* It is so nice to have someone visit from the outside world." Her lips harbored a sly smile as she leaned toward him. She lowered her voice. "Before you go. Tell me. Who told you about Clive?"

He blinked at her, not understanding. "Forgive me. What?"

She tsked, still keeping her voice to a whisper. "Clive's little secret. You found out. Otherwise, I doubt he would have given you entrance into the house against Maybelle's orders."

Alexander let out a laugh. "You already knew?"

She rolled her eyes and waved her hand about. "Och, everyone in this house knows! Everyone except for Maybelle, that is. Clive fancies himself to be a bit of a father to her and would never forgive any of us if we changed that between them. Not that Maybelle would mind. She is most tolerant of such things. But he insists. And so we never say anything. Now, do tell Madame. How did you ever learn of it? He is, after all, most discreet."

Alexander couldn't help but grin. "I paid several chaps to watch the house."

"I expected nothing less from you." Madame de Maitenon sighed wistfully and settled back against the pillows again, closing her eyes. "It is best you leave, Lord Hawksford. I am tired and need rest. I have busy days ahead."

"Forgive me." Alexander leaned toward her and kissed her forehead lightly, wishing her not only rest but a full recovery. "You are a surprisingly lovely woman, and I cannot even begin to thank you for taking care of my Charlotte all this time."

Madame de Maitenon reached up, with eyes still closed, and blindly patted the side of his face. "Now it is your turn, *oui?*"

He nodded and straightened, filling his chest with a renewed sense of hope. Yes. It was his turn. And he could hardly wait.

Lesson Twenty-Four

Shagging in and of itself is not love.
You do know that, yes? Because if you
don't, well then you'd better. Or it will
all end without so much as a letter.
                    —*The School of Gallantry*

The Rutherford ball
Two days later, evening

Being a widow certainly had its merits. For one, she didn't need a chaperone to make an appearance at a London gathering. She also didn't have to worry about appeasing the whirlwind known as the marriage mart.

Thank goodness for that much.

Of course, when a woman *didn't* have a chaperone, there were other complications. Like having no one to talk to. Or not having someone to fend off all the unwanted men. Or gossip.

When the line before her dwindled and her name was finally announced, Charlotte gathered

her honey-colored crape evening gown, which
Madame had gifted to her for the occasion, and
headed toward the large ballroom. She only hoped
the noeud of expensive gauze ribbon and white
satin, which her chambermaid had sewn around
her waist to hide the dress's imperfect fit, would
stay in place.

She tentatively entered the ballroom, the
merry strings of violins fluttering right along with
her heart. It was all so exciting and frightening at
the same time. For even when she had been married to Chartwell, she rarely made public appearances. She enjoyed dancing and people, simply
not all at once.

An endless array of candles flickered from the
solid gold sconces attached to the paneled walls.
Gilded crystal chandeliers graced the high, arched
ceilings. Flames from every candle glittered and
multiplied in the mirrors decorating the ballroom.

It was indeed the most beautiful home she had
ever had the pleasure of being invited to. She
wistfully sighed, trying to enjoy the sense of freedom she felt knowing that she had no one to
answer to but herself.

Charlotte walked past a small group of lightly
rouged faces and overly coiffed ladies draped in
expensive, colorful evening gowns. They leaned
against the wall, waving their delicate fans in
unison before their faces, all appearing completely and utterly bored.

And yet, as she passed, she could feel their
eager little eyes following every step she made.
Even heard a few rushed whispers touch her ears.

It was how the *ton* always liked to play. Appearing indifferent at all times, when really, they were anything but.

For the most part, she was quite happy to have no further association with that aspect of London society. It kept her life simple. For the most part.

Charlotte made her way toward a portrait on the far wall before her, then settled below it and waited, watching the throngs of people dancing and talking as all respectable people did at such events.

Though she wasn't terribly nervous about meeting Madame's prospective student, who was to replace Alexander, considering she was standing in a room full of people, she did find it all odd. It wasn't as if she could publicly discuss the school and its benefits during a ball. But Madame always knew what she was doing.

After the third song and dance passed, Charlotte sighed, leaned back against the wall, and glanced at the dancing card dangling from a velvet string on her wrist. She turned it over in her hand and read the list of dances. How strange. She couldn't even remember the last time she had danced.

She paused. Well, no, she could. But she preferred not to remember it. Seeing it had been with Chartwell.

A movement beside her made her drop her card and turn. Her eyes widened as she drew in a sharp breath.

For Alexander leaned against the wall beside her, arms crossed over his chest, casually looking out toward the dance floor. He was dressed in a formal black evening jacket and a bottle green waistcoat with a matching cravat that had been perfectly tied ballroom style. Nothing about him was out of place. Even his bronzed hair had been meticulously combed back with tonic, as if he had put a great amount of thought and care into his appearance.

Clearly, this was the new prospective student. "I take this to mean you're reenrolling?"

He didn't respond. He didn't even glance at her. He merely continued to stare out before him, appearing bored out of his mind. But then, without warning, he slid the entire length of his muscled body in her direction and settled himself close. Close enough that the heat of his body penetrated the small, sacred space a person usually called their own. Close enough that she could smell the tantalizing scent of leather and lemon floating off his heated skin toward her.

All this time, he'd been trying so desperately. And yet, he still hadn't quite figured out that all she really wanted from him were three little words. Three. Little. Words. Words that she wanted to not only hear, but believe that he meant with all of his heart.

She supposed she might as well give him a sporting chance after all his efforts. Besides. She had missed him. A bit too much.

Charlotte closed the remaining gap between them, firmly setting her exposed bare shoulder, just above where her beret sleeve dipped down the length of her arm, against him.

"Have you ever made love before a crowd?" he suddenly whispered.

An unexpected shiver trickled through the length of her body. "No," she whispered back.

"Would you like to?" he whispered again.

Her pulse jolted. He couldn't possibly be serious. There was no respectable way a man and a woman could . . . was there? She nervously wet her lips. "I wouldn't know how."

"Allow me to demonstrate." He uncrossed his arms. His gloved fingers found hers. He buried their hands into the folds of her gown and rubbed a finger on the inside of her palm. Slowly. Up and down.

She didn't know why, for it was nothing but his finger against the inside of her glove, but the touch was so overwhelming and evocative of what more she could have, it awoke every inch of her body.

She trained her gaze ahead of her and tried not to slide down the length of the wall in utter bliss. To keep herself from getting too lost in the moment, she focused on a young, pretty woman with strands of glistening pearls fashionably woven through her gathered blond curls. The woman affectionately released the hand of a handsome dark-haired gentleman.

The scene was as beautiful and romantic as she felt in that moment. The gentleman bowed gallantly to the woman, his dark hair cascading across his forehead. His lips moved, conveying something briefly to her before he finally turned and walked away.

The woman paused, as if still yearning to be with him, then turned, her emerald silk gown shifting against her slim body as she moved in the opposite direction.

"I am ardently making love to you, Charlotte," Alexander murmured, his voice practically melting into the hum of the violins. "And might I also add that you look absolutely beautiful. I hardly recognized you in that gown."

His finger continued to slide up and down the inside of her gloved palm, increasing its steady rhythm. Creating an erotic friction and heat. She tried to slow her breathing, but all she could imagine was him thrusting into her. With that same rhythm. With that same intensity.

The lady in the emerald gown she had been admiring in a half daze, suddenly reappeared into view. Only much had changed. Charlotte blinked, then froze against Alexander's amorous touch.

The woman struggled against a blond-haired gentleman who ruthlessly held her by both wrists, forcing her to remain close to him. The same dark-haired gentleman who had earlier escorted her off the floor stormed upon them and a clear exchange of heated words commenced. The woman was now smashed between the two, the look of horror on her face reflecting Charlotte's own. And what was worse, no one around them seemed to care.

Charlotte sucked in a sharp breath, snapped her head toward Alexander, and yanked her hand away from his. "You'd best do something, Alexander," she demanded, panic edging into her voice. "Now."

He blinked down at her in utter astonishment.

Then leaned his shoulder into the wall to face her. Grinning, he adjusted his evening jacket around what was a more than obvious erection. "What exactly did you have in mind?"

"Oh, for heaven's sake!" Charlotte reached up, grabbed hold of his chin, and snapped his head toward the commotion. "That woman is being assaulted! Do something!"

Alexander yanked away her hand, pushing himself away from the wall, and jumped to attention. "Don't use this as an excuse to leave!" he ordered, then sprinted off for the drama.

Charlotte bit down on her lower lip and watched as Alexander pushed his way through the people around him. Just as he came upon the tiff, the dark-haired gentleman snatched the blond man by the collar, yanking him off of the woman completely. With one full swing, he smashed a fist into the side of the man's head, sending him senseless to the floor.

"Oh God!" Charlotte let out an astonished cry and smacked a gloved hand to her mouth.

The young woman scrambled back and away from them, but her scrambling feet caught and pulled on the hem of her full skirts. She tipped backward, her arms flailing.

Charlotte cringed.

That was when Alexander, *her* Alexander, swooped in and effortlessly caught the woman right before she hit the floor.

Charlotte blew out a breath and set a heavy hand to her chest. "God love you, Alexander," she whispered. She watched in complete adoration as he gently assisted the blonde back onto her slippered feet.

The woman turned, stepping outside the circle of his arms, and momentarily blinked up at him. As if acknowledging that Alexander was not only handsome, but *very* handsome.

Charlotte crossed her arms over her chest, raising a brow in their direction. She only hoped that the woman hadn't entirely forgotten about her suitor. Or the man laying motionless on the floor.

Alexander adjusted his evening jacket around himself, as if he were still under the influence of their earlier romantic adventure, then grabbed up her satin-gloved hand and kissed it. He then turned and walked away.

He strode cockily toward Charlotte, looking quite pleased with himself, and eventually settled before her with a grin. "Is there anything more I can do for you before we elope tonight? I have a carriage waiting out front. It is ready whenever you are."

He wanted to elope? Tonight? Her heart fluttered. That is why he arranged all of this.

This had to be it. The moment in which he would profess his undying love to her, then sweep her off into the night in a grand romantic scheme. A grand romantic scheme Chartwell had never been capable of.

She lovingly met Alexander's gaze and smiled, knowing that if she was ever going to give him a chance, this most certainly was it. He had to love her. He simply had to. Why would he go through all this effort if he didn't? Perhaps all he really needed from her was a nudge. "I love you, Alexander," she finally said, not caring what the ballroom of people around them thought. "You know that, don't you?"

His grin, along with the laugh lines around his green eyes, faded. "I . . . yes. You told me. That one night. Thank you. It, uh . . ." He cleared his throat and glanced at the people around them. He smoothed the front of his waistcoat. "*So.* Do you care to dance? Or shall we simply elope?"

Her eyes widened in horror and disbelief, feeling as though he'd slapped her. On both sides of her cheeks. *Yes, I know, you told me and thank you? And do you care to dance or shall we elope?*

What on earth was wrong with him? He could bloody make love to her hand in a ballroom filled to the ceiling with people, had no qualms about making a scene at the Row, had sent sonnets and choirs and everything else to her door, but when it came to the simple subject of *love,* he had absolutely no words to impart except yes and thank you and do you care to dance or elope?

"I don't dance," she retorted icily, trying to keep herself from punching his arm. "And I certainly have no interest in eloping with a man who does not love me."

Charlotte gathered up her skirts and whipped away from him. She marched straight for the entrance, wishing she could rid herself of the humiliation she felt. What was even more heartbreaking in that moment was that he wasn't even calling out her name or running after her, begging her to stay. He was letting her walk away.

Inwardly she heard herself screaming and felt herself crumbling. She should have known. She should have known that a man like him was not in any way prepared to hand over his heart. At least not the way she wanted it.

Charlotte slid to a halt and tried to get around a group of older men blocking her path to the front entrance. "Pardon me," she insisted. "I should like to pass."

Each of them ignored her and continued to talk animatedly amongst themselves. As if she hadn't said a single word. As if she wasn't even there.

Damn them and all of their stupid brass waistcoat buttons! She wasn't going to stand about and beg for an outlet. Charlotte shoved her way straight through the group of men, pushing their arms and bellies out of the way.

"I beg your pardon!" a heavyset, balding man snapped down at her as she passed through. "Don't you see us all standing here?"

"Oh, pop off!" Charlotte snapped back at him, eliciting a wave of gasps.

Men. Why, they even thought they owned the floor everybody walked on.

Lesson Twenty-Five

*Clearly, you have much to learn. Which is why
you will continue to suffer, yearn, and burn.*
　　　　　　　　　—The School of Gallantry

11 Berwick Street
Two days later, early morning, the classroom.

Though Mr. Hudson and Harold had been
anything but friendly, and Charlotte was not *at
home,* Alexander knew he was officially taking his
first step toward becoming a new man. The sort of
man that Charlotte wanted him to be. The sort
of man Charlotte needed him to be. The sort of
man who knew *how* to confess his love when she
needed to hear it most.

Indeed, it had been in very bad taste to ask her
to elope with him without even assuring her of
his love. The truth was, he'd been overwhelmed.
For he had wanted that moment in which he
confessed his undying love to her to be monu-
mental. He didn't want to simply toss it out at her

before a room full of judging faces and a man still lying unconscious on the dance floor behind him.

At least now he knew what he needed to do. And he intended to turn it into a very special night for her. Tonight.

As for now, he intended to have some fun and pass away the time. In class. As he'd promised Madame.

Alexander strode into the room, toting along his old nightshirt from his days as a rake. The garment had seen far too many women, and it was time he retired the damn thing. In the name of Charlotte. He tossed the nightshirt onto the pile of other nightshirts that had been set on the desk, then turned to all the men. He paused, surprised to find not only Brayton, Banfield, and Caldwell, but also a newcomer, as Madame de Maitenon had earlier intimated.

Though not just any newcomer. It was the Duke of Rutherford himself, the man who had smashed a solid fist into his own guest at the ball just a few days earlier.

Alexander grinned and approached the man, extending his free hand. "Your Grace. You honor us with that wicked right hook. How is the lady I swooped in on? Good, I hope?"

The duke grasped his hand firmly and inclined his dark head toward him. "Maybelle is doing quite well, thank you. Many thanks. I would have never forgiven myself if any harm had come to her."

Alexander slowly pulled his hand away from the duke's and gawked at him. "Wait. *Maybelle?* As in

Maybelle de Maitenon? Madame de Maitenon's granddaughter?"

The duke's sharp, dark eyes met his. "Is there a problem, Hawksford?"

Obviously, they were already on friendly terms. In a manner of speaking. Alexander laughed and put up both hands. "No, no. Not at all, Rutherford. Not at all."

"Good. Because I hate complications."

"Yes. So do I, Rutherford. So do I." Alexander let out a laugh, seated himself in a chair, and shook his head. Now he understood why Madame had opted to call London quaint and small. Because it was.

Caldwell leaned far forward in his seat and glanced at Alexander. "You're not planning to propose at my house tonight, are you? You know how wild those gatherings can get. It'll hardly be romantic. Hell, half the time even I don't know who's coming."

"There's no need to worry. The whole point of this party is to show Charlotte the sort of life I am permanently leaving behind. I'm trying to be metaphorical. Women love that sort of thing. Afterward, I intend on whisking her away to my country estate and proposing beneath the night sky. It'll all be perfect. I've planned it all right down to the minute. Now, you're certain she's coming?"

Caldwell gestured cockily toward himself. "If I were any more certain, I'd be God."

Now there was a scary notion. "And what about you, Almighty One? How are your wedding plans coming along?"

Caldwell gruffly laughed, dropping his hand back to his knee. "Caroline still hates me."

Alexander grinned. "Glad to hear it."

"You would be."

A petite blonde stepped into the classroom, wearing a simple, light blue muslin gown. The very same blonde he had rescued from kissing the floor. Her firm stance as she stood in the doorway called attention to the fact that she was anything but petite in nature. Her sharp blue eyes, very similar to those of Madame de Maitenon, scanned them all in silence.

Alexander rose to acknowledge her.

The other men followed suit.

She smiled with overconfidence, and Alexander sensed she was anything but.

Which would indeed prove to be fun.

The duke stepped forward and bowed. "Madame."

She inclined her blond head toward him. "Good morning, Your Grace."

Caldwell bowed sweepingly, causing his wavy blond hair to fall across his forehead. "I am Lord Caldwell, at your service."

"Good morning, Lord Caldwell," she offered. "I have heard so much about you."

Alexander inwardly cringed at the thought. God only knew the sort of things Madame had told her granddaughter about each and every single one of them.

Caldwell's half smile broadened. "I am quite certain you have."

The bastard. He sounded rather proud of himself.

Brayton stepped forward next and bowed curtly. Serious as ever. "Lord Brayton."

"A pleasure, My Lord," she intoned. "Are you always this cheerful? Or is it the early hour?"

Caldwell grinned and smacked Brayton on the back. "From what we have gathered, this is as cheerful as he will ever be."

Alexander coughed into his hand, trying to disguise a laugh. Yes, leave it to Caldwell to make a man feel his best.

Brayton shifted his scarred jaw, placed his hands behind his back, but otherwise remained quiet and detached despite the stab at his honor.

"Any other man would have been quick to draw blood on less," Miss Maitenon delicately offered. "It seems you have a talent for self-control, Lord Brayton. I have no doubt it serves you and your lady well."

She shifted her gaze to Alexander. "And you are?"

This was the moment he'd been waiting for. Sweet, succulent revenge in the name of Charlotte. He instantly caught Maybelle de Maitenon's gaze, knowing full well that the staunch types, like herself, were always easily ruffled when it came to overt male attention. Which is exactly what he planned on giving her.

She froze. As if suddenly remembering him from the ball.

He strode toward her, slowly, moving with a suave, steady intent well deserving of the situation. He stopped before her, took hold of her gloved hand, and brought it up to his lips, his eyes never once leaving hers.

Hovering over her glove, he answered indulgently, "I am Lord Hawksford." He traced his thumb over her knuckles, hoping he was making her squirm. "You shall have my undivided attention. At all times."

She quickly drew her hand away. "Try not to overdo the kissing of a lady's hand, My Lord. It leads a woman to think that you are desperate, and we all know a man should be anything but."

The men behind him refrained from laughing, several of them opting to clear their throats instead.

If Alexander had had any doubts, any doubts whatsoever, there wasn't a single one left. For not only was this woman indeed Madame de Maitenon's granddaughter, but it appeared every single one of them were about to get spanked. But he'd be damned if he'd bend over for anyone else but Charlotte from here on out.

Lesson Twenty-Six

What happens next in this little game called love?
My goodness. Don't you already know?
You suffer a bit more. But of course!
     —The School of Gallantry

Lord Caldwell's
Evening

"Hawksford!" someone yelled out from across the overcrowded parlor. "Are you really getting married? Or is that just piss flying about the room?"

Alexander swiveled toward the dark-mustached man who held up a glass of gin in one hand while nestling a very large-breasted brunette closer to himself with the other.

Despite the fact that he didn't know either the man or the brunette, Alexander pointed at the two and grinned. "It's not piss! I am getting married."

"Then may you and your future wife fuck to a hundred!" The man tossed back his drink, threw the glass aside, shattering it against the wood floor, then turned and kissed the woman beside him.

"Uh . . . *thank you!*" Alexander called out to the man, despite the fact that he was no longer the center of attention. "Thank you very much. I appreciate your kind and warm thoughts."

That was the eighth person tonight who had congratulated him in their own bizarre manner. And all of them were people he didn't even know. Caldwell's doing, he was sure.

Alexander finished his port, gave his glass to a passing servant, and strode back toward the entryway, knowing Charlotte would be arriving at any moment. He couldn't wait to pull her into his arms and make her feel loved and wanted the moment she walked in through that door. He only hoped that she was prepared for the chaos around them. Not that they'd be staying.

Seeing Caldwell was occupied with greeting all the incoming guests by the main entrance, Alexander strode farther back into the foyer's corridor and out of the way. He settled against one of the walls that had a clear view of the main entrance and waited. And waited.

He didn't know how long he'd been standing there, but he assumed it was at least fifteen minutes. He shifted against the wall and looked over toward the entryway again.

He paused at seeing Madame de Maitenon's granddaughter. He'd almost forgotten that Caldwell had invited her. And though everyone in the classroom seemed to have taken to her firm, blunt ways, he still didn't know what to make of her. Especially after that whole lecture on dildos. Complete with demonstrations.

Maybelle de Maitenon continued to stand in the foyer just outside one of the large receiving rooms as if uncertain as to whether she should stay or go. She then glanced down at the modest lilac lace neckline of her gown and quickly looked up again, looking rather concerned.

He bit back a smile. For here she was, the grand-daughter of a great French courtesan, teacher of sex to men, with the nerve to demonstrate the placement of a dildo in her mouth before the entire class, and yet she appeared to feel out of place amongst all the risqué women around her.

It was downright curious.

A chestnut-haired woman dressed in a black velvet gown that provocatively clung to her siz-able breasts and corseted waist paused before Maybelle. A cigar was tucked between her raised bare fingers.

Cleopatra, as Caldwell liked to call her. The queen of all things erotic, whose sole pleasure was licking the cunt off every woman who'd let her. And occasionally even those poor women who would normally never let her unless a bit of music and wine was involved.

Cleopatra seductively drew in a long puff from her cigar, cocked her head, and blew out a tuft of smoke in Maybelle's direction. She pointed her half-smoked cigar toward Maybelle's neckline and said something.

Alexander's brows rose at the interaction.

To his astonishment, Maybelle quickly turned away and adjusted the front of her bodice, trying to maneuver her corset in a way so as to shove her breasts farther up and out into the open. She hesitated, peering down at what she'd done, then turned back to Cleopatra.

Alexander shook his head and pushed himself away from the wall. The woman was likely to get raped doing things like that with Cleopatra. Fortunately for his new teacher, he was around to assist. And, of course, being the noble gentleman that he was, he was going to do it without her even knowing.

He strode toward them just as Cleopatra wrapped a slender arm around Maybelle's waist and yanked her against herself, draping their front sides seductively close.

This would certainly prove to be yet another amusing little rescue. He paused behind them, then wrapped his arms around both their shoulders and gathered both women to his wide chest. "Is there adequate space for one more?" he drawled down at each of them, grinning. "I brought my dildo."

Maybelle scrambled out of both his embrace and that of Cleopatra. She smacked his arm hard, then pointed rigidly at him in warning. Yet couldn't utter a single word in her defense.

All that mattered, despite her obviously being miffed, was that she was no longer in Cleopatra's grasp.

He laughed at his own brilliance, smacked his hands together, then turned and swaggered down the corridor back toward where he'd originally been waiting for Charlotte.

Indeed, the way he felt right now was downright dangerous. For he was in such cocky high spirits, he almost felt like going around and helping whoever else needed assistance.

But then again, he had to first see to his *own* success. Which should be arriving at any single moment.

Late evening and still waiting around at Lord Caldwell's

Despite the fact that rat bastard had assured him Charlotte would come, and he had ardently and patiently waited, going around and talking to complete strangers and making an idiot of himself throughout the evening by announcing his upcoming marriage, she never came.

He'd long given up on the port and had since moved on to the gin. Though he was beginning to realize that even all the gin in the world could never possibly take away the feeling that his time for miracles had finally run out.

Through a haze that he prayed would never lift, Alexander staggered among the blurring faces around him, toward the mahogany table that was cluttered with decanters of brandy, wine, port, and gin. The empty glass he held out before him seemed to be the only thing balancing him. The only thing keeping him sane.

Didn't the woman realize she was killing him? Ever. So. Slowly? He slammed his glass down onto the table, causing all of the crystal decanters on it to chime against one another.

He frantically rubbed the top of his head, trying

to clear his muddled thoughts, and then stripped off his cravat and tossed it aside. Still feeling bloody hot, he unclasped his starched collar and stripped it away from his neck and drew in a deep breath.

Gripping the edges of the table, he leaned heavily against it. Now what? What was he supposed to do? Wait a bit more?

"Thirty pounds says Hawksford won't survive a single one past twenty!" a man called out across the room.

He knew he should have never made that boast about being able to stand upright after twenty drinks.

"Oh, come!" another man countered, sounding rather annoyed. "He's already lasted past eighteen. And look! The son of a bitch is still standing! Like he said he would. I say he's got another good ten in him. That's where I'm placing my thirty pounds! Another ten!"

Alexander gurgled out a laugh as more male voices floated around him, placing more bets. He once used to be Alexander the Great. Capable of saying and doing the right thing at the right time with any woman. But now? He was Alexander the Not So Great. And he was completely foxed. What was worse, the men around him were eagerly placing bets on the last of his crumbling kingdom.

Alexander released his hold on the table and pushed himself away. Blowing out an exhausted breath, he reached out a heavy arm and grabbed another crystal decanter filled with brandy.

He poured another glass of the amber liquid. Splashing it everywhere.

He tossed it back, then slammed it down on the table and turned for the doorway. He'd had enough of this waiting. This abuse. He was going straight to her house, and, Harold or no Harold, was going to demand that she give him an audience.

A familiar blond-haired woman in a lilac lace and silk gown marched past the doorway and toward the foyer. His brows rose. Ah, now *there* was a person who could help him. His *teacher!* The one who had all the answers about dildos and bedside manners and nightshirts and God knew what else. Perhaps she had a solution. Someone had to have a solution. For he certainly didn't.

"Madame de Maitenon!" he called out. It was only fitting he call her that after that brilliant lecture she gave on dildos.

She paused, then slowly turned to him.

He staggered for a moment in the middle of the crowded parlor and grinned.

She hurried over to him and set her hands on her hips. "Do not make life difficult for me."

"This'll only take a moment. I assure you." He grabbed her waist and yanked her toward him. Needing something to balance him. "I am in need of advice," he drawled down at her. "*Female advice.*"

Taking hold of his arms, Miss Maitenon tried to ease out of them. "I do not think my advice will do you any good, as clearly, you won't be able to remember a thing come morning."

Ignoring her protest, he wrapped his arm

heavily around her shoulder and swayed as he looked down at her. "Does love truly exist? Or is it something we . . . want to exist?"

She froze against him. "Really, My Lord, this is far beyond my level of . . ."

Her face and words blurred, the room grew dark, and his arms and his body suddenly ceased to exist.

So much for female advice.

Lesson Twenty-Seven

At last.
— *The School of Gallantry*

11 Berwick Street
Seven o'clock in the morning, next day

Charlotte was downright curious as to what sort of female could have possibly won over Mr. Hudson. The man never accepted visitors at unconventional hours. Nor would he ever dare to summon her from her sleep.

She paused outside the parlor and blinked in astonishment at seeing the oldest of Alexander's sisters, Caroline.

Caroline was openly admiring all of the nude male statues, tilting her head slightly to one side, as if a different view would somehow change them.

Charlotte bit back a laugh and entered the room. "I have found that the middle one is the most endowed," she chanced, guessing that they were both naughty at heart.

Caroline jerked toward her, placing a gloved hand to her chest, and let out a laugh. "So I noticed."

Caroline grinned, a small dimple appearing on her left cheek, and moved closer to her. Her simple royal blue morning gown brightened not only her entire face but her very eyes. "I'm so pleased Mr. Hudson obliged me. Forgive me for calling upon you at such an early hour."

"You are always welcome here, no matter the hour." Charlotte gestured at the lone chair. "I hope this will do. I only recently acquired funds from my husband's estate and have yet to properly furnish the house."

Caroline glanced toward the gilded chair, then turned back to her. "No worries. This shouldn't take long. I am merely here on behalf of my brother."

Charlotte blinked, and though she tried to keep a blush from creeping into her cheeks, it was no use. "Yes?" was all she could manage.

Caroline sighed heavily and shifted from one slippered foot to the other. "As I am certain you know, Alex has been relentlessly trying to win your hand in marriage. And I'm afraid it has finally taken its toll. I usually don't worry about him, but I must say I genuinely fear for him. From what I understand, he waited for you all of last night at Lord Caldwell's home. He had plans to ride off with you into the country and propose. But when you didn't make an appearance, he drank himself into a state of obliteration and is still lying unresponsive on the sofa where he was deposited by God knows who last night."

Oh, poor Alexander. She'd ruined him. Completely ruined him. And here she was worried about what he'd done to her.

Caroline eyed her. "I am here not to preach, but rather to inform you of his current state. I pray that if you do not love my brother that you inform him of it. For he most certainly loves you. And though he may not have been able to verbalize it properly, surely his behavior should count for something."

Charlotte's pulse skittered uncontrollably. For she realized the truth in Caroline's words. A proclamation of love meant nothing without a fire burning behind it. No one knew that better than she. "Forgive me," she finally whispered. "I knew nothing of his true feelings or that he was waiting for me. Had I known . . ."

"I thought so!" Caroline let out an impish laugh, grabbed hold of Charlotte's hands, and shook them excitedly. "Come with me! Let us put the poor sop out of his misery, shall we?"

Charlotte squeezed Caroline's hands, still trying to cope with what she was saying. Alexander loved her. *Her.* She let out a laugh in disbelief. "I'd love to put us *both* out of our misery, actually."

Caroline grinned and leaned toward her, her blue-green eyes sparkling. "Welcome to the family. I can't *wait* to have another sister."

Charlotte let out a shaky breath and willed herself not to cry from the joy bursting through her. Family. At long last. She had a family. And not just any family. *Alexander's* family.

* * *

"Is he dead?"

"If he were dead, Mary, he wouldn't be snoring."

"Yes, I know, but what if—"

Alexander groaned and pried open his eyes, feeling as though he *were* going to die. How downright fitting that Mary truly thought he was dead. He only hoped she hadn't already sent out invitations for the funeral. Or ordered his casket.

"Alex!" Mary exclaimed. A pair of small, sloppy lips smacked his cheek, leaving a cool spot against his burning skin. "Oh, thank goodness! You're alive!"

"I'd rather not be," he muttered, shifting toward her and Anne, who were both sitting on the walnut coffee table across from him. "How long have you both been sitting there staring at me?"

"*Well* . . ." Anne jumped up to her feet and rubbed her hands into the sides of her morning skirts. "Seeing as you are alive and all, I ought to go. Have fun!" She waggled her brows at him, then dashed out of the room.

He blinked. *Have fun?* Hell, when she was old enough, he'd give her a jug of gin and then see the sort of fun *she* had.

Mary slowly cocked her head, so as to better see him in his horizontal position. She wrinkled her freckled nose. "Who was that man that brought you here last night, Alex?"

Alexander groaned. Still not feeling comfortable against the cushions of the sofa, he shifted his sore body again. "Please don't expect me to remember anything, Mary. Because I don't."

"Try to remember. It's important."

He blew out a breath, wishing he could blow

out the pounding headache and nausea gripping him. One would think a man would learn not to overindulge after all these years. "Why? It was probably Caldwell. I was at his house all night." Drinking the very thought of Charlotte away.

Mary shook her head, still keeping it cocked to one side. "No. It wasn't Caldwell. The man who brought you home had dark hair and dark eyes. *Very, very* handsome. Not to say Caldwell isn't. I just don't care for blonds. Do you suppose you can put out a marriage offer on this dark-haired gentleman so that he'll wait until I'm eighteen?"

Alexander jerked up into a sitting position. The room momentarily spun, his stomach whirling. God save him, who had he brought to the house last night?

All he needed was Mary to fall in love with a thirtysomething-year-old man. He was still recovering from the whole ordeal with Caroline and Caldwell. "How do you even know the man was handsome? Weren't you supposed to be in bed last night?"

She leveled her head once again and shrugged, her lips tugging into a frown. "I couldn't sleep. When I heard voices downstairs, I knew you were home and wanted to say good night. Only I never got past the top of the stairs. You see, this incredibly beautiful man was standing in the hall foyer. Looking up at me. For a moment, I thought Charon himself had come and almost fainted at the sight of him. And what is more . . ." She lowered her voice as if imparting a great secret. "*He saw me wrapped in my linens.*"

His eyes widened at the admission. "Whoever

the bloody hell he is, I assure you that if he so much as mentions you *or* your linens, I'll change the color of his skin. Permanently. Furthermore, I highly doubt you were feeling faint because of him."

Alexander noted with annoyance that her face looked even more drawn than it had the previous week. "It's because you aren't eating. Caroline told me all about what you're doing, and enough is enough. You need to eat. Do you hear me? You *will* eat."

Glaring, she crossed her arms over the ruffled front of her pea green morning gown. "If you gave me back all of my dresses, I wouldn't *need* to starve myself. Now would I?"

Oh, for the love of mother and child! He'd had enough. Enough of fighting the inevitable. Enough of trying to change those around him. Enough of making everyone into something they simply were not! For it was pointless. Absolutely pointless. And only he and he alone suffered.

"Go!" he barked. "They're all upstairs in a trunk hidden beneath Mother's bed. Take them. Take them and wear them all at once if it'll so please you. Arrange a few funerals while you're at it, invite all the neighbors, and *die*."

Her face brightened as her thin brows popped up. "Truly?"

"Yes. Truly. Only before you hurry back to dying, be sure to eat breakfast."

She rolled her eyes, leaned toward him, and smacked his knee with her hand. "Silly. Don't you know it's already past one?"

She sprang to her feet, clapping, and then

skipped out of the room. "Alex says I can wear my dresses again!" she sing-songed for the entire household to hear. "I told you he wouldn't last!"

Alexander closed his eyes and groaned at the misery of it all. He simply didn't have the makings of a man who could run a household. With propriety, that is.

A heavy female sigh echoed within the room as the slow clicking of heels left the far corner of the room and rounded on him. "You'd better be a bit more firm with *our* children."

Alexander whipped toward the voice behind him in disbelief. "*Charlotte?*"

She stood behind him, her hands on her hips, dressed in her usual black finery. She quirked a dark brow at him. "Do you have anything to say to me?" She coughed suggestively. "Anything at all?"

He bloody wasn't going to waste any more time, that was for sure. What did he care about making it special? It *was* special. And he now knew that. "I love you," he blurted out. "I love you, Charlotte. *Very* much. So much, I don't think I could possibly love you any more. But I'll spend the rest of my life trying to prove it." He paused. "Do you want me to go on?"

She laughed, rounded the sofa, and slowly sat down beside him. She took his hand and kissed it with those soft lips he had missed so dearly. "I apologize I didn't come last night. I didn't realize you were waiting until Caroline called on me this morning."

"Caroline called on you? You mean . . ." He furrowed his brow. "But Caldwell said he spoke to you. He assured me you were coming."

She lowered her chin. "He spoke to *Mr. Hudson* and slipped the man ten pounds. And well . . . as protective as Mr. Hudson has been as of late, I never received the message. Or the ten pounds."

Mr. Hudson had clearly taken his earlier words too much to heart.

Charlotte grabbed his hand, set it onto her lap, and slowly and purposefully traced her finger up and down the inside of his palm.

He swallowed and watched her bare finger, hypnotized by the seductive movement that produced a slow heat against the width of his palm. Not to mention the rest of him.

"I'm making love to you, Alexander," she whispered to him ever so softly. "Most ardently."

The air around him seemed to grow hot. And if his head weren't pounding and his stomach weren't roiling, he would have thrown her onto the sofa and made love to her for the rest of the day. And then for the rest of his life.

Stifled giggles erupted from the doorway.

"Now *that* is quite enough, you two," Victoria drawled.

"Yes," Elizabeth added. "If you must know, this is a respectable household."

"*And*," Mary mocked, lowering her voice to a deep tone that matched his, "there are individuals here under the age of nineteen."

Alexander's heart stopped as he glanced up to see all five of his sisters and his mother grouped together in the doorway. Every single one of them was grinning at him. As if he had not only done right by them, but by himself and Charlotte. Without a doubt, it was the most amazing moment he'd ever experienced in his life.

His mother's arched brows playfully rose. "Does this mean we're all allowed to be Hawksfords in our home again?"

He laughed. "Yes. But only in the house."

"I can live with that." Caroline clasped her hands together. "Ask her, Alex! Ask her, before anything else ruins it."

Nothing could ruin it. Ever.

Alexander cleared his throat, pressed his other hand atop Charlotte's, and squeezed it tightly.

Charlotte shyly smiled up at him, her cheeks flushing, making her even more beautiful.

Though the moment of his proposal was not as he had imagined, for he had wanted to do it in the country, it was more. He stood, and seeing that there was no room for him to kneel beside the sofa, he lifted his booted foot and shoved the small table back and away.

He kneeled and took Charlotte's hand again in his, meeting her dark eyes. "Charlotte . . ." He hesitated. "Hell. I don't even know your birth name. And I'm certainly not calling you by Chartwell's name anymore."

"It's Charlotte Jane Sutton," she offered, still shyly smiling.

"Charlotte Jane Sutton." He grinned. "Will you honor me by becoming my wife and giving me sons so that I may never be outnumbered again?"

Charlotte burst into laughter, a single tear trickling down from the corner of her eye. She swiped it away with the tips of her fingers and grinned back. "Yes, Alexander. Most certainly, yes."

Lesson Twenty-Eight

*Depending on how you went about collecting
your happily ever after, know that it may
cost you a good thing or two thereafter.*
—*The School of Gallantry*

Two days later

Alexander knew Madame de Maitenon would
one day ask that he pay his dues for favors
rendered—for the French were like that—but he
simply hadn't expected that the request would
come so damn soon. Or with such ridiculous
expectations. Especially when he was so mindlessly
preoccupied with setting the last touches on
Caroline's wedding before he could start to plan
his own.

"What is it?" Charlotte, who was visiting his
family for afternoon tea, swept into the study. Her
dark brows rose inquiringly. "You look harried."

Alexander blew out a breath, leaned far back
into his chair, and waved at the letter sitting on his

desk. "Madame is calling in favors. And what is worse, she wants me to do the impossible."

Charlotte rounded his desk, sat on his lap, and lovingly wrapped an arm around his neck. "Madame would never ask for the impossible."

"Is that so? Then perhaps I ought to read this little missive to you." He reached around her, firmly pressing her softness against his chest with one hand, and grabbed up the letter with the other.

He snapped the paper stiffly up before them and read aloud in his best forged French accent, "*Lord Hawksford. Unfortunately, school will not be in session this upcoming week due to unexpected complications. Hence my little letter. As I once helped you, I know you will help me. I want you to arrange a rendezvous between my granddaughter and the Duke of Rutherford. Sometime by the end of this week. As you may know, I am still in a very delicate state of health and refuse to be subjected to the further theatrics that we all know love creates. I have faith that you will see to my request accordingly. Do not disappoint me or my granddaughter. Merci. Madame de Maitenon.*"

Alexander tossed the letter toward his cluttered desk. "And here I thought winning your heart was an undertaking."

Charlotte let out a small laugh, grabbed the sides of his face with both her hands, and soundly kissed him right on the lips. "Considering all that she's done for us, we really should try and help." She paused, a thoughtful look crossing her features. She tilted her dark head to one side, a small smile now playing on her lips. "No one really knows about our engagement just yet. Aside from Madame and your family, that is."

"And a few others at Caldwell's party," he added.

She met his gaze for a long moment. "Actually, I have a rather brilliant idea on how we can bring them together."

He slowly leaned toward her, wrapping his arms possessively around her waist. "Is it devious?"

She slid her hands from his face and let them playfully and seductively travel down the length of his chest. She lowered her chin. "'Tis *very* devious. For we would be forced to play the only game that ever truly prompts results. You'll have to make me jealous, and I'll have to make you jealous. And in turn, we will make Maybelle and her duke jealous. Of course, it would probably involve drinking, scheming, and unforgivably crude behavior that the *ton* would never approve of."

Alexander grinned. "I can do that."

Charlotte's mouth curved into an equally big smile. "Yes, I know you can."

"Do you want to know what else I can do?" Alexander waggled his brows and caught his tongue between his teeth, squeezing her tightly against himself.

Charlotte giggled and playfully smacked at his shoulder. "Save it for our wedding night, you relentless beast."

He leaned slightly back, appearing somewhat concerned. "I am *not* waiting that long. I have needs. Hell, don't you?"

Charlotte paused, shifting slightly in his lap, and glanced back at the open doors of the study behind them. Turning back toward him, she poked him in the chest and quickly whispered, "I'm supposed to be having tea with your mother and Caroline in twenty minutes. Which would only really give us ten."

"A lot can happen in ten minutes, I assure you."

"I'll hold you to that." She gave him a pointed stare. "The cellar. In exactly four minutes."

He blinked. She already knew where the cellar was? Hell. He quickly rose, lifting her up and off his lap, then growled down at her, "Make it two minutes."

"Two it is." She blew him an enchanting, amorous kiss, then hurried around his desk and disappeared out of the door and into the hall.

Alexander straightened, carefully smoothed back the sides of his hair, and strode determinedly right after her. Now *this* was what a Hawksford would call a very happy ending.

And a very happy ending it was for him, indeed.

Romantic Suspense from
Lisa Jackson

See How She Dies	0-8217-7605-3	$6.99US/$9.99CAN
Final Scream	0-8217-7712-2	$7.99US/$10.99CAN
Wishes	0-8217-6309-1	$5.99US/$7.99CAN
Whispers	0-8217-7603-7	$6.99US/$9.99CAN
Twice Kissed	0-8217-6038-6	$5.99US/$7.99CAN
Unspoken	0-8217-6402-0	$6.50US/$8.50CAN
If She Only Knew	0-8217-6708-9	$6.50US/$8.50CAN
Hot Blooded	0-8217-6841-7	$6.99US/$9.99CAN
Cold Blooded	0-8217-6934-0	$6.99US/$9.99CAN
The Night Before	0-8217-6936-7	$6.99US/$9.99CAN
The Morning After	0-8217-7295-3	$6.99US/$9.99CAN
Deep Freeze	0-8217-7296-1	$7.99US/$10.99CAN
Fatal Burn	0-8217-7577-4	$7.99US/$10.99CAN
Shiver	0-8217-7578-2	$7.99US/$10.99CAN
Most Likely to Die	0-8217-7576-6	$7.99US/$10.99CAN
Absolute Fear	0-8217-7936-2	$7.99US/$9.49CAN
Almost Dead	0-8217-7579-0	$7.99US/$10.99CAN
Lost Souls	0-8217-7938-9	$7.99US/$10.99CAN
Left to Die	1-4201-0276-1	$7.99US/$10.99CAN
Wicked Game	1-4201-0338-5	$7.99US/$9.99CAN
Malice	0-8217-7940-0	$7.99US/$9.49CAN

Available Wherever Books Are Sold!
Visit our website at **www.kensingtonbooks.com**

Thrilling Suspense from
Beverly Barton

__**Every Move She Makes** 0-8217-6838-7 **$6.50**US/**$8.99**CAN

__**What She Doesn't Know** 0-8217-7214-7 **$6.50**US/**$8.99**CAN

__**After Dark** 0-8217-7666-5 **$6.50**US/**$8.99**CAN

__**The Fifth Victim** 0-8217-7215-5 **$6.50**US/**$8.99**CAN

__**The Last to Die** 0-8217-7216-3 **$6.50**US/**$8.99**CAN

__**As Good As Dead** 0-8217-7219-8 **$6.99**US/**$9.99**CAN

__**Killing Her Softly** 0-8217-7687-8 **$6.99**US/**$9.99**CAN

__**Close Enough to Kill** 0-8217-7688-6 **$6.99**US/**$9.99**CAN

__**The Dying Game** 0-8217-7689-4 **$6.99**US/**$9.99**CAN

Available Wherever Books Are Sold!

Visit our website at **www.kensingtonbooks.com**